The Sphelix

Jay Flaherty

To my mom, Alice.

TABLE OF CONTENTS

1. THE ORB

I finished it. Come tonight.

Irene slipped me the note after class with a hug. The paper was sweaty, folded neatly, but I didn't dare open it there. Not at school, with so many watchful eyes.

On the walk home it pressed against my thigh, like a rock in the pocket of my gray pants. I tried to focus on what Peter was saying, but my thoughts kept coming back to it.

"Leo!" he finally shouted, slapping the back of my head. "You in there?"

"Man, I got more important things than listening to you," I said with a smile.

He continued talking, but I stopped trying to concentrate on what he was saying.

When we got home to my aunt and uncle's, I sprinted upstairs to the room I shared with Pete.

I finished it. Come tonight.

My heart jumped. She'd done it. Finally.

That night, after dinner, I sat by the window, reading the note by the Orb light. It glowed like an emerald sun atop the Propa building, keeping watch over the city.

The bathroom toilet flushed, and a few seconds later Peter walked in, flossing his teeth, his blonde hair damp.

"Your parents asleep?" I asked.

"Think so."

I slid open the window gently, just hard enough to unstick it. Summer heat always made the window expand into the sill. Just as I finished sliding it, our door opened once again. Jenna, my sister, stood there, her long brown hair neatly brushed. She took in the scene quickly, her eyes darting around.

"Go away," I whispered.

She shook her head and closed the door behind her. "I'm coming with."

"No you're not. Go to sleep."

"Let me come, or I'll tell Lester and Helen."

Peter smiled, knowing the outcome. "My parents will kill us if they hear we're nightwalking."

I turned to Jenna. "Go get dressed. We'll wait." Jenna was always latching on to me and Peter, wanting to come with us to the gully after school or play cards with us in our room. She was terrible at taking "no" for an answer. Peter, who loved seeing me annoyed, always egged her on.

Slightly behind schedule, we finally made it onto the cobblestoned street of the Desoway. Rats crawled in and between trash cans, and a few homeless stirred beneath tarps.

"Where are we going?" Jenna asked.

"Shh...keep your voice down. You don't get to ask questions."

"Yeah, but—"

"Jenna, you know what happens if we get caught, right?" She nodded. "Shut up then."

We inched up against a house to peer around the corner. Peter paused and looked back at me. "Where are we going?" he whispered. I hadn't told him for a reason. Mainly because I'd hoped to go alone. "This better not be some stupid nightwalk so you can make out with Irene."

"You really think I'd do this for a make out?"

"You really want me to answer that?"

"Good point. But it's not. It's something else."

"Then what?"

"Can we not do this right now?" I said. "Was it at all unclear that I didn't want you to come?"

"You know me," he said. "I'll do anything for the story."

It was true. Peter wanted to be a writer, and he spent every class dreaming up stories to tell our friends. Usually they were about our nightwalkings: when we'd thrown some rocks through the window of an abandoned house only to have to run away when the blackhats showed up, since it turned out the house hadn't actually been abandoned; or when a homeless guy had been getting beaten up down in the Bugs and we'd stepped in. Peter had a knack for the dramatic, even if he also had a knack for exaggeration.

We took off at a sprint at 19th Street since it was clear of blackhats, me leading the way, staying low and close to the homes lining it. After a few blocks, I ducked into the alley between the Pennyway and Lucinda's, the grocery store. A mound of trash bags filled with old produce sat right next to the side door, giving off an awful stench.

"How much farther?" Jenna whispered. Her cheeks shone red,

like they'd been freshly scrubbed. "Leo, we should get back."

"Look," I said, my frustration bubbling, "I didn't ask either of you two to— "

A voice sounded from around the corner, gruff and loud: "This war better end quickly. Trussel shouldn't be a threat, and if they can put up this kind of fight, well, I'd hate to see what Vacson does to us."

I grabbed Jenna and Peter. Together, we carefully crawled under the bags of Lucinda's trash. I covered myself completely, except for a peephole, trying not to gag on what smelled like spoiled tomatoes. A few blackened bananas spilled out onto my shoe, smearing it with goop.

Two police officers, black batons hanging from their fingers, walked past. They wore all black. A single silver sash cut across each of their chests, gleaming in the Orb light. Their boots crunched against the gravel.

"We've only been fighting them for a few months," said the other officer. "Give it time. Trussel will surrender eventually. They always do."

Just then, a little wretch came from the bag covering Jenna. The officer closest to us turned on the spot.

"You hear that?" he asked his partner.

"Hear what?"

"Sounded like…" He paused, inching closer. I held my breath, my heart thumping. The officer squinted directly at me. "Guess it was my imagination," he said, turning and continuing on.

We didn't dare move. Finally, after a couple minutes, Peter

stirred.

"Bleh—that smelled worse than your body odor, Leo," he said, peeling off a trash bag and tossing it aside. Strands of lettuce still clung to his hair.

Jenna appeared a second later, pinching her nose. "Lucky the blackhat didn't check under the bags."

"Try not to cough next time," Peter said. "I'd rather not spend the night in jail."

"It wasn't a cough—it was a sneeze," Jenna said. "And besides, you'd probably love to spend a night in jail. Would give you something to tell all the girls about."

I didn't wait for Peter's response. Irene's was just a few blocks away now. We passed the offices for the Arcton Gazette, a few windows still lit up, and found ourselves amongst three-story homes. Bigger than Uncle Lester and Aunt Helen's, these were reserved for high-ranking officials in the Propa, Conservation, and Citizen Protection Departments.

Finally, we got to Irene's place. A porch swing swayed gently in front of the yellow-and-white brick home. All the lights were out, but I knew which room was hers. I tiptoed through the side to the back, where the fire escape was. Jenna and Peter followed.

"Be quick," Jenna said. "Uncle Lester could be checking our beds as we speak."

"Why did you come if you're just going to nag me the whole time? You're worse than Aunt Helen."

"Someone has to look after you," she said.

I climbed the fire escape, careful not to shake it too much. It creaked with every step until I reached the top floor, where Irene's bedroom was. I tapped on her window, peering inside the darkened room. Almost instantly, a small flame appeared and moved quickly to a lamp. Irene climbed out of bed carrying a book. Her light-blue nightgown clashed beautifully with her almond skin.

She slid open the window, poked her head through, and gave me a quick kiss. "I thought you were going to be here an hour ago," she said. "I was worried."

I climbed through the window and closed it behind me. Her room was stuffy, but cozy. Family photos were arranged on her dresser, a mass of huge blankets and quilts covered her bed, and a few pillows even sat uselessly on the floor—something that would never happen at my house.

Irene's black hair shone in the lamplight. Her skin had darkened a few shades thanks to the summer, her light blue eyes searching my face. She smiled wide. I kissed her again.

"Is that it?" I said, reaching for the book. She pulled it back.

"Of course not," she said. "What if my dad had come in? It's over here."

She went over to her bureau and opened the bottom drawer from which jeans and sweatpants overflowed—another sight you'd never see in Uncle Lester and Aunt Helen's place. She reached underneath them and pulled out a large book with the title A Population History of Arcton.

"Irene," I said, putting a hand on her shoulder, "I don't know how to put this to you… but that's just a school textbook."

She put her hand on my cheek, staring up at me mock-seriously.

"Leo, I don't know how to put this to you…but you should never judge a book by its cover."

She swung open the front cover, and I took a deep breath, well aware how hard my heart was beating, feeling beads of sweat trickle down my armpit. Inside was fresh stitching where the old pages had been taken out and the new ones put into place. The first page read *Dasher's Revenge*.

2. DASHER'S REVENGE

"Clever, right?" Irene smiled, her face lighting up.

"Had me fooled. What'd you think of the book?"

"It was incredible. Wanna know what it's about?"

"Don't spoil it! You sure your dad won't find out?"

"Even if he does, it won't be for ages. And what's he going to do, turn me into the blackhats?"

Dasher's Revenge felt heavy in my hands, like it was made of stone. I flipped through the pages, inhaling the musky, ancient smell.

"I can't believe you were able to steal this from your dad's library," I said.

"First off, I *borrowed* it," she said. "Besides, he brings home so many Nefa books from the Propa, he'll barely miss this one."

"This is only the second Nefa I've ever seen," I said.

Irene nodded. "I'm well aware. Your dad would be glad you got to read this."

Her feverish eyes bore into me. I fought back tears.

"I'm just...I don't know what to say."

"You can say thanks, and then get home safely," Irene said. "Don't get caught nightwalking with that."

She walked me to the window and gave me another kiss before I ducked out, *Dasher's Revenge* tucked tightly in my arm.

"See you tomorrow," I said, heading down the fire escape.

Jenna and Peter were waiting at the bottom, sitting with their backs against the house.

"How was the make out?" Peter said, standing up and brushing the dirt off his butt.

"Best I've ever had," I said with a smile. Nothing, not even Peter's bad jokes, could bring me down.

"Is that a book?" Jenna asked.

"It is," I said. I considered but then rejected the idea of telling her the truth. Nefas were dangerous to carry around, but she wasn't the one that had it. If she knew I did, she'd just pester me to throw it away. "We have a lot of geography homework, and Irene had it all done already."

Peter eyed me. He knew I was lying since we had all the same classes together, but he kept quiet.

We started off down the street towards the Pennyway, again staying close to the houses in case we needed to make a quick escape. Any sound out of the ordinary—a rat scurrying, a far-off window closing—made me jump about a foot in the air. *Dasher's Revenge* made the journey back infinitely more dangerous than the trip to Irene's – for me at least. Hopefully Jenna and Peter wouldn't be punished if we got caught, but you never know with the blackhats.

"What time is it?" I whispered to Peter.

He checked his watch, an old silver one that his dad had given to him last year. "One-fifteen," he said. "It's going to suck getting up for school tomorrow."

"At least it'll be a good story." I could already imagine him telling our friends at lunch about the nightwalk, probably making the run-in with the blackhat a closer call than it actually was. After all, he was the writer; I was just the reader.

"Yeah, this'll be the best one yet," Peter said sarcastically. "We snuck out, and Leo got a textbook!"

I couldn't help but to smile. From his perspective, it must have been a boring night. No trips to the river, no meeting up with friends to roam the park, just me getting a boring, boring book. If only they knew…

Jenna led the way back without acknowledging our conversation. She had to be peeved that she was out of bed, but she wouldn't have been able to sleep knowing I wasn't home. I knew why she'd come.

Last year, Peter and I had snuck out one too many times—on what turned out to be the same night the war started with Trussel. There were blackhats everywhere, and every person in every house in the city was wide awake, listening to the radio to hear what Arcalaeus, our president, had to say. Peter and I almost got caught three separate times that night, having to hide in clumps of bushes and dart down alleyways to avoid getting caught. When we'd finally made it back, we'd had to face the wrath of my aunt Helen, my uncle Lester, and, worst of all, Jenna.

The moment we walked through the door, I could still see how red her eyes were. She'd wasted no time in shoving me in the chest. "Where were you?" she'd screamed. "You're lucky you weren't killed!"

Later that night, after everyone had gone to bed, Jenna and I had stayed awake on the couch together. "Don't leave me alone," she'd said, as we'd watched the sun rise. "Not you, too."

And I hadn't. Not on a nightwalk, anyway. She'd been out with us every time since— which made me less inclined to go in the first place.

The Pennyway turned into 43rd Street, and the Desoway was in sight. Our footsteps were slightly masked by The Orb, buzzing like a white noise from the massive black tower on which it sat a mile away. I followed behind Jenna, though I wished we could move faster. Once we were home, I could finally read another Nefa.

Out of nowhere, a black object ripped through the night and knocked into Jenna's chest. She collapsed to the ground, her breath coming in short gasps. The blue emerald necklace Mom had left her fell to the ground, broken.

I picked it up and placed a hand on her shoulder. "Jenna!"

Through gasps of breaths she managed to point to a spot behind me. I turned in time to see two blackhats sprinting at us full-speed. One wound up and threw his baton. I watched it come toward me on a crash-course for my skull, but somehow it veered past me at the last second. Peter and I each grabbed one of Jenna's arms and yanked her up.

"Run!" I said, pushing her toward a side alley. The footsteps behind me grew louder, and I turned just in time to dodge a pudgy blackhat's extended hand and take off down the street, away from Jenna and Peter. I cradled the book in one arm, extending my strides, and shoved the necklace into a jacket pocket. When I turned again, the blackhat was still after me, red in the face and clutching his baton.

I turned a corner and searched for a place to toss the book. It was too dangerous to keep on me, but there were no garbage cans or even fences around. I made to throw the Nefa into a cluster of blackberry bushes, where the officers might not find it or, if they did, would have a hard time proving it was mine. But as I wound up, my legs went out from under me. *Dasher's Revenge* went flying. As I scrambled to my feet, a black baton landed next to me on the ground. I turned in time to see the blackhat lunge toward me. When we collided, my chin hit pavement and split open. I could barely breathe as he shoved his knee into my back.

"You little snock!" he said, clasping handcuffs to my wrists. "I oughta beat you senseless for making me run like that." He picked up the baton with which he'd tripped me and secured it to a rung in his belt. Then he took out a long wire and tied one end through the handcuffs and the other to a streetlight.

Three more blackhats marched Jenna and Peter in a minute later. Neither said a word as they sat down next to me, hands cuffed. Their faces were stony, unreadable.

They were here both here because of me. Out past curfew, hands cuffed. But it could be even worse.

Please, don't let them find the Nefa.

The blackhats stood together in conversation. I couldn't pick up what they were saying, other than that one of them was radioing for a truck to get us. If they didn't find *Dasher's Revenge*, we'd probably just be in jail for the night and end up on probation. That was nothing. Peter and I had been caught before. I forced myself not to look toward the bushes, even though I kept wanting to reassure myself that no one was anywhere near the book. If they did find it... Well, it would mean at least a five-year stint in The Pit for me. And worse, Jenna and Peter could be implicated.

"How'd they catch you?" I asked the two of them.

"Ran straight into two of 'em in a blind corner," Peter said. "He clotheslined me, and I didn't really have a chance after that. By the way, what happened to—"

"Shut up!" hissed Jenna. She glanced nervously at the officers, but none of them seemed to have heard. "Don't bring it up."

Did Jenna know what it was? Why else would she be so concerned?

An officer came over. Freckles covered the bridge of his nose, and he wore his cap down low, covering his eyes. "I.D. cards," he said. "Hand 'em over."

"It's in my front pocket," I said. Wasn't like I could reach it with my hands tied behind my back. The officer reached in and took out my card, scribbling notes on a pad of paper.

A gentle rumble sounded in the distance, followed by blinding light coming from a massive truck painted black and silver. I hadn't seen a car in weeks, and the headlights were even stronger than I remembered. A few neighbors poked their heads through their windows to check out the commotion.

"Where are we going?" I asked. But I knew. Or at least was pretty sure.

"The station," the officer said, returning my card to my pocket.

"You're lucky it's not the Pit. War time is no time to go sneaking around. We put three kids younger than you in the Pit just last week. A little full at the moment, though," he said, clearly bummed out they wouldn't be able to fit any more.

Relief flooded through me. Jail for a night we could handle. The officers untied the wire from my cuffs, and I followed Jenna and Peter into the back of the truck.

As the freckled officer went to close the door behind me, I saw a hand clasp his shoulder. He stepped to the side of the door and turned to face the pudgy officer.

"Hold on a second," he said, looking past the freckled officer and right at me. "*That* one was carrying something." My head started spinning as he trotted off toward the bushes. My heart raced. *Please don't find it. Let it have fallen down a storm drain. Or a dog grabbed it and took it far away.*

The cop came waddling back, huffing and out of breath.

"This is it," he said, grasping the book with his sausage fingers.

"It's just a schoolbook," said the freckled officer.

"Look inside."

The freckled officer opened to the first page and his lips curled into a thin smile as he looked at me.

"Well now, this changes everything."

3. HELEN & LESTER

I stared at the large crack on the ceiling in the corner, one of the few things to look at in the sad gray cell besides the small square window protected by metal bars. The few lonely candles on the walls did nothing for warmth. My butt had gone numb when I'd sat on the steel chair, which felt more like a block of ice, so instead I paced and focused on the crack.

How long had it been there? The gray paint had chipped, revealing damp wood above it. Probably rotting away.

Jenna and Peter were in similar cells because of me, though I'd told the officers that they knew nothing about the book. I could only hope that they wouldn't share whatever punishment awaited me. I was definitely off to the Pit to spend the foreseeable future peeling fire ants off my body, or being tortured, or whatever it was they did to prisoners in there.

My stupid infatuation with Nefas. Why had I risked everything for one? It was just ink on paper, definitely nothing worth spending an entire life behind bars over. Those books had been deemed nefarious for good reason. Was reading one really worth Jenna and Peter sitting in cold cells—was it even worth me lying to them?

A door opened down the hall, and footsteps rang out through the hallway. I stood, expecting a guard to peak through the window to check on me, but instead the cell door swung backward and

Uncle Lester and Aunt Helen walked in. I wasn't sure whether to hug them or run away—this was their worst nightmare realized, and I'd been the cause of it.

Aunt Helen rushed over and squeezed me into a hug that did more than just provide warmth, it provided comfort. I couldn't stop tears from rolling down my face. There were bags under Helen's eyes and her white hair was a frazzled mess.

"I'm so sorry," I said. "It's all my fault. I should've never brought Jenna and Peter."

"That's okay, sweetie," Aunt Helen said, clasping her hand to my cheek. "Mistakes happen. We're glad you're alright."

I pulled away, relieved to hear the kindness in her voice. I thought she'd be furious; I thought she'd hit me, but she was as gentle as ever. I looked over her shoulder to Lester, who hadn't moved away from the door. He stood with his arms crossed, his beard face frowning at me. His brown eyes were still, taking in the scene.

"I'm sorry, Uncle Lester," I said. "I know everything you've done for me and Jenna, and I screwed it up."

His jaw moved side-to-side, as though he were chewing gum. Could you chew on anger?

"Uncle Lester," I begged, "say some— "

"Don't you order me to do anything," he said. "Out past curfew AGAIN! And this time with a Nefa. I thought you were smarter than that. I thought Peter and Jenna—me and Helen—meant more to you."

It was like I'd been slapped. I felt frozen. What little comfort

Aunt Helen's hug had given was yanked away. Venom leapt from Uncle Lester's cold voice, and goosebumps formed on my shoulders.

"Do you have any idea what Helen and I risked by taking you and Jenna in?" Uncle Lester said. "Any idea?"

"Lester, of course—"

"I could've left you in a shelter. Plenty of people told me I should, instead of taking in two extra mouths to feed when I already had three of my own. But you know what I said?"

I nodded.

"I said I had a duty to protect the children of Geoff Belfin. That they'd go hungry only after I'd starved to death. And this is how you repay me?"

Helen put a hand on my shoulder. I leaned into it. "Leo," Helen said, "Things are going to work out okay. I promise."

"Are they?" I asked. "I'm going to the Pit, and Peter and Jenna might be too. Did the guards say anything?"

"Lester's working on it," she said. "You're not going to the Pit. Jenna and Peter, well, they're in just as much trouble as you. The blackhats don't believe you were acting alone."

"How did you get that book?" Lester said. "Who gave it to you?"

"I...I found it," I said, but it sounded like a question. How come I never learned to lie?

Lester strode up and pushed me up against the wall. Whiskey rolled off his breath and into my face as he glared at me.

"Tell me where you got the book," he said. "This isn't up for discussion."

"I can't," I said. "I won't."

Helen pulled Lester back by his collar with surprising strength. "That's enough!" she said. "Enough!" Lester finally let go of me. "Leo, you're not going to the Pit, and neither are Jenna and Peter. Lester's been able to see to that, at least. But, you're joining the Verdean Guard. All three of you. It's a chance to win back your freedom…" Her voice cracked, but she took a deep breath and finished. "If you perform well in the war."

My knees started to wobble. Jenna, Peter, and I were going to war?

I tried to steady myself, get my feet under me, but my mind was racing. Jenna was being forced to join the Verdean because of me, and so was Peter. They were going to have to fight Trussel, risk their lives, all because of me.

"Do Jenna and Peter know?" I asked.

"Peter was surprisingly upbeat about it," Aunt Helen said. "We haven't told Jenna yet, but she'll only be a nurse. She won't be in any danger."

"How—how come they're not putting us in the Pit?"

"I have a friend in the Justice Department," Uncle Lester said. "He took pity on you."

"They were able to get an altered punishment," said Aunt Helen. "The Pit is always so filled up these days. Plus, the Verdean can always use more able bodies."

"How long do we have to be in the Verdean for?"

"Long as they want," said Lester. He spat out the words.

"Should teach you some discipline at least since I sure wasn't able to."

Knuckles rapped on the cell door. "Gotta get going," a guard's voice said. "Almost time for departure."

"We're leaving *now*?" I said, looking to Helen. Tears welled in her eyes as she nodded.

I'm sorry, Leo," Aunt Helen said, "But it was the only way." She hugged me again, kissed my forehead, and then brought me close once more. She was shaking, but her voice was steady. "You're going to be okay. Don't try to be the hero out there. You, Jenna, and Pete need to look after each other. You'll be fine if you stick together. You hear me? Don't run towards danger. Get home safe."

She zipped up her coat and turned to walk out with Lester, who didn't say goodbye. The door clanged shut, leaving me alone with an uncomfortable, lonely silence.

I'd betrayed their trust for a book. We were going to war over some ink and paper... Why?

If I was honest with myself, I knew why I wanted *Dasher's Revenge* so badly. It would've been the second Nefa book I'd ever read. The first had been with my dad. After my mom got sick, he'd wake me up early every morning, we'd have a bowl of cereal, and he'd read me *Gestalt Diary*.

I hated it. Waking up early, even on the weekends, just so he could read me a book. I was eight years old and wanted to go outside and play with Pete or the other neighborhood kids. But he'd make me read it until mom and Jenna woke up.

Every morning he'd say the same thing. "You can't tell anyone what we're reading. Not mom, not Jenna, not anyone. You need to remember. And you need to focus on the book. This is important."

But I would daydream while he read, longing to play kickball outside, or go swimming in the river. I was too young to understand why it was important. And then, one day, he died.

We never saw his body, but Uncle Lester said he'd gotten into the wrong crowd thanks to his frequent trips to Tony's, one of the bars off the Pennyway. My mom was around a few months longer, but, well…she'd been fading for a long time.

So Jenna and I went to live with Uncle Lester, Aunt Helen, Peter, and our youngest cousins, Jexter and Flora.

I never saw the banned book again. Drowning in guilt over not having paid it the attention my father had asked, I'd snuck back into our house to look for it after a few months living with Aunt Helen and Uncle Lester. I picked through trash, tore up the desk drawers in my dad's room, flipped over beds searching for it. But there was nothing.

For someone who used to slather shaving cream on his face and jump out to scare me, for someone who would make funny faces at me while my mom wasn't looking, *this is important* wasn't something he often said.

And now I couldn't remember anything about the Nefa other than its name: *Gestalt Diary*.

4. BASE CAMP

"Not exactly the happiest meeting I've ever had with my parents," Peter said as he boarded the truck and sat between Jenna and me. "I mean, usually my mom saves the tears for her birthdays. Bit dramatic if you ask me."

I shook my head, smiling in disbelief. Peter and Jenna should've been furious at me: I'd lied to them, and that lie was sending them to Base Camp and, soon enough, into war. Yet they were far from angry, and neither seemed scared, although, like me, they were probably hiding it. Lester had to have asked them who had given me the book, too, but they hadn't ratted out Irene.

"How are you making a joke out of this?" I said. "We're going to war!"

"Yeah, but imagine the stories we'll have!" Peter said. "And anyway, our dads went to war, too. And survived. Besides, girls freak out over war heroes."

Jenna rested her head against my shoulder. "I lost mom's necklace," she said without looking up. "I lost it. After all this time."

I shrugged off her head and bent down to grab the necklace out of my sock, where I'd been hiding it. I handed it to her without a word.

"Leo," Jenna said, giving me a hug. "I thought the blackhats had taken it."

"Lucky I found it," I said.

"Thank you." She stuffed the still-broken necklace inside her jacket. "I would've never forgiven myself for losing it."

I felt the same way about bringing her and Peter into this mess.

The open-backed truck drove along. It was the fourth time I'd ever been in a truck, and none of those other occasions had been happy either—getting caught playing hide-and-seek with Peter behind the gated community that held the Orb, trying and failing to steal a bag of oranges from Lucinda's market, and making one too many jokes to a passing blackhat (though that one was on Peter, not me).

But we'd made it through those times. Some harsh words from Aunt Helen, maybe a punch or two from Uncle Lester. Nothing we couldn't endure, and then things had gone back to usual. Unlike today.

The dawn sunlight peeked over the city skyline, casting Jenna's face in a gentle orange glow.

We hadn't been able to sleep all night, and now we had a day-long trip to Base Camp. But that was better than a day-long trip to the Pit.

"You still happy you came along?" I asked Jenna.

She sighed, nodding. "You see how I'm able to close my eyes and actually breathe?" she said. "If I was back at home, without you and Peter, I'd be hyperventilating. Sleep-deprived. So, yes, I'm happy I came, but you should've planned the nightwalk better – and you definitely should've told us about the Nefa. You can't just go diving into things without telling us the real story."

"You knew, though," I said. "You told Peter to shut up when he mentioned it in front of the blackhats."

"A textbook, Leo?" she said. "You'll come up with any excuse *not* to do homework — there's no way you'd let me come on a nightwalk with you for a textbook."

"Fair point," I said. "And…I'm sorry for—for, you know, getting you both stuck in this. I should've just gone alone."

"That was never gonna happen," Peter said.

"Ever," said Jenna. "Now enough talking. I need to get some beauty sleep." She dug her head into my shoulder and fell asleep within minutes. Not long after that Peter conked out, too.

The sun rose quickly over the city, but the warmth spreading through me had nothing to do with it. I was lucky to have them both. Extremely lucky.

The truck rumbled down the Pennyway. A few old-timers sitting inside coffee shops watched us pass. Most had the morning *Gazette* open on their laps and hot coffee on the tables in front of them. I stared at the steam rising from the cups and longed to just hold one in my still-chilly hands.

We continued south until we got to the city limits, where a few blackhats searched everyone going through the checkpoint either way. Without waking Jenna or Peter, I retrieved their ID papers and handed them, along with my own, to our driver. Minutes later, I was officially outside of Arcton City for the first time in my life.

Could the rumors about Base Camp possibly be true? That they made soldiers fight lions, swim through crocodile-infested waters, kill other soldiers in the Verdean Guard before they even reached war...

I shook my head. There was no way. Maybe we wouldn't even make it to war – maybe the war would end early. But when had anything I'd wished for ever come true?

The Pennyway gave way to dirt and rocks, making the drive that much bumpier. Pine trees lined the roads, covering hills and gullies as far as I could see. We drove alongside the Semantie river, which wound its way down from the city, its waters calmly churning forward.

Suddenly the Orb glow vanished. A green tint was removed from everything—the sky became bluer, the crashing water of the Semantie was whiter... and even the trees seemed to give off a stronger scent. It was stunningly easy to breathe, my lungs filling with fresh air.

The transition was as easy and seamless as diving into water. It was so intoxicating, though, that like too many of Aunt Helen's chocolate chip cookies, it made me want to pass out. I rested my head on the top of Jenna's and my thoughts blurred.

When I woke up, the sun was overhead and two new passengers were staring at me. One was a dark-skinned boy with short black hair, a flat nose, and glasses who looked no older than us. He stared politely over the thick book in front of him. For a second it crossed my mind that it could be *Dasher's Revenge*, but of course it turned out to be an actual textbook. The second boy was flimsy and small, with tan skin and brown hair, a tuft of which stuck up in the back. He had freckles and appeared to have only just reached puberty. Judging from his scowl, he wasn't too happy about it.

I poked Jenna and Peter awake. Peter let loose a long, drawn out yawn before he realized we had company.

"Who are you?" he said, as way of an introduction.

"Name's Langston," said the dark-skinned boy. He closed his book, careful to mark his page. "How about you?"

"Peter," said Peter. "This is Jenna and Leo."

"Nice to meet you guys," said Langston. He got up and shook our hands.

"And your friend?" said Jenna.

"Just met him—his name's Willie," said Langston. Willie nodded but did not speak. "Long night?"

"You have no idea," I said. "You volunteers or forced?"

"I'm uh…I'm forced," said Langston. Willie nodded in agreement. Their hesitance was understandable. Volunteering was seen as selfless. Your family received a stipend for more food and a couple extra rations of water. Being forced simply meant you were a criminal.

"Us too," I said.

No one asked what anyone had done. In fact, no one spoke much at all for the rest of the trip. The dense tree-line of pine trees gave way to rolling farmlands as we went further south. The sun beat down on us, navigating through its orbit. Corn stalks zoomed past, glowing in the sun.

The sun had almost set by the time I could hear the ocean's waves crashing. We all stood, even Willie, to get a view. The truck climbed a large hill covered in golden-brown grass, taking a slight left turn near the top. When it came around the bend, there, stretched across the entire horizon, was water. Only water. Far below, white caps crashed into sand and rock; the sounds of breaking waves and seagulls' calls meshed together.

I'd only ever read about the ocean in textbooks – a strategic landmark in war that required boats to cross. The water was crucial in a country's defense, something generals weighed heavily in any wartime decision. But now, seeing how massive the ocean was, I was in awe…

I licked my lips, tasting the salt, and tossed my head back to let the wind flow through my hair. Beside me, Peter and Jenna took in the view, their faces bathed in sunlight. Willie and Langston moved next to me.

"Haven't seen that before," said Langston. "No one where I'm from has."

None of us had either.

"What're those?" Jenna asked, pointing. "Are those islands?"

Langston squinted. "I think it's the Foxtails," he said. "They're completely uninhabitable for humans, but a herd of foxes have lived there for ages, apparently. When I read about them, the book said they're impossible to see unless the weather's perfect…. we got lucky, I guess."

Luck wasn't a word I'd use to currently describe our situation, but the islands were beautiful all the same.

The trucks turned left once more around a bend, and the view was lost. The road took us down and away from the sea. By the time we started climbing another mountain – a finger separating from a fist – the sun had set. When we reached the top, we passed into a green glow just like in Arcton City.

The emerald tinge entered everything. Jenna and Peter both involuntarily put their hands to their chests. Breathing became difficult, like when Uncle Lester smoked cigarettes in the living room.

Down below, thousands of lights glowed up at us through the darkness. Base Camp. In the center of camp stood a massive tower with a green Orb atop it. It was identical in size and color to the one in Arcton City.

Langston let out a soft whistle. "Incredible," he said. "Those are all barracks, huh? And the big building with the lights still on must be the Captains' Offices. You can see everything from here."

"What's this mountain called?" I asked. I had a feeling he'd know.

"Mount Brentwood," he said, without a second thought. "And the Pit is across those few smaller peaks over there."

"How'd you know that?" Jenna asked.

Langston shrugged and held up his book. "I read about it."

The truck wound its way down the mountain, stopping briefly outside of a checkpoint. The Verdean officers, who were dressed sharply in dark-green with swords at their hilts, asked for our I.D. Papers, and the gates opened up.

Small one-story barracks dozens of rows deep bordered the dirt road. Barely anyone was outside; curfew had probably gone into effect hours ago. The driver pulled straight into a huge, white barn.

Inside it was all pavement and metal. A group of nurses with dark-green aprons came forward as we got off.

Without so much as a hello, the nurses' hands opened and a white powder was thrown into my face.

"Hey!" I called, coughing out a few clouds of it. "What's that for?"

"We need to make sure you're sterile," said an officer with a handlebar mustache, striding towards us with a rigid walk that he clearly practiced. His dark-green cap sat perfectly on his head, not an inch to either side. He didn't show any teeth when he spoke. He didn't smile either.

"I'm Lieutenant Yawkey," he said, "and I'll be escorting you through your introduction to Basic Training. The powder is to limit any bed bugs or diseases that might be brought into Base Camp. The last thing we need is a sickness spreading. Now, follow me." He turned on his heel and walked straight out the door from which he'd come.

As we followed him, he kept up a constant stream of words. "Tomorrow you will be up and at the obstacle course at 0500 hours. Sleep well, and don't bother eating anything before physical training. Make sure you're not late—it doesn't bode well on your first day.

"These bags," he said, motioning to a group of plain green duffels resting against an office door, "contain every piece of your uniforms, your toiletries, and your required reading while with the Verdean. Take them and follow me."

I grabbed a bag with Belfin written in tidy white print, swinging it over my shoulder and nearly collapsing under the weight. Lieutenant Yawkey didn't wait up. The constant flow of words continued as we made our way outside and walked past the other barracks.

"The Verdean Guard isn't for everyone," he said. "But my understanding is that none of you have a choice in the matter—which makes it all the more imperative that you perform to the highest standards, especially in these two weeks of Basic Training.

"There have been plenty of soldiers forced into the Verdean who performed admirably and went on to launch very successful careers at every level of government. You have that same opportunity.

"That being said"—he came to an abrupt stop outside a barrack with the number 19 painted on the door— "we are in the midst of a very bloody war, one that, should it go badly, could mean the end of Arcton. That means your loved ones back home will meet their deaths. To prevent that, you will risk your lives on numerous occasions. No doubt you are scared right now, wondering how you ended up here. That's natural. But every great story starts with something terrible at the beginning. Remember that."

He opened the door.

"I'll see you at the obstacle course, fully dressed, at 0500 hours."

"Sir," interrupted Jenna, before Lieutenant Yawkey could leave, "am I sleeping in the same bunk as the boys?"

"You are," said Lieutenant Yawkey. "Is there a problem with that?"

"Not at all. I just wasn't sure what happened with nurses."

"Ah, yes. The lieutenant of your squadron will explain tomorrow." He turned and left.

The single light hanging from the barrack's ceiling swayed slightly from the breeze of the door closing.

"Does anyone know what time it is?" Jenna asked.

Langston, again, was the one to answer. "Twelve-thirty," he said, looking at a silver watch on his wrist. "We have about four hours before we need to get up."

Three sets of bunk beds lined one wall of the uncarpeted room, with desks and a blackboard on the opposite wall and a single window on each of the others. Other than us and our duffels, it was empty. I chose a bunk right above Pete's. Langston picked out one beneath Willie, who still hadn't said a word, and Jenna took one to herself after pulling the string on the light, drowning the barrack in darkness.

Sleep came as easily as flipping a switch, but before long there was a banging on our door to wake us up.

I searched the barrack, taking a moment to get my bearings. I wasn't in Arcton City anymore, at Uncle Lester's and Aunt Helen's. There was no smell of coffee filtering through our bedroom door. I pulled off the flimsy blanket that covered me, and tried to rub the goose pimples out of my frozen thighs.

Basic Training was here.

5. CARL

"Listen up!" Lieutenant Yawkey yelled at our group of over two hundred soldiers—or wannabe soldiers in my, Jenna's, Peter's, Willie's, and Langston's cases. Rope walls loomed in the background, along with a field of mud with low-hanging wire, huge logs, a series of massive wooden boxes, and a murky pool. My breath fogged in front of me, clouding up in the dawn light.

"The Verdean Guard is only as strong as its weakest link," Lieutenant Yawkey said. "And since that is the case, we have split you up into teams based on which barrack you're in. Each member of that team must complete the obstacle course, one after the other. Once you've gotten through the pool, you'll take each of the obstacles in reverse until you reach the starting line again. The weakest link—the last place team—gets to clean out the lavatories every day for the rest of the week while everyone else is at Mess Hall for breakfast. Understood?"

"Yes, sir!" we said in unison.

"Good. Now form a line with your squad."

We scrambled into a line, one of dozens that spanned the length of the field. Willie stood in front, and I was in the very back. On Lieutenant Yawkey's whistle, Willie tore off down the field, his tiny legs pumping furiously, easily outstripping everyone on his way to the rope wall. He looked like a squirrel as he scaled it, his arms furiously gathering up rope.

"Who is this kid?" I asked. Willie was in first, yards ahead of anyone else.

Langston, two in front of me, shook his head. "You wouldn't believe how hard it was to get him to even tell me his name. Boy, can he run though."

A few other soldiers caught up to Willie at the log roll—his small body a liability while he tried to push it forward. I lost sight of him after he went over the box jumps – four up, and four back down. When Willie appeared again after going through the mud crawl, swimming through the pool, and then doubling back through the previous obstacles, he was firmly in the top five.

Willie slapped Langston's hand, and Langston took off down the course. Willie put his hands above his head, breathing heavily.

"You were awesome!" Peter said, clapping him on the back. "You're a freaking cheetah out there."

Willie nodded, smiling slightly, his face painted in mud.

Langston's athletic skills were, unfortunately, the exact opposite of his intelligence. Slowly but surely, other soldiers sped by him, and by the time he returned and collapsed onto his back, his chest rising and falling rapidly, we were among the bottom three teams.

When Peter went next, I did my best to be heard cheering him on over the screaming from the other teams. He nimbly climbed over the rope wall, practically swam through the mud crawl, and was at the pool before we had gotten done congratulating Langston. By the time he'd doubled back and slapped hands with Jenna, we were back in the middle of the pack.

Jenna shot out like a bullet. She was quick through the rope wall, but, like Willie, struggled with the log roll thanks to her small frame. She stumbled on the first box jump – barely catching her balance – but hurried easily over the other boxes and out of sight. There were only a few girls competing, and I swelled with pride that she bested almost all of them and a few boys as well. By the time Jenna got back, there were only five teams ahead of us.

I took off in a dead sprint towards the rope wall and jumped as high as I could, snaring the rope between my hands, the rough nylon peeling off while I climbed. Above me, there were only a few other soldiers dangling on the wall, but I was faster than them. Peter and I had climbed trees every day one summer, pushing one another to see who would be willing to go higher. He'd won, of course, but the training had stuck with me. I gained ground on each of the soldiers ahead, and before I knew it my legs were straddling the top of the wall.

I jumped down the other side, and started pushing the log as quickly as I could from the blue line on the ground to the red one roughly one hundred feet away, my back aching with every push.

Next came the box jumps. You weren't allowed to climb or use your hands in any way, but had to instead jump from each box to the next. I was gasping and exhausted once I reached the top, but I caught my breath on the blocks leading back down.

I dove into the mud crawl, keeping my head and butt low as to not catch them on the barbed wire. Mud filled my mouth. I spat it out in disgust and pushed forward. I was behind only one soldier, a tall guy who picked himself up out of the mud a few feet in front of me.

We could win.

The other guy and I jumped into the water simultaneously. It was so cold that I gasped, the temperature constricting my chest. I tried to remember the tips Aunt Helen had given me in the community pool: breathe steadily and let your legs do the work. I kicked furiously, trying to breathe on every fourth stroke. But white bubbles floated up ahead—I was still behind.

I came up on the edge of the pool, touched it, and kicked back the other way.

Quicker. Just stay close. Other swimmers passed me in the opposite direction, and I dug in harder, only taking one breath the entire length of the pool this time.

I touched the other end, and quickly hoisted myself out of the pool, water dripping down. The first-place soldier was only a few feet ahead. I dug my elbows through the mud furiously, like little crutches. At the end of the obstacle, my shoulders bounced off the other soldier's.

We sprinted to the box jumps side by side. One, two, three...I took the first jumps in quick succession, but as I bent down to jump up to the fourth one, I tripped and stumbled on the jump, barely getting six inches off the box and teetering very close to the edge.

A hand came into my peripheral vision. On the blocks to my right, one step above me, the soldier, his dirty-blonde hair half-covered in mud, flashed his white teeth.

"It can get pretty slippery up here," he said, reaching for my hand. I took it gratefully.

He hoisted me up, but then, a second later, something hit my chest and I fell backwards. I flailed in the air, trying to put something beneath me and the ground ten feet below.

I crashed down hard. My head whiplashed back as I hit the dirt, and every ounce of air left my lungs. I tried lifting my legs, but they refused to move. Soldiers passed, jumping onto each box in quick succession. No one stopped.

Gingerly, I finally managed to turn myself from my back onto my stomach. I got to my knees and then to my feet and started the long walk back to the others.

All eyes were on me. Everyone had finished. I forced myself to jog in, each step seeming to bring me further away from the group instead of closer. Tears welled in my eyes, but I refused to let them fall. Crying would be the only thing that could make the situation worse. When I finally reached Jenna, Peter, Langston, and Willie, they patted me on the shoulder as I got in line behind them.

Five rows down, the soldier who'd offered to hoist me up and had instead pushed me off the block stood with his own group. They all looked identical, each taller than me, with huge biceps and the same stupid grin plastered across their faces. The soldier himself, who wouldn't have been discernable from the rest except for his cleft chin, gave me a wink.

It took everything in my power not to rush after him and clock him in his smug face.

Lieutenant Yawkey stepped up to the group. "Squad 19, with me," he said. "Everyone else, breakfast."

The stench of the lavatory hit me before I even walked through the door. I lifted my elbow to cover my nose. Troughs lined the walls, with a few stalls at the end.

"You're lucky I'm only making you do one of them today," Yawkey said before handing us brooms, mops, and damp rags.

I took some of the rags and began wiping down the trough. The crusty yellow stains came off easily enough, but then I had to figure out a way to fold the rag over without getting the dry urine on my hands. Bending over wasn't easy, either, with my bruised tailbone, so I finally gave up and knelt onto the damp floor to wipe down the underside.

"So what happened?" Peter asked in between mouthfuls of egg. "You were way out ahead of everyone."

I didn't want to relive it, but they deserved to know. After all, it was because of my naïveté—or sheer stupidity, depending on how you looked at it—that they'd had to clean up other people's poop. So I told them everything.

"You could've been seriously hurt!" said Jenna once I'd finished.

"Why didn't you report the little snock?" asked Langston. "His squad shouldn't have won. And we definitely shouldn't have come in last."

Jenna sighed. "Leo doesn't believe in tattling. He thinks he can handle everything himself."

"No one saw it happen," I said. "It would've been my word versus his."

"We'll get him back later," Peter said. "Don't worry. Oh, Leo, I think you missed a spot over there."

"Feel free to take care of it for me," I said.

"Ah, I would," said Peter, "But I don't have any rags."

"You're welcome to lick it up," I said.

Peter flashed a smile, the same one that made all the girls in class swoon over him. It was beyond annoying. "Think I'll save my appetite for the next trough," he said.

When we finally finished—my arms sore, my legs aching, and my tailbone throbbing as though someone had jabbed a hot poker into my lower back—there were only ten minutes left for breakfast. We rushed into the Mess Hall, a massive overhang covering hundreds of metal tables, with three separate buffet lines packed with eggs, hash browns, and cereal.

"Can we—can we eat as much as we want?" said Langston.

The soldier in front of him piled three servings of eggs onto his plate and topped them with a generous serving of hash browns.

Langston seemed to take that as a yes, as he did the same. When no one came over to reprimand him, we all followed suit. Even tiny Willie stacked ten strips of bacon onto his plate.

We chose an empty table near the back entrance. I scarfed down three eggs and two strips of bacon within minutes.

"You should chew at least," Jenna said. "We're not done training for the day. You're gonna throw up."

Dun care," I said, a few crumbs of cornmeal falling out of my mouth. "This is incredible."

"Hey Leo, is that him?" said Peter, nodding to his left. I turned just in time to see the cleft-chinned soldier walking by with his crew of tall, jacked friends. He must've felt our eyes on him because he turned abruptly, caught my eye, and smiled. He came over.

He extended his hand. "No hard feelings, eh?" he said.

"I shook your hand once," I said. "Didn't work out so well for me."

"Oh, come *on*," he said. "Don't be such a little girl. It was a competition."

"Like nearly kill someone? Get out of here, man."

His group of cronies moved closer to our table. Until this moment I hadn't realized just how small Willie—who was glaring up at all of them—really was in comparison.

"Gonna have your friends do all the fighting?" said Peter as he stood.

Carl-the-cleft-chin turned to me. "What was your name again? Belfin, right? My dad said there was a new crop of Forcies arriving today. Didn't think they'd have such a mouth on 'em."

His friends laughed and a few heads from surrounding tables turned in our direction. Their eyes narrowed at us.

"Forcie?" I said.

"*Forcie?*" Carl mimicked. "You don't even know what you are?"

I clenched my fists, suddenly overheating.

"Why don't you tell us what—"

Carl rolled his eyes as though he were telling a seven-year-old what two plus two equaled for the tenth time.

"You were forced into the Verdean," he said. "You're too much of a chicken to volunteer for battle on your own. I would fight you, but what does that really prove? That we can beat up a bunch of snocks and a girl?"

Willie stood up, fork in his hand, glaring. Jenna grabbed his shoulder, pulling him back. Carl grinned. "Real soldiers sign up for the Verdean, they're not forced. Real soldiers are trying to save this country from being taken over by criminals like you. Luckily, you won't last long. My dad says squads of Forcies tend to die off quickly."

With that they walked away, but the effect was immediate. Soldiers at nearby tables stuck their middle fingers up at us. Others flicked bits of hash browns our way.

"Ignore them," Jenna said. "It's not worth it."

As one we picked up our trays and made for the exit, avoiding the outstretched legs trying to trip us but unable to drown out the hisses.

6. BOWS & SWORDS

After breakfast, we were supposed to meet in the archery range, according to Langston (who had our schedule memorized). On our way there, though, a tall, broad-shouldered woman with her hair tucked into a Verdean cap stopped us.

"Jenna Belfin?" she said. Jenna nodded. "You're to break off and train with the other nurses. You'll rejoin this squadron later in the day."

"But I want to shoot," Jenna said.

"I don't care," said the woman.

"So am I going to be with a squad or in the hospital with the other nurses?"

"You're one of the field nurses, but until your squad is deployed, you'll participate in mandatory nurse's training every day. Your squad lieutenant will explain to you more fully."

Without another word, she turned on her heel. Jenna had no choice but to follow.

"I hope our squad lieutenant is good," I said.

"Probably a pretty bad one," Langston said. "Doubt they'd give a group of Forcies anything resembling good leadership."

"Well, that's nice to hear," Peter said. He smiled at us. "I mean, it's only our lives at stake."

My eyes drooped while we walked down the dirt road. The sun

had now fully risen and combined with the Orb light. I couldn't believe we'd only just finished breakfast.

What was Irene doing right now? Had she found out we'd been caught with the Nefa? Had the blackhats been able to trace it back to her? Hopefully she wouldn't blame herself for what had happened to us.

There were already a few squads at the archery range when we arrived. Thankfully, Carl's wasn't one of them. Straw targets with bullseyes were stretched out along the range. Standing in front of it was a short, stout man with biceps the size of my entire body. His muscles were practically tearing through his shirt.

"For those that don't know, my name is Lieutenant Wes, and I'll be your shooting instructor. Listen carefully. We're going to be going through an expedited training since you boys will be heading off to war in only a couple weeks. Usually, I prefer months or even years of training before you see action, but we need you out there yesterday. Got it?" His voice was squeaky and cracked a couple of times.

"Yes, sir!" we called in unison.

"The key to shooting a longbow is your breath," he said. He inhaled deeply, his massive chest rising, before exhaling again. "An even breath makes for an even shot. While shooting, it's important to stay calm. Otherwise your aim will be thrown off. This is true both while shooting from a stationary position and when shooting on the run."

Beside me, Peter took a huge breath through his nose before letting out a low, fake snore, pretending to fall asleep. I kicked him.

Luckily Wes didn't notice.

"The second most important thing is your base," Wes said, widening his stance. "You want your feet to be slightly wider than shoulder-width apart, and you need to keep your posture straight, like so. Finally, pull the arrow back, right against your cheek. Steady, and release."

The arrow hurtled through the air, sinking a half-inch from the center of the bullseye. Peter wasn't making fun of Lieutenant Wes anymore. His mouth was open.

We broke off into our squads and took turns trying to shoot the bullseye. The weight of the arrow was foreign to me, and I fumbled trying to knock it into the string. Finally, with the string secured inside the nook of the arrow, I aimed at the target, brought the string back close to my cheek, and loosed...

The arrow wobbled immediately and struck the dirt just ten feet in front of me.

Peter keeled over with laughter.

"I really hope you're better with a sword than a bow," he said.

I shot a few more times, getting progressively better. On my tenth shot, my arrow finally reached the target—but then sailed about twenty feet further.

Peter still wore an annoying smirk as I handed him the bow.

Peter stepped up to the range, and with one quick motion fired his first arrow, barely missing the target. He reloaded and within seconds was back in position; his back and shoulders were much stronger than mine, stretching easily, and the arrow whipped through the air once again. He hit the target on third try and then didn't miss again.

He passed the bow to Langston and grinned at me. "I must have the *steadiest* breath," he said. "We can do breathing training later if you want some extra practice."

"You're an idiot," I said. "But nice shooting."

Langston's first shot didn't even leave the bow—he didn't knock the arrow properly, and it simply fell to his feet when he let go. The rest of his shots weren't much better, with the furthest one only reaching halfway to the target. Each of his movements was stiff, like those of a creaky old man.

I patted him on the shoulder. "That's alright," I said.

"I'm not worried," he said, matter-of-factly. "I'll get better. Just need a couple books and some more lessons."

Willie took the bow from him and immediately eyed the target, stretching the string back, an arrow nestled between his fingers. He released with a *thwang* and the arrow hurtled towards the target, hitting dead center.

"Woah," I said.

"How did you—?" Peter stammered.

Willie, as usual, didn't say a word. He re-strung his bow, and took aim again, shooting another arrow just outside the first. By the time he was finished, all ten of his arrows were inside the smallest ring of the target.

He turned around, his face betraying no emotion. Absolutely none. I would've been bouncing off the walls, rubbing it in Peter's face, but not Willie. He didn't say a word, just sat the bow down next to the post and walked over to us.

"Where did you learn to shoot like that?" Langston said.

Willie shrugged.

Lieutenant Wes had us repeat the exercise four more times, and I eventually put an arrow on the outer edge of the target. Langston managed to get one nearly all the way there, and Peter continued to get better, though never quite besting Willie, who was nearly perfect.

Next was the archery obstacle course. Makeshift dirt piles and garbage cans stood at increments throughout the course, along with a series of targets. The object: hit as many targets as possible while running over and around obstacles.

I stood at the starting line, sweat sliding down my forehead. My hand gripped the curved wood of the bow. Lieutenant Wes gave me the go-ahead, and I took off down the course, shooting arrows at the targets as I went. I missed badly on the first few, but finally hit the target as I was running past a garbage can. Stunned, I came to a stop and admired my marksmanship. Only when Lieutenant Wes yelled at me – jerking me back to the present – did I remember I still needed to finish the rest of the course.

After everyone had gone through once, Lieutenant Wes called for our attention.

"This is something we don't usually get to for a few months," he said. "So listen carefully: speed is paramount when shooting on the move. Your accuracy will go down no matter what, so shoot as early and as often as possible. To do that, you want to have easy access to your arrows."

He removed three arrows from his quiver and slid them

between the fingers of his right hand. He held his hand up, the arrows dangling. He raced down the course, firing an arrow every two seconds. When he'd fired each one in his hand, he grabbed three more from his quiver, again nestling them between his fingers. He darted between dirt mounds like a jackrabbit, firing three more arrows in rapid succession—all nailing the target. After he finished the course, he jogged back to us, breathing heavily but smiling.

"Don't worry about shooting through your stock of arrows," he said. "You have enough in your quiver, and you can always pick up more later."

We all went through the course a few more times, but no one, not even Willie, was as skillful as Lieutenant Wes at getting through the course.

After archery we went to the fighting pit, a sandy area surrounded by a wooden fence. Racks of blunt wooden blades stood on one side. We were one of the first groups there and got a good look at the lieutenant waiting. On his green uniform was the name tag *Lt. Ulysses*. Unlike Lieutenant Wes, who was built like an ox, Lieutenant Ulysses was, well…pretty normal. He was tall, and had long fingers, but he wasn't anywhere near as intimidating as Wes.

When the other squads finally gathered around, bringing with them a musky body odor, Ulysses pointed at me. "You," he said in a husky voice. "Grab a sword."

I looked from side to side at Langston and Peter. *Me?*

"Uhh, lieutenant, are you…are you sure?" I said.

"Grab a sparring sword," he repeated.

Peter shoved me, and I jogged to the wooden swords, all of which were dinged up with scratches and kinks. I grabbed one and turned to face Lieutenant Ulysses. The blade felt heavier than a tree trunk. Ulysses' mouth curved into a thin smile.

"It's just wood," he said. "Nothing to be afraid of. Now, I want you to attack me like your life depends on it."

I nodded but stood still. I didn't want to go anywhere near him.

"Can't expect a Forcie to be much of a fighter," someone called out. A round of laughter rang out.

"Attack me!" Ulysses said, more forcefully.

I ran forward, swinging the blade at him. He blocked the swing easily and parried my sword away.

"The fighters with the showy moves," he said to the group, "and those with intimidating muscles, aren't the ones to be scared of."

Ulysses parried another of my blows.

"They are often overconfident, which can be used against them."

He faked low before switching his stance and swinging high. I managed to block it with my sword, but my feet dug a few inches into the sand.

"The key is to allow your opponent to think he has agency. So when I fake left"—and he did—"you think to block and come right." Which I did. "You believe that you are reading my every move, that you are acting of your own free will."

He faked right this time, and I parried his blow. Quickly, I spun and swung, backhanded, into where Ulysses stood—or where he had stood a split second before.

His wooden blade rested firmly against my neck, sending shivers down my spine. "But really," he said, "I am the one telling you what your next move will be. *I* have the agency."

An hour later, we jogged over to the Mess Hall for lunch. Thankfully we didn't see Carl and the rest of his squad, and I got to enjoy all three of my turkey sandwiches in peace. Jenna met up with us shortly afterward, carrying her own plate packed heavy with food.

"How was training?" she asked.

"Not going to be able to move tomorrow," said Langston. "But other than that it was good. What did they have you doing in nurses training?"

"Just listened to a bunch of people give speeches. They said we'll be learning how to make ointments, do proper sterilization techniques, all that stuff."

"Are you going to be transferred to a hospital?" Willie asked.

I nearly spit up my half-chewed bite of turkey sandwich. He had finally spoken. Langston and Peter stared at him, stunned.

Willie looked around. "What?" he said.

"Nothing," said Jenna, giving me an annoyed look. "Most nurses are stationed in hospitals around the country. A few, like me, are with squads. So I guess you guys are stuck with me."

Willie nodded and said nothing more. He chewed on his sandwich thoughtfully and then took a long swig from a glass of milk.

"Are you going to go through Tactics and Strategy with us," I asked. "Or—"

"I think they're going to let me go back and forth, so long as I pass these nursing quizzes," Jenna said. "I'm with you the rest of the day."

"Did they tell you anything about who our squad lieutenant is going to be?" Langston asked Jenna. "We're supposed to find out today."

Jenna shook her head.

"Hopefully he's okay with us beating the crap out of Carl," said Peter.

We scarfed down the rest of our lunch and walked over to the looming brown tower filled with classrooms. The brown paint was flecked with black soot, and the bricks were on the verge of crumbling. Flocks of soldiers passed us in every direction, some doing physical training, others making their way to the mess hall or another classroom. Everywhere, a sea of green-uniformed bodies swam past each other.

A stern man walked past with three silver stars on his chest. "What are those for?" I asked, pointing in a way I hoped was discreet.

Naturally it was Langston who answered. "The stars are for rank," he said. "One star is special officer, followed by lieutenant, corporal, captain, and, finally, general. With each bump in rank, you get privileges."

"Like what?" I asked.

"Some are big—like better quarters so you don't have to share a room with anyone, or a higher monthly stipend. Some are small like permission to grow a mustache or beard."

Lieutenant Yawkey's mustache floated through my memory.

"How do you get bumped up?" Peter asked. "Like, what if I wanted to be a general? How long would that take?"

"Really long," said Langston. "I've heard it can take twenty years. Sometimes longer. But once you're a general, you get to sit in on high-level meetings, strategize military plans, live in the generals' village in whatever city you want. It's pretty luxurious."

Arcton City had its own generals' village, close to the Orb. It was gated and under high security, with blackhats monitoring every entrance, but Peter and I had snuck in a couple times just to check it out. All the generals drove these slick black cars, smoking cigarettes out the window.

"It'd be nice if they gave us at least one star to start," said Peter.

I picked at the cloth on my shirt. There was never going to be a star there, and I could never imagine having a car. Only the generals and a few high-ranking government officials did.

"Our handbook says we don't have any title because we haven't earned it yet," Langston said. "So instead they just call us by our last names."

"Have you read the *entire* handbook already?" I asked.

Langston nodded sheepishly.

"We need to find you a girlfriend," Peter said.

"You can lend him one of yours," said Jenna.

"I would, but they're all back in Arcton City."

We finally found our way through the faded, yellow-tiled halls and joined the group of people standing outside our classroom. I recognized a few faces from the Mess Hall – they were the ones who sneered and flipped us off. Thankfully the door opened and the calls of "*Forcie*" subsided as everyone filed into the classroom.

I followed Langston into a cluster of seats in the third row, while the corporal shuffled some of his papers at the podium up front. Just as the corporal cleared his throat to address the class, the door opened abruptly and a lieutenant walked in. He looked at no one but the corporal.

"Corporal Daniels, is Squad 19 in this classroom?" he said.

Annoyed, the corporal combed the list in front of him. "Yes," he said. "Squad 19?"

We all stood. "Yes, sir," we said in unison.

The lieutenant spoke. "With me," he said, walking out the door without an attempt at an explanation. Confused, we gathered our backpacks and went out into the hall.

"You are to report back to your barrack," the lieutenant said once we got outside. "Your squad leader requested you be taught in private, with him." He walked briskly away.

"What kind of lieutenant wants to teach us in our barrack?" Peter asked.

"Probably doesn't want to trek all the way across Base Camp," I said. "Figures we'll be dead in a few weeks anyway, so why waste the energy?"

The sun beat down on us and my shoulders sweated where the straps were as we made the long journey back to Barrack 19. Our door was slightly ajar, and standing in the classroom portion, with the desks set up in a neat semi-circle, was a man with his back to us, a long black ponytail lying flat against his uniform.

He turned to face us. "Hello," he said, pushing up his thick-cut glasses with his finger and giving us a wide, bright smile. "I'm Memo. Please, sit down."

7. MEMO

"Please, sit down," Memo repeated again, motioning towards the desks. "We have a lot of work to do, and not much time to do it."

I took a seat in the center desk. Memo's smile was broad and genuine—the first such expression I'd seen from a superior all day.

"It's great to finally meet you face to face," Memo said. "I've been anxious to get to know you all. No doubt you've had a tumultuous couple days. I'm sure your heads are spinning at the moment, but you'll get used to life at Base Camp soon enough."

His voice was soft, but he pronounced every word perfectly, each syllable crisper than a knife cutting an apple. I'd never seen a uniform so perfectly fitted—the collar was straight and orderly, his belt shiny and new. There were no wrinkles on his shirt, and his pants were perfectly pressed. He was clearly someone who followed the rules.

I shifted in my seat, trying to get comfortable. Peter sat to my right and Willie to my left, our elbows grazing in the cramped desks. Willie sat with perfect posture, his hands folded neatly in his lap. Pete had never seemed so focused in his life; he took in every word Memo said. No wisecracks, no sideways glances at me.

"Your Tactics and Strategy training is going to be a little different from that of the other squads," Memo continued. "I've been granted permission to teach you rather than have you in the lecture with everyone else."

Jenna's hand shot up.

"Yes, Jenna," Memo said.

"How come you're our leader and not a lieutenant?" she said. Just then, a ray of light reflected off one of four stars on his chest. Why would a *captain* be teaching us? I sat up a little straighter.

"There were reasons," Memo said. "Several. But the only one relevant to you is that I was tired of my typical duties. I wanted to be closer to the action."

"You're fighting with us?" Peter asked. My hopes immediately perked up—we'd be invincible with a captain in our group.

"I actually offered, Peter, but unfortunately the line was drawn. They don't want me to be the oldest Verdean soldier ever to enter into battle."

I raised my hand.

"Yes, Leo?"

"How do you know our names, sir?"

He smiled. "There's a reason I'm a captain. But I'd like you to hold off on questions for a second. I'll explain everything in due time. First, I want to ask you all a question: What is war?"

I raised my eyebrows. That was kind of a dumb question. *What is war?* People killing each other seemed like too obvious an answer. Fighting for food and resources did, too.

Langston gave it a go. "War is an armed conflict between two groups."

"A very good answer, Langston," Memo said. "In the literal

sense, you are absolutely right. But in order to understand what something *is* you need to understand what *causes* it. And in that case war is actually a lack of understanding. It's the inability between two groups to peacefully coexist. Does that make sense?"

"Yes, sir!" we said in unison. Our response together felt rigid, out of place.

Memo smiled again, warmly and widely.

"I appreciate the enthusiasm," he said. "But there will be no need to say *Yes, sir*, unless you actually do understand what I'm saying. I'm more interested in a conversation than absolute obedience. Understood?"

"Yes—sorry, sir," I said. "Understood."

"Good," said Memo. "A second question, then: Why are you fighting this war?"

"'Cause I was dumb enough to follow Leo on a nightwalk," said Peter.

A more reluctant smile from Memo this time. "That's true. And the reason Arcton is fighting this war with Trussel is because a peace treaty was broken. Trussel got greedy and decided to raid a few of our oil reserves. Which brings me to my next question: How is this war different from others, say, a war one hundred years ago?"

"No guns," said Langston. "No planes, rifles, grenades. The technology has regressed over the past few decades."

"Exactly right. The technological devolution has transformed the battlefield from one fought thousands of miles away to one fought close up with swords and bows. And because of that, we've had to adapt our fighting style, our tactics, in order to succeed. Last question: What is success?"

"Winning the war," Peter said. I nodded in agreement.

"Not in this case," said Memo. "Success is staying alive. Success is everyone here completing their prescribed term of service and getting back to their families."

I wasn't the only one that raised my eyebrows this time.

All I'd ever heard about was sacrificing for the good of Arcton. Putting your country before self. Yet here Memo was, telling us that staying alive was the most important thing. And why was a captain leading a squad of Forcies? None of this made sense.

"Success is sending five soldiers out and having five soldiers return," Memo said. "Is that clear?"

"Yes, sir!"

"Good. Now let's get started."

Memo pulled down a map of Trussel from the blackboard. It was only half the size of Arcton but had just as many inhabitants.

"Does anyone know the name of this city?" he asked, pointing to a large black dot on the map.

Of course only one person did. "Wendwerth, sir," said Langston. "The biggest port in Trussel."

Memo did this for every city, river, strategic stronghold, and port in Trussel. Langston knew every last one of them. Memo would point to a place on the map, Langston would recite its name, and then Memo would discuss why it was key for Trussel and why combat would likely take place there. After two hours of this, it was on to attack and defense strategies.

"You'll be employing a guerrilla warfare style," said Memo. "Which means it'll just be you five out there—maybe with another squadron or two—on most of your rangings. You'll be gone for a week or two at a time, possibly longer. The goal is to…"

"Stay alive," we recited.

"Yes, and to do that you need to engage the enemy when you're in a position of power." He pointed to another spot on the map. "Now, let's pretend you're in between a mountain and a river. And, let's say there's a Trusselian food envoy here. If you attack right away, your retreat path is arduous, either up a mountain or crossing over water. Not to mention you'll already be tired from the attack."

He pointed to another spot.

"But, if you wait until the food envoy moves a mile further down the road, you can attack coming from the mountain—a position of power—and trap the enemy beside the river. Remember: always use your surroundings to your advantage."

We went through dozens of these scenarios—how to infiltrate a village, the best way to retreat after an open field attack, drawbacks of fighting during the day rather than at night—with Memo discussing every possible angle, anything that might happen. Once or twice, Langston actually suggested another strategy that could be used. I thought for sure Memo would yell at Langston, remind him that he was just a Forcie. But, instead, he asked Langston to explain himself. Each time Memo agreed with him.

Every hour Memo gave us five-minute breaks, but still I started dozing in my chair, looking longingly at the bed waiting for me just a few feet away. I poked myself with my pencil every five seconds, trying to stay awake.

"I think that's enough for today," Memo finally said. "But before I leave, I'd like to spend some time meditating. I don't think any of you have done this before."

"What is it?" I asked.

"It's thinking of nothing while still having intention."

"So, sleeping?" I said hopefully.

"Not quite," said Memo. "It's another way to rejuvenate and strengthen your mind and body, though."

"Sounds a lot like sleeping to me," whispered Pete. He had bags under his eyes.

"If you all would sit up straight in your chairs... Now, close your eyes, and I want you to focus on your breath. Breathe in through your nose and out through your mouth... Good. Now, again... Don't focus on anything but your breath. Breathe in, breathe out..."

I jerked awake with a start, quickly looking around the room. Peter was laughing, and Jenna was shaking her head in disappointment. Langston and Willie both smiled.

Memo's face was unreadable. On the very first day of Basic Training, I fell asleep.

"Would you like to splash some water on your face?" Memo asked.

"Huh?"

"You're tired. Would you like to go splash some water on your face to wake up?"

"I'm okay… Thanks," I added hesitantly.

"Okay, let's continue."

We practiced meditation for another thirty minutes, during which it took everything in my power not to doze again. Finally, Memo dismissed us for dinner.

"How could you fall asleep, Leo?" Jenna asked. "I can't believe he didn't punish you." The sun had set. Lights on posts lit up the road. We were some of the few people heading towards the Mess Hall. Everyone else seemed to be walking back to their barracks.

One girl passed us, with dark skin and her hair tied in a long braid, that looked no older than ten.

"There's no way *she's* in the Verdean," I said. "She's younger than Jexter."

"She's not," said Langston. "Probably a daughter of one of the captains or generals."

"Speaking of, Memo seems…different," said Peter. "Did anyone else get that?" We followed the road past a wash station and the commissary. The Mess Hall finally came into view.

"He's the first captain we've met," said Jenna. "Maybe they're all like that?"

"I don't think so," Langston said. "Lieutenants want to be like captains, right? No lieutenant we've met would offer Leo cold water rather than a punishment."

Peter chimed in. "And no lieutenant would let Langston run his big mouth like that, correcting what he was saying."

"That's actually a good point," Langston said.

"I don't know if I can do another day of this, let alone two weeks," groaned Jenna. "My feet are killing me."

"First day's the toughest," I said. "It'll get better from here on out."

I kept my tone upbeat even though I was feeling anything but. After all, Jenna was here, miserable, because of me.

When we finally reached the doors, it felt like I hadn't seen the Mess Hall for days. The hall was only a quarter full of soldiers, each carrying a metal tray. We got into line, stuffed our plates with chicken, rice, and corn and sat down.

"Leo!" someone yelled. I turned in time to see a long mane of black hair, and then a giant hug knocked the wind out of me.

No. It couldn't be. She shouldn't be here.

"Irene…"

Her smile was wide and contagious when she released me, and her blue eyes twinkled. My heart soared before it came crashing down again. I wanted to kiss her then and there, but I didn't. She was wearing a white nurse's uniform. And I was heartbroken.

"You shouldn't be here," I said.

"I had to," she said. There was no self-pity, no sadness in her voice. She spoke matter-of-factly. "Dad turned me in. I didn't have a choice in the matter."

"Your own dad?" said Jenna.

"Didn't want to risk getting thrown in jail—imagine that." Irene's smile faded a little.

"What a prick," I said. "Never liked him."

"Shut up and scoot over," she said. She held out her hand to Langston. "I'm Irene, who are you?"

Langston and, surprisingly, Willie both greeted her warmly. She hugged Peter and Jenna, who were both just as surprised to see her as I was.

"Are you in the field or hospital?" Jenna asked.

"I'm going to be in the Base Camp hospital, unfortunately," Irene said. I sighed with relief. At least she'd be safe. "I wish I could be in the field with you guys, though."

"I wish Jenna was at a hospital," I said.

"I would've volunteered to be with you, anyway," Jenna said. "No way was I going to be left back while you were all fighting."

"I tried to volunteer for the same," said Irene, "But apparently my dad's love carries just far enough to keep me out of the field. How's your first day been? I only just got here."

I let Peter fill her in. He didn't stop talking until we'd finished dinner. On our way back to the barrack, I stayed behind with Irene while the others walked on.

"I missed you," I said. "I didn't know if you'd heard what happened."

"My dad found out pretty quickly. You should've seen how pissed he was, throwing lamps, breaking plates."

"He didn't hurt you, did he?"

"Not physically, no." She barely met my eyes.

I pulled her into a hug, running my fingers through the back of her hair. Somewhere near us, machines churned in the background, a low hum disrupting our silence. Her dad had betrayed her.

"I'm sorry," I said.

"For what? My dad? I should be the one that's sorry. You,

Peter, and Jenna are all in the Verdean because of me."

"I wanted that book just as badly—"

"You guys are actually going into the field." Irene's eyes watered as they searched my own. "I'm just sitting back in a stupid hospital, in no real danger. And you might die."

"I'm not going to die, and this isn't your fault," I said. "I wanted to read *Dasher's Revenge* more than anything. I was just... We were stupid. It should just be me here, not anyone else."

"At least I get to see you still," she said, kissing me. Her lips were a welcome warmth, but the feeling didn't override my guilt. It was my fault that the people I cared about were here. I'd been the one desperate to read *Dasher's Revenge*. And all because of *Gestalt Diary,* a stupid book of which I couldn't even remember the plot.

We broke apart as we neared the nurses' barracks. The Orb light gave her shadow a green tinge as she walked away.

I returned to Barrack 19 and quickly got my washroom pouch out of my duffel. Peter and Langston were already waiting at the front door. Willie stayed on the bed.

"You coming?" I asked him.

He shook his head. "I'll shower later."

It was the third time he'd spoken all day.

"Weird kid," said Peter once we'd gotten outside.

We showered and brushed our teeth quickly and were back in bed in no time. Willie was still in bed, playing a harmonica, having apparently decided he didn't want to shower at all. I climbed into the top bunk, right above Peter. I was as almost as good as asleep as I slipped under the covers, but when my head hit the pillow, I heard a crinkling sound. I reached under and pulled out a long, yellow slip of paper.

My heart started racing. I turned it over in my now sweaty palms. On it, in scratchy handwriting, was a note:

Section 342, number 2-5.

8. ARCALAEUS

"What does it mean?" I asked Langston, showing him the paper the next morning. If anyone knew the answer, it would be him.

He held it up to the light and then brought it to his nose, inhaling the scent. He rubbed the paper between his fingers.

"No idea," he said, handing it back.

"Oh, come on! You know every President in Trussel's history, but you can't tell me what this stupid message means?"

"Sorry, Leo." He shrugged. "Just not that much to go on. Best I can say is it looks like a kid wrote it, and it smells like someone spilled lemon juice on it."

Big help. I finished tying my boots, and Langston and I jogged to catch up with the others, already on their way to the obstacle course. I was eager to get another chance at Carl, but when we reached the course, his squad wasn't there. I stood on tiptoe, trying to see over the heads of everyone next to us. No sight of Carl or his group.

Lieutenant Yawkey yelled at us to get into position. Our group was even better this time through the obstacle course, and without anyone there to trip me, we easily finished first. Still, we needed to go clean the lavatories afterward as our punishment for having come in last yesterday. On the walk over, I took the opportunity to show the others the note.

"But…how did someone get that into your barrack?" Jenna asked. "We were there the entire afternoon."

"Weren't there during the morning or for dinner," Peter said. "Would've been easy for someone to sneak a piece of paper in."

"But what does it mean?" I asked. "Section 342, number 2-5?"

Everyone was stumped.

Over the remainder of the week, I became obsessed with it. Trying to figure it out and wondering where Carl's squad had gone took up most of my waking thoughts. The rest went to remembering Memo's teachings.

Each afternoon, sore and exhausted from the obstacle course, archery, and sword fighting, we got to sit inside hot and stuffy Barrack 19, where Memo would greet us with a most un-Verdean smile and begin throwing a tornado of information at us to memorize: the thirty-two different edible plants in Trussel (and what they looked like), the specific outfits civilians wore (simple white shirts and jeans for the girls, the same but black shirts for the boys), diversion tactics, retreat formations, and solutions and mixtures to cure poisons. For five or six hours every afternoon.

From what we heard in the Mess Hall, it sounded like other soldiers' Tactics and Strategy sessions spanned a few hours a day at most. They learned about fighting formations and maybe some diversions tactics, but they weren't forced to memorize anything. In fact, most of their Tactics and Strategy sessions were spent back in the fighting pit or archery ranges.

Stab, stab, overhand blow. I blocked and backpedaled, trying my best to keep Peter in front while clouds of dust kicked up between us. Peter was getting faster—stronger, too—he poked at my legs and I jumped away. He grinned, poking again, playing with me.

"You think you're funny, huh?" I said. It had been two weeks since we'd arrived at Base Camp, and as usual, Peter was running circles around me in the fighting pit. Langston and Willie had left a little earlier for lunch, but Peter and I had wanted to get some more work in. A number of pairs from other squads were still sparring as well.

"I just like seeing you dance," Peter said. "Never knew you were so nimble."

My footwork was getting stronger, and I was able to side-step a few of Peter's blows and get a strike in now and then. Every once in a while Lieutenant Ulysses would give us some pointers – demonstrate countermoves like blocks-into-lunges, parries-into-spins, side-steps-into-punches.

"The sword is not your only weapon when fighting," Ulysses said. "Your leg, your free arm…everything is fair game."

"Sir, why don't we get shields?" I asked.

"We don't have the steel for it," Ulysses said. "But don't worry, neither does Trussel."

It seemed like there was plenty of steel in Base Camp or in Arcton—there were enough trucks and swords to go around—but maybe it was a different kind of steel?

Peter slashed out again, nailing my arm with the blunted blade. A searing pain shot up my biceps, leaving my arm limp.

"Ow!" I said.

"You alright?" said Peter.

"Yeah, fine. I wish I could just spar Langston."

"Wanna spar me?"

I turned. Leaning against the outer edge of the fighting pit with some of his friends and a few nurses was Carl-the-cleft-chin. He looked taller than I remembered, and his sleeves were rolled up to show bulging biceps.

No, I didn't want to spar him either.

"Where've you been?" I said. "Thought we'd get another shot at you on the obstacle course."

"We were on a ranging," Carl said. His dirty-blonde hair was perfectly combed in a curl over his forehead; his teeth gleamed in the sunlight. He crossed his arms. "When you survive in battle, the Verdean lets you come back to Base Camp for a bit to rest up. You won't have to worry about that, though, since it'll be one-and-done for you."

His friends laughed loudly.

Peter raised his eyebrows. "Do they actually think that was funny? Or is this one of those things where because you're the leader everyone has to laugh at everything you say?"

"You've got quite a mouth on you," Carl lashed out. "I'll shut it up after I beat your friend." He tossed a white tablet into his mouth, jumped down into the dirt, and picked up a spare sparring sword from a rack. "It was Belfin, right?" he said, rounding on me. "Tough to keep track. I get all you Forcies mixed up."

Without waiting, he heaved his sword high and brought it swiftly down. I reached up and blocked it, but before I had time to think, his sword was on its way down again. I parried and spun into him, shoving him back and slashing out. He swung my sword aside with a flick of his wrist.

I wiped sweat from my forehead and shifted my weight back and forth, waiting for the next blow.

Carl grinned up at the others. "Not bad for a Forcie," he said. "Should I finish him now?"

He didn't wait for a response. He swung his sword sideways, connecting with my shoulder before I could react. Wood hit bone, it felt like my arm could be broken, but I didn't hear a crack. He gathered again and slashed at my chest, knocking the wind out of me with the blunted blade. I fell to a knee and looked up in time to see him swinging again.

Out of nowhere, Peter stepped in and blocked his blade. He kicked at Carl, pushing him back.

"You got him," Peter said. "He's down. Why are you still fighting? We're on the same side."

"I'm not on your side," Carl said. "I volunteered for this. You didn't. I'm going to be a General one day. You're all cowards heading for an early grave."

Peter smirked as he pointed his sword at Carl, challenging him. "Should be an easy for you then."

I got to my feet and backed up against the wall, still clutching my arm.

Carl charged Peter, swinging swiftly at his head. Peter dodged the blade, and poked out his own, nipping Carl in the chest.

Carl recoiled, looking stunned. He twirled his sword around his body, a showy move but one that really just meant he wanted time to recover.

Peter wasn't having it. He rushed forward, feinting left before switching and coming from his stronger right side with a furious blow. Their swords met, letting loose a loud, dull thud.

Peter had the momentum and swung out again, this time low, clipping Carl's leg.

Carl hobbled, grimacing in pain. His once-perfect hair was now a scraggly mess. Without pausing, Peter came forward with his blade raised. Carl dug his left foot into the ground and kicked up a cloud of dirt straight at Peter. When he reflexively covered his eyes, Carl danced around and struck Peter in the back.

Still wiping the dirt out of his eyes, Peter slashed out behind him, but missed Carl by a good foot.

The snock had called us cowards, yet here he was kicking dirt in a sparring session.

"You've got it, Pete," I said.

With his face covered in dirt, Peter charged one more time. Carl was able to block his swing, but he couldn't block Peter's body, which slammed into Carl at full speed. Carl crashed hard to the ground and his sword went flying.

Peter leaned over him, his sword aimed at Carl's head.

"That's enough, Herbert," a voice called. Lieutenant Ulysses jogged over. "Enough. Magner, this isn't your time to spar. You can get out of here. You two, with me," Ulysses said, pointing to Pete and me. Carl gingerly got to his feet and climbed out of the fighting pit to join his squad, several of whom glared at me and

Pete as we walked away with Lieutenant Ulysses.

I slapped Peter on the back. "That was awesome! Carl didn't stand a chance. What a little snock, kicking dirt up at you like that."

"Everything's fair game in battle," said Ulysses. "It might seem dirty to you now, but if your life is on the line, you'd better be willing to do whatever it takes." He turned to face both of us, his brow furrowed, suddenly serious, his long blonde hair flowing in the wind. "And you need to be careful with Magner over there. He's a pain in the ass, but his family is even worse. His dad's a general and can make your life miserable if he wants to. I'd stay away from Carl if I were you."

We both nodded. I wasn't going to avoid Carl, though. If he wanted to fight, we weren't backing down.

"Now head to lunch."

Dark gray clouds began to roll in over Mt. Brentwood, funneling down the coast into Base Camp. Peter and I walked briskly, reliving the fight but eager to get under cover of the Mess Hall before the rain hit.

"I guess that's why he thinks he'll be a general," I said. "His dad's one."

"Wish my dad was a general," said Pete.

I didn't say anything. Truth be told, I was more likely to become a general than Uncle Lester. He never exactly inspired loyalty. Most nights he fell asleep on the couch, a glass of whiskey in hand. On the rare occasions he showed any interest in me or Pete, it was to insult us.

My dad could've been a general. He worked at the Conservation

Department, and was pretty high up. But that came with consequences: working late into the night, people showing up at our house with requests for even more work. He was well-liked, though – at least that's what Aunt Helen told me.

Geoff Belfin would smile and wave at everyone on the street, and, even crazier, everyone would wave back.

Peter continued. "Remember when my dad asked my mom to make chocolate chip cookies for his birthday?"

"Oh, yeah. And Jenna wanted to help, but she had no idea what she was doing and used pepper instead of salt in the mix?"

"And my dad started sneezing like crazy. He had that fit, remember? Couldn't stop sneezing and finally went outside…" He started laughing.

"…And walked straight into the rake, which came up and hit him in the balls," I finished for him. We were both cracking up as we entered the Mess Hall. The others had apparently finished lunch, so we ate quickly and left for the usual routine with Memo in Barrack 19.

"I can't wait to get out into the field," Peter said. "I'm done sweating my face off in that room all day. Every time you raise your arm, it smells like a cow farted."

"You're the one with a pool of sweat next to you every day," I said.

He smiled. "You'll know what it's like once you mature and get armpit hair."

"Two months!" I said. "You get armpit hair two months before me and you go walking around like you're some Supersoldier."

Memo and the others were outside Barrack 19 waiting for us. "Heard you had an interesting sparring session," Memo said.

"How did you hear that already?" I asked.

"I overheard Carl talking about a fight in the sparring pit," Langston said. "He looked pretty bloodied up. Didn't take much to figure out he fought Peter."

"It could've been me that fought him," I said, offended.

"Judging by your bruises, you fought him first," said Langston.

I expected an overly protective comment from Jenna, but she and Willie were in quiet conversation behind Langston. They'd been hanging out a lot over the past two weeks. Apparently Jenna was the only one Willie felt comfortable enough to talk with at length. It looked like there could be…something…starting between them, but there was no way I was going to say anything. Jenna was vicious when it came to my being overprotective.

"What are we doing today?" Peter asked Memo.

"I know you'll be deeply saddened to hear that we won't be doing Tactics and Strategy today," Memo said. "There's been a special speech called, so we're going to the amphitheater instead."

"Who's giving the speech?" Jenna asked. "You?"

"I'm not nearly important enough. No, it's Arcalaeus."

"*Arcalaeus?*" I immediately perked up. The president was going to give a speech for *us?*

"Why's he here?" Langston asked. "Doesn't he have more important things to worry about?"

"I don't know the reason," Memo said, "but we don't want to be late."

The amphitheater was squeezed between the Captains' Offices and the beginning of a long stretch of trees that shot up Mt. Brentwood. Hundreds of soldiers stood on huge stone ledges in a semi-circle around the main stage, each wearing the Verdean green. Conversations buzzed in anticipation of Arcalaeus's arrival. The gray clouds had followed us to the amphitheater and were now closing in, threatening rain.

I'd never seen the president in person, only pictures—a portrait of Arcalaeus hung over every entryway to a government building. He had a lined face with wispy white hair and sunken eyes. He always wore a soft smile that didn't reveal his teeth and made his cheeks look sunken. I'd heard him speak a few times, of course, on the radio after major events, like when we first went to war with Trussel. Despite his feeble looks, he was youthful in the way he spoke, even through the crackling radio. There was energy, confidence. I often didn't know exactly what he was talking about, it always sounded right.

Memo left us at the top of the amphitheater and went to stand with the other captains. The five of us were able to squeeze our way into a far corner on one of the upper stone ledges, where a few clumps of grass had managed to grow through the stone. Raindrops landed on the back of my neck, and I shuddered.

A short man wearing a suit walked out of the right corner of the amphitheater. Even from this high up, I could see him adjust his tie as he walked slowly to the podium on stage. A hush went through the crowd.

Peter elbowed me unnecessarily. "That's him."

Arcalaeus at last reached the podium, bracing himself against it with both hands. He took in the scene for a few seconds, apparently in no rush.

Arcalaeus held out his hands in a wide embrace. "Comrades," he said. "I stand before you, a humble servant. Your strength, your indomitable spirit, has been so admirable over the past few years that I feel lucky to be called your president. In fact, it is the single greatest honor of my life.

"I did not enter into this war lightly. The taking of lives is no easy thing, and yet the courage you all have shown has been nothing short of legendary.

"Unfortunately, in war, and in life, we sometimes lose those we love. Our friends and family members pass away. Whether it be by old age or disease, or through fighting to preserve the safety of your families and the integrity for which Arcton stands, we must endure these hardships.

"Yes, we have lost lives in this war. But those we have lost will not be forgotten—they will forever be remembered in the Gilded Library, where captains, generals, and lieutenants will read about their heroics that helped save the future of Arcton."

A huge roar burst out from the crowd. The rain fell heavier now, water soaking my hair and my back. Langston grabbed my arm.

"What?" I said, keeping my head trained on Arcalaeus.

"The library!"

"Yeah?"

Arcalaeus raised a hand, and the roar died down quickly. He

waited for complete silence before he continued.

"*Section 342, number 2-5*," Langston whispered. "That's a reference to books. The Gilded Library. It's here in Base Camp."

"Of course!"

"Shh!" Jenna said.

"...Be honest with you," Arcalaeus continued. "The war is not going well right now. Trussel is a worthy opponent who hit us first and hit us hard. They are pushing in on our perimeter, getting closer to our oil reserves and our cities. They are getting closer, every day, to our friends and families that we love so dearly.

"But when we fight as one, we are invincible. When every general can rely on his captains, when every captain can rely on his lieutenants, and when every lieutenant can rely on his subordinates, the Verdean's outlook for the war and for the future is one of hope and success. That *oneness* is the key to the order around us. It sows the fields we use to grow crops, forges the steel we use to fight, and harbors the love we use to protect one another.

"So we will continue to fight. And in these dark times, we look to our soldiers to show us what it means to be an Arctonian. We look to our soldiers to be brave and fight not for themselves, but for Arcton and what Arcton stands for: togetherness, selflessness, and the good of the people!"

All around, soldiers were stomping their feet, creating a buzz.

"Live faithfully! Fight bravely!" Arcalaeus yelled.

"Live faithfully! Fight bravely!" we all echoed, and then the rain from above turned into a torrential downpour. Everyone began yelling, jumping up and down, though I couldn't tell if it was in response to the speech or, for some reason, the rain. Unsure what to do, I joined in. Next to me, Peter's face was wild with excitement, water matting down his hair and drops spilling down his cheeks.

The scene continued for a few minutes with Arcalaeus staying on stage, welcoming it like a father does his son. Finally, with no hint that the yelling and screaming and rain would ever die down, Arcalaeus gave us a wave before leaving the podium.

I turned to Langston.

"We've gotta go find the Gilded Library," I said, pushing my way through the sea of soldiers filing out of the amphitheater.

"Right now?" Langston said.

"Yeah, right now! Someone wanted me to find those books – I need to know what's in there."

"Squad 19," I heard from behind us. I turned. Memo had gotten back to us quickly. His glasses had fogged in the rain, and water bounced off his jacket. "Let's meet back at the barrack. I have one more lesson before your first ranging tomorrow."

I groaned. Tomorrow? But what about the rest of our training. What about the Gilded Library? And what about Irene? I'd been so busy the past couple weeks that I'd barely gotten a chance to see her. Would I be able to say goodbye?

Still in a fog of my own thoughts, I followed the others into the Mess Hall to eat dinner. We headed straight to the barrack afterward. Darkness had fallen and the curfew would soon be in effect. Memo stood just inside the front door, beads of water still clasping onto his forehead, his shirt fully buttoned.

"Please come in and take a seat," he said, smiling widely at us.

The room immediately seemed off when we walked in, though it took me a minute to figure out why. Then I saw it: rather than arranged next to the chalkboard like usual, the desks formed a circle right next to our bunk beds.

Memo closed the door. "We're doing something a little different," he said. "You've worked extremely hard the past few weeks, so rather than a typical lesson, I thought we should discuss my own fighting days. Back when I was a member of a small squad called the Sphelix."

9. THE SPHELIX

"The Sphelix?" Peter said, as though tasting the words on his lips.

"The Sphelix," said Memo. Before he could elaborate, a knock came at the door and, without waiting for an answer, a skinny officer with the beginnings of a mustache walked in. Without so much as a hello, he began to blow out the candles in each of their sconces.

"Would you mind leaving those?" Memo asked politely.

"Rules are rules," said the officer, not bothering to check who he was talking to.

"Rules are indeed rules," Memo said, "But I wish to speak with my squad, and doing so in the darkness will likely make that endeavor needlessly difficult."

This time the officer, a long-nosed pasty man about six inches shorter than Memo, took the time to see who dared talk back to him. He stopped dead in his tracks when he saw the four silver stars attached to Memo's breast. "I'm sorry, sir, I—I didn't realize you were in here."

"Perfectly understandable," said Memo with a nod. "Now, if you'll please excuse us."

The officer's face turned a deep red as he left, and the rest of us sat down. Memo closed the door behind him and walked over with a slight smile on his face. His uniform was soaked through.

"As I was saying," Memo continued, "back when I was just a little older than you, I fought in the Verdean with a group of soldiers that eventually became my best friends. We hated referring to ourselves as Squad 571—it felt like we were a shipment of grains, not people—and after a while, our lieutenant began calling us a different name. The Sphelix – which, he said, he learned from his grandma's stories. The Sphelix was an ancient group of warriors that fought hundreds of years ago.

"Anyway, when I was lucky enough to start leading my own squads, I made a point to give them all different, more familiar names as well.

"For many bureaucratic purposes, you will continue to be Squad 19. When you're out in the field amongst other squads, or back in Base Camp talking to other soldiers or any higher-ups, you will still refer to yourselves as Squad 19. But amongst yourselves I'd prefer you to use the name I give you. It's more unique, more personal."

"What is it?" said Langston. "What's our squad's name?"

"The Sphelix," said Memo.

"But that was your squad's name," said Jenna. "Do you give it to all of your squads?"

Memo shook his head. "You're the first one to receive it since my own."

"How come?" Willie asked.

"Because you're the only squad for whom I have felt as much pride and reverence. You are one of the strongest groups of people

I've ever seen. It seems fitting."

I raised my eyebrows. I mean, sure, we did fine in the obstacle course, and Willie was great at archery and Peter was a strong swordsman, but we were far from the strongest squad at Base Camp right now, let alone the strongest one Memo had seen in years.

"I'm serious," Memo said. "I don't take this name lightly. And neither should you. After all, Leo and Jenna, your father was in it with me."

I met Memo's gaze. His eyes were sad. He'd known my dad. Then that also meant...

"I fought with your dad, too, Peter," Memo said, shifting his gaze to Pete. "We've stayed in contact ever since, and when you were arrested a few weeks ago, he wrote to tell me what happened."

"That's why you gave up the duties of a captain?" said Jenna. "So you could come teach us?"

Memo nodded. "I wanted to make sure you received—forgive my inflated ego—the best training possible. I felt I owed that to Lester and Geoffrey."

I'd only heard my dad's name spoken by three other people— my mom, Lester, and Helen, and they rarely mentioned it. Jenna and I only ever called him Dad.

Langston and Willie," Memo continued. "The Sphelix isn't in your blood, but you're both natural soldiers worthy of the name."

They both nodded, and Willie even gave a small smile.

"Now, about tomorrow..." Memo said.

The atmosphere in the room immediately changed—my stomach constricted, the room feeling ten degrees hotter.

"The first thing you need to know is that you'll be just fine. I've never been more confident in a squad. However, it is war. You'll be going on a simple mission as protection for a food envoy well within the boundaries of Arcton. Battle is unlikely, but it is of the utmost importance that you be ready for anything. At all times.

"When I was starting out in the Verdean, we were just as nervous as you are now. We had no idea what to expect. Battle puts you in intense situations, and people react differently. That's just a fact. But—and you're going to have to take my word for it—I've prepared you for everything. Trust your instincts, trust each other."

No one said anything. We sat in silence, and my mind flashed back to that truck ride two weeks ago when we'd stood next to each other, watching the sunset over the ocean, with the Foxtails in the distance. It had been the first time any of us had seen the massive expanse of water. I was still reeling from the arrest then, and I'd just met Langston and Willie. Now they were closer friends than any I had back home.

"Are there any last questions for me?" Memo asked.

I had tons: What was my dad like? Did you know my mom? Was it okay to be scared? Was it okay to miss them? How do I deal with knowing Peter and Jenna are going to be put in harm's way because of what I did? Will I ever see my family again? Will I ever see Irene again? What's in the Gilded Library? What's it like to kill someone?

But I stayed quiet.

"What time do we meet tomorrow?" Langston asked.

"0700 hours," Memo said. "I'll be there to see you off."

10. THE RANGING

A cold wind swept through Barrack 19 as I tied the sheathed sword around my waist. It felt lighter than the sparring ones, thinner but also sharper. I plucked a handful of arrows and stuffed them in the quiver at my back. I stowed the crumpled paper with *Section 342, Number 2-5* written on it into my breast pocket. I carried the bow in my left hand, using my right to keep the sword from getting caught between my legs.

Butterflies leapt in my stomach, fluttering around and threatening to race straight out of my mouth. We weren't going to the Mess Hall. And even if we had been, I wouldn't have been able to eat.

Jenna stood before me, her face pale, Mom's blue emerald necklace around her neck. She must have found a way to repair it – she'd always been the one in charge of creating a makeshift bandage when someone fell from the rope swing at the gully in Arcton City. Jenna tucked the necklace beneath her shirt. She hadn't worn it since the nightwalk, keeping it stowed away in her dresser. After catching my eye, she gave me a nervous half-smile.

Please, just let her be safe.

Willie stood at the door, his hood thrown up and his sword hanging at his waist, running his fingers up and down an arrow. He'd been fully dressed when I woke up, and had patiently watched us get ready. The entire time he'd shown no emotion.

Langston was in the corner fumbling with his backpack, trying to stuff a book in with the food and extra clothes we'd been told to bring. His hands kept slipping on the zipper, whether because of nerves or the cold I couldn't tell, and he said little.

Peter finished packing and stood with Willie. When he'd combed his hair today, I'd told him that it would get messed up in battle anyway, but he'd said it was part of his preparation. "When I tell stories about our fighting days, I wanna make sure everyone knows I was the good looking one."

"Well, you can always just lie and say you're actually handsome," I said.

"The word *handsome* doesn't do me justice," Peter said. "I need details. I want the girls listening to be able to see my beautiful hair, combed perfectly. I want them to see how my green eyes lit up when the morning sunlight hits them, knowing full well that battle would take place that day."

"When you're telling the story," Jenna said, "Make sure to remember the part where Willie saves your butt."

"Let's just try and live to tell that story," I said.

Outside, in the crisp pre-dawn morning, voices rang out from the obstacle course. Other soldiers walked briskly to the Mess Hall, trying to beat the pre-dawn gloom. We were some of the few carrying bows and swords. The handle from my blade kept jabbing me in the hip.

Memo met us outside the truck depository to go over the ranging. While he gave us details of the route and food envoy we'd be protecting, I couldn't help but think about how much better off we'd be if he were fighting with us.

He finished up just as a flatbed truck with the driver's window completely tinted pulled up outside the depository. We climbed in the back, where a larger squad of ten soldiers—Squad 1579, Memo said—sat waiting. They didn't say a word to us as we got in. Memo wished us luck.

The engine roared to life. We pulled out onto the street, turned a corner, and reached the outer border in no time. The guards quickly waved us through without checking our documentation, and we were officially on our first ranging.

The dirt road rumbled beneath us as the truck climbed. When we crested the hillside, an expanse of rolling hills stretched before us, covered in pine trees as far as I could see. The trees were jumbled together, but each was of similar height, none soaking up more than its fair share of sunlight. Togetherness, just like Arcalaeus said.

At the very bottom, a river twisted down and out of sight, like a snake. The rising sun dazzled upon its surface.

After another few minutes, we passed outside of the Orb's glow, and for the second time in my life the trees and hills brightened. Without a tinge of green intertwined, the sky was a pristine baby blue. The piney air hit me like coffee, and my head immediately lightened. Everyone else seemed to perk up as well. Jenna gave me a lazy sort of smile.

I looked down at my sword and bow between my legs. They felt awkward, like they had no business being there. I didn't want to use them. Hopefully I wouldn't have to.

Stay in the moment, I could practically hear Memo urging me. *What comes will come.* There was no use fretting about something you had no control over, and right now all I could control was how long I stared at the river, trying to imagine its path around the hills, where it dumped out into the bay.

Less than an hour later we arrived at port. They checked our papers, and we passed through the gates. The harbor was chock full of docked boats, all bearing Arcton's vermilion "A" against a stark-white flag, a green whorl circling the top. When we arrived, our shipment of fruits, vegetables, and about sixty cages of live chickens being offloaded onto its own truck, behind which we would drive to ensure nothing went wrong.

While we loaded the shipment into the truck, a rat-faced sailor hocked loogies beside it and spoke loudly to one of his comrades about rumors of Trusselian units behind enemy lines.

"They don't eat or sleep," he said. "I heard they're like Supersoldiers – they just wander through the night, like shadows, picking off unsuspecting squads. They've been wreaking havoc all along the western border. I feel sorry for this lot." He nodded at us. "At least we get to stay inside the gates."

I couldn't tell if he was being serious or just trying to spook us. Either way, I was thankful once the truck was loaded and we left. The tarp covering the fruits, vegetables, and chickens flapped in the breeze, revealing the poor birds packed together so tightly that their feathers poked out of the cages.

"Wouldn't it just be easier to kill them before transporting them?" Jenna asked.

"You want fresh meat, don't you?" a soldier from the other battalion said.

"Couldn't they at least get bigger cages?" I asked.

"What, so they can run around?" The same soldier said. "Nah, bigger crates would just mean more chickens in 'em. Every inch of space is an inch wasted. Besides, they're all heading to die aren't they? Who cares if they're uncomfortable?"

"I'm going to die someday, too," said Langston. "And I'd prefer to be able to at least stretch my arms before doing so."

A burst like someone smashing a trash can lid rang out. I jumped out of my seat, throwing my arms above my head for cover. But when I looked up, there was only bright blue sky. A couple soldiers from the other battalion laughed.

Willie gave me a hand back up into my seat.

"Engine must have backfired," said Langston.

"Happens all the time with these trucks," one of the other soldiers said. "You'll get used to it."

The passenger side door opened and a soldier hopped out, disappearing behind the hood. The chickens clucked from their cages. I was still on edge, but everyone else seemed at ease. I scoped out our position, something Memo had apparently succeeded in drilling into my skull, and searched for the quickest way of retreat. The river seemed like it could be a good spot to drive the enemy, and close by was a cabin with a big water tank next to it.

I took a long swig from my canteen, letting the cool water run down into my mouth. Just as I was about to screw the cap back on, a bird flew right over my head. A moment later, another flew past.

"What the—"

"Incoming!" Someone yelled.

An arrow hit the soldier working under the hood, and he collapsed, screaming.

I ducked just before a swarm of arrows—not birds—flew past, a couple thudding heavily into the guard rail on which I'd been leaning. An arrow pierced the driver-side window, and the car screeched to a halt. Soldiers from squad 1579 took out their swords; a couple of smarter ones got out their bows. Langston took out his bow and glanced through a slit in the guardrail.

"Where are they?" I asked.

"Embankment thirty yards behind us," Langston said. "I think."

Willie unhinged his own bow and snagged three arrows. "We're sitting ducks here," he said.

A few of the soldiers from the other squadron were firing arrows blindly.

"Stop shooting," I hissed. "You're wasting arrows."

"You got a better idea?" one yelled back. "At least we're doing something!"

An arrow pierced one of his comrades through the chest. Screaming in agony and grasping at the quiver, the soldier fell back onto another squad-mate, who shrugged him off quickly without a second look. Jenna crawled over and began examining him, blood spilling onto her lap. More arrows came whizzing past without warning, the truck reverberating with thick thuds as steel hit wood.

"Come here," I said to the others over the yelling. Squad 1579 was still firing blindly over the guardrail, and only the Sphelix listened. My heart was thumping. The adrenaline gave me a new clarity. "I saw an outpost fifty yards from here. We can get cover."

"Screw that," said one of the other soldiers. "We're from Arcton! We don't retreat. *Live faithfully, fight bravely!*"

A manic grin plastered across his face, he reached into his pocket, pulled out a white tablet, and popped it into his mouth.

"Prepare for a counterattack!" he yelled to the rest of the comrades in his battalion.

Everyone in the Sphelix was looking at me now. By yelling about the water cabin outpost, I'd accidentally assumed the role as leader.

"We're not going with them," I said. They all nodded in agreement. Jenna was busy trying to stop the bleeding of the wounded soldier, whose battalion seemed to think he was a lost cause. "How's he going to do?" I asked her. The arrow protruded from his chest and blood was still seeping everywhere, but he was alive.

Jenna shook her head. "Leaving him here is his best chance to survive. I've done what I can to the wound. If we can get him back to Base Camp soon, he might have a chance."

The boy clasped Jenna's hands. "Please, don't leave me," he gasped.

Jenna looked stunned as she met his eyes. "I…I'll be back soon. We can't take you with us, though. And you'll be safer here."

Tears flowed down his face. His own battalion was starting to creep out of the back of the truck. Meanwhile arrows kept flying in at us. The longer we waited, the truer their aim.

"We've got to move—now!" I said. "Follow me!"

As the other battalion got out of the truck and veered right, I veered left towards the cabin. The sounds of steel clanging together and soldiers crying out in pain rang through the air, but I didn't look back. Only one thing mattered: getting to cover. I sprinted toward the cabin and water tank, pressing my bow and sword close to my body to keep them from swinging wildly.

When I turned to check that the others were following, I saw two Trusselian soldiers, dressed in dark red, standing atop the embankment and launching arrows our way. Calculating their flight trajectory was easy since I was looking for it. I yelled to warn the others. Jenna, Peter, and Willie turned and sprinted away just in time. Langston didn't.

One of the arrows caught him in his leg, and he came up lame before staggering face-first into the dirt.

None of the others saw him, his yell just one of dozens ripping through the crisp air. They were all running as fast as they could after me, toward the cabin.

The archers had retreated behind the embankment – maybe the other squad had engaged them? It was the best and only opportunity to grab him.

As I sprinted towards Langston, Peter, Jenna, and Willie all looked confused. "What are you doing?" Jenna yelled, as she ran by me with the others in the opposite direction.

"Langston's hit," I yelled back, not breaking stride. "Go on. I'm right behind you."

Langston had rolled over and was examining the back of his thigh, grimacing. The arrow had pierced through one end, and the head showed out the other. He went from tenderly trying to slide it out to getting frustrated and aggressively jerking the shaft.

"Langston, stop!" I yelled, catching my breath. He turned, looking surprised to see me. He was breathing heavily. His eyes flashed to a spot behind me, and his eyes went wide with fear. "Guys, get to the cabin. What are you doing? Leave me!"

The rest of the Sphelix had followed me back to Langston.

"Shut up," said Peter, before I could open my mouth to speak. "Both of you guys," he said. Together, we bent down, each wrapping one of Langston's arms around us and lifting him up.

"Langston, hold on," I said. Peter began dragging him back to the cabin.

"Their archers are back," said Willie. "And there's—oh crap, there's more."

There were no longer just two red uniforms on the embankment. Now, there were at least ten, their bows knocked and ready to loose. I looked around for a safe spot to hide—some type of shelter, anything.

There was none.

We were in an open dirt path, the nearest trees a good fifty yards away, and I realized that those first two archers hadn't disappeared because they were under attack from the other battalion, a battle that now seemed to be raging out of sight. It was to lure the rest of us back into the open.

Peter and I picked up the pace, now practically carrying Langston, who did everything he could with his healthy leg to help us.

But one after another arrows soared in the air again.

"Leave me!" Langston said, trying to shrug off our arms. Peter and I held tight and kept moving. Jenna and Willie were just ahead of us, unable to help but unwilling to leave. The arrows arced terribly downwards...

"Jenna, get out of here!" I yelled. She shook her head.

I'd never see Irene again, never know what was in the Gilded Library.

I stopped walking and steadied my breath. Memo's meditations came to me, now of all times, and I felt my mind go blank. I looked up at the arrows, black birds of death soaring through the crystal blue sky.

They looked pristine. My vision was acute, as if it had increased ten times over. Every nick, any splinter in each arrow was clear to me. And yet my whole line of vision was also wavy, like I was viewing the arrows through a fishbowl.

Just before they came down upon my flesh—our flesh—I raised my hand and imagined an invisible barrier forming between us...

They stopped in midair—every last arrow—like they'd run into that invisible wall.

A moment of complete silence drowned out the distant yells. The world went deathly quiet. I stared at my hand in disbelief...

Langston had his hands over his head, still awaiting impact. The

Trusselian archers were too far away for me to make out their faces, but a few lowered their bows.

"What the…" said Peter, breaking the silence. He was staring at me with a mixture of adoration and shock.

"What happened?" Langston said, having only just released his hands from over his head.

I looked behind and saw Willie with his mouth wide open. The dozen or so arrows still hovered in the air, completely still. I let them drop to the ground.

"Go!" I said. "They're getting ready to fire again."

Willie sprinted up and collected the arrows, stuffing them into his quiver. Peter and I carried Langston, a trail of blood tailing us.

"You're gonna be alright, Langston," I said.

My heart was thumping. What just happened? How did I… Was I really the one who'd stopped those arrows?

"How did they miss us?" Langston asked. His voice was weak, his eyes drooping.

"Don't talk," I said. "Save your energy."

Jenna sprinted ahead to open the cabin door. The archers sent another round of arrows, but they didn't have the strength to reach us. Peter and I rushed Langston inside, his leg hitting the threshold painfully. Willie came running through right after us, carrying an armful of arrows. Jenna slammed the door shut.

Peter turned to me, eyebrows raised, leaning back as though seeing me for the first time.

"What was that?" he said.

11. I DON'T KNOW

I shook my head. "I don't know."

"We can talk about it later," said Jenna. "We need to get Langston taken care of." She fumbled around inside her aid kit, pulling out various ointments and bandages. Willie closed the curtains. A lonely cot sat in the far corner. Hastily, Peter and I dropped Langston onto it. I threw aside an oak table and carried over a rickety wooden chair next to the cot for Jenna to sit on.

She set to work immediately on his leg. His blood slowly stained the white sheets, seeping across the fabric like spilt water.

I was sure the Trusselians had seen what happened with their arrows, and I hoped it might make them a little hesitant to attack again. But still, Peter, Willie and I barricaded the front door with an overturned bookcase and a couple remaining chairs.

"Leo, what was that?" Peter asked again as he pushed over a heavy oak bureau to reinforce the bookcase.

"I don't know," I said. "I have no idea."

"It was incredible," said Peter. "The way they just stopped like...like they were frozen in midair. I've never seen anything like it. We should be dead."

Willie ignored him, peering through the blinds. "We can't stay in here for long," he said. "We're sitting ducks. We need to fight back."

"Yeah, but how?" I said. "We can't just run at them like that other squad did. They got slaughtered."

"Agreed," said Langston through gritted teeth. Jenna dabbed an ointment around his wound. "What do we know about where they're hiding out?"

"They're on an embankment," said Peter, "So they have a downhill retreat, but it's quickly cut off by the river."

"Good point," I said. "If we can get them to give ground, we'll have the higher position. How many are there, though? Seemed like fifty or more. And they looked as big as Supersoldiers."

"Supersoldiers aren't real," said Langston. He bit down on his sleeve and took a deep breath before speaking again. "They ambushed us...that made it seem like there were more of them than there actually were. These are supposed to be small, quick-strike groups built to attack and disappear in enemy territory. I don't think there was more than twenty."

"Still means we're outnumbered," Peter said.

"If we can create a diversion of some sort," I said, "something to get them retreating down the hill towards the river, that should give us enough of an advantage to take 'em out."

"What kind of diversion?" Peter said. "We don't exactly have anything that will make them scared of us—other than your ability to stop arrows."

He was right. We were stuck. How did you force twenty soldiers to retreat when there were only five of you?

Beside us, Jenna was still working on Langston's leg. She cut off the arrowhead on one side and the fletching on the other, leaving a small portion of the shaft still inside. The wound kept bleeding, but she was able to tie a tight bandage around it. Red splotches soaked through the white cloth, but, all things considered, Langston seemed to be doing well.

She held his head, forcing him to take small sips of water like a mother feeding a child.

"I have a way," Langston said, gasping in between mouthfuls. "Along the trail are a bunch of siren sensors. They used to be used as warning devices. If any part of Arcton was under attack, whoever was closest to a sensor could set it off to let areas nearby know."

"So we set it off and wait for backup to arrive?" I said.

"If we sit and wait, yeah we might still survive, but the Trusselian squad would be able to retreat and hide before the backup arrives. If we set off the right sensor, though, they'll run down the hillside and toward the river. Perfect spot for an attack."

"How do we know where those sensors are?" Willie asked. He hadn't moved from his spot keeping watch at the window. "What do they look like?"

"It's the moss on the trees," Langston said, finishing another sip from the canteen and gently pushing it away. "On the side of the road we were driving on, there are a bunch of cypress trees."

"And?" I said.

"Well, that's unusual," said Langston. "Most of this area has pine trees, not cypress."

"I can barely tell the difference between broccoli and green beans," Peter said. "I don't know anything about trees."

Langston smiled. "I'm well aware, Pete. But Willie can." He

turned to Willie. "I saw one right before we got ambushed, down closer to the port. Look for it and pull the siren, and the Trusselians will head for the river."

"How'd you find out about this?" Willie asked.

"I asked Memo if he had any books he thought I should read, and he came back with about ten high-level Captain textbooks. I've been sifting through them ever since. The sirens were planted so long ago, though, that I just hope they still work."

Knowing Langston, "sifting" meant reading each one cover to cover and memorizing every word.

"Should we go now?" Peter asked. "I mean, does it make sense to wait?"

"Definitely now," said Jenna. "They know we're in here and could try and attack us any second. Langston can't go anywhere for a while. He has to stay behind."

"I can go," Langston said. "Just help me up." He tried standing, but the pain quickly overwhelmed him and he fell back down.

"You're staying here," Jenna said.

"So are you," I said.

Jenna narrowed her eyes. "Oh, really?"

"It's not because I'm trying to protect you," I said, although that was a plus. "Someone needs to stay with Langston. If he's here all alone. He's defenseless. Not to mention he just lost a ton of blood."

"I feel like my baby sister," Langston said. His eyes were watery from the pain, but he looked determined too. "Next thing I know Jenna will be reading me nursery rhymes and heating up some milk."

Jenna and Langston both eventually agreed to stay in the cabin. Willie, Peter, and I moved the makeshift barricade at the door, peeking through the windows to make sure the Trusselians weren't planning another ambush when we left. The trees obscured most of our view of the trail, but we went for five minutes without seeing any movement.

We edged our way out, one in front of the other, ready to pull back at a second's notice before sprinting from one tree to another. Each time we moved out from behind a tree, I expected an arrow to go whizzing past.

Finally, we got close enough to the main road to get a vantage point on the embankment, where a few heads poked out. Trusselians.

Though the area had been a full-fledged war zone thirty minutes earlier, it was now completely silent. Bodies lay on the path—most of them in Verdean green.

"Stay here," Willie said. It was always a shock to hear him talk. "I'll get the sensor. After I pull it, I'll meet you on the path."

"You sure?" I said.

"Give me five minutes." He was off before I could respond, crawling in between a clump of bushes. He disappeared out of sight in less time than it would've taken me to draw my bowstring.

"I'm starting to like Willie more and more," said Peter as we waited. He stretched his arms out in front of him. "I think he's said more words in the past ten minutes than he did the last two weeks."

"Maybe," I said. "Seems to be a little too comfortable with Jenna, though."

"Speaking of, she probably saved Langston's life just now. Not to mention that soldier from squad twenty-two-hundred-or-whatever."

"Won't do any good if we die going after the Trusselians," I said. "Langston got lucky that arrow only caught his leg. A few more inches up and well…"

"He wasn't the only one that got lucky," Peter said. "We should be five bodies in the dirt right now—and instead…you have this *power*. Wait till the girls hear about this at Base Camp."

"It was weird," I said. "I don't know, I just—I just saw each arrow, but it was like I was seeing them underwater. They were moving in slow motion. It's hard to explain. And I was able to just…stop them after that."

Peter smiled. "Were you *at one* with the arrow?" he said. "Memo would be very proud."

"I was actually doing those meditation tricks Memo taught us when it happened," I said. "Maybe he was onto something."

Peter shrugged. "Who am I to say? I'd be dead otherwise. Still corny. But the Verdean will be talking about this forever."

WHOOOOP! WHOOOOP! WHOOOOP!

A siren erupted somewhere to our left. I covered my ears, trying to drown out the sound, before realizing this was what we were waiting for. Willie had found the sensor. Behind the embankment, the heads dropped from view, and I hoped it meant they had turned to retreat. We were counting on it…

Peter and I took off in a sprint. I was scared out of my mind, always fearing a red uniform popping up to take us out.

Just before we crossed, Willie rushed into view. The three of us scrambled over the muddy road where the Trusselians had been a minute earlier. All of them were now retreating across the grassy knoll towards the river.

I whipped out three arrows from my quiver and steadied the first on the string while continuing to give chase. I lost it and watched its flightpath towards, and over, the burgundy caps; it cleared the leaders by a few feet and hit the ground. One of Willie's arrows soared through the air and nailed a soldier in the back. I launched my next two arrows in rapid succession, each faring better than the first and taking down a soldier.

The others were still running away from us, none of them taking the time to look back at who was giving chase or aware that they outnumbered us at least three to one. When we came upon the fallen soldiers, all of whom lay face down with arrows piercing them, we stabbed our swords between their backs, blades crunching into their bones and ending any doubt.

I shivered but kept running—there was no time to think about the deaths. Adrenaline flooded my mind, and instinct took over. The Trusselians were up to the river now. They ran alongside it, heading for a cluster of pine trees a half mile off. Once they reached the woods, we'd never be able to find them.

"Just keep shooting?" Peter yelled.

"Yeah," I said. "Hard for them to shoot up the hill."

We veered parallel to them, maintaining our current distance, firing arrows as we went. A minute later, though, they seemed to realize it was only three of us, not the army of reinforcements that the siren had indicated. Immediately halting their retreat, they flipped around and started advancing toward us.

Each of their arrows, fortunately, fell rather lamely to the side or in front of us, never posing a real threat. Our own shots were aided by slope and, since we'd expended far less energy than they had, came out of our bows like bullets.

One by one the red uniforms fell, each body a few feet closer to us but never close enough to pose a real threat. Finally, there was one left—a boy no older than I was. He pulled out his sword, yelling in a drawl, "Fight me one-on-one, cowards. Bring out your swords."

An arrow tore through his jacket, directly underneath his right armpit. His eyes grew wide with the pain, and he took a great, raspy breath. He tried to swing his sword, but he could barely lift his arm. I turned and saw Willie knock another arrow and loose it straight into the soldier's chest. He collapsed to his knees and finally fell over.

Willie lowered his bow calmly. He looked at the soldier without any emotion. He then walked up to him and stuck his blade through his back.

The adrenaline rushed out of me and my legs started to wobble. I leaned on Peter, throwing my arm over him to prevent myself from falling over.

He patted me on the back. Blood and mud were streaked across his brow. "You alright?"

"Yeah, just a bit woozy."

Willie eyed us curiously. "Back to the cabin?" he said.

I struggled to stay up, but I nodded. "Let's get Langston and Jenna and go back home."

12. THE GILDED LIBRARY

"Leo, how did you…?" Jenna asked.

I shook my head. Since we'd gotten back in the truck, I hadn't been able to think about anything but those arrows stopping in mid-air.

Both drivers had been killed in the ambush, so Peter was in front driving. Jenna, Langston, Willie, and I were in the back, along with the injured soldier from squad 1579, who was fast asleep. "I have absolutely no idea," I said. "Maybe it was one of you guys, and you didn't realize it."

"It was you," said Willie.

"Langston, do you have any idea what happened?" I asked. If anyone knew what I'd done, it was him.

"I've never read about it," he said, "Never heard about anything like it… There's no physics theory that supports it, no weapons from the past that could do that same thing. It's an anomaly."

I kept replaying it over and over in my mind. One second the arrows were flying through the air, on their way toward us, and the next they were just…frozen. It didn't make any sense.

The truck lurched forward. "Sorry!" Peter called back to us. "No idea how to drive."

Despite Peter's horrible driving, we crossed back into the Orb's range within a few hours. Not long after, we arrived at the outer gate to Base Camp, where Peter immediately told the guards what had happened and urged them to send out a rescue group for the other soldiers.

We woke up the wounded soldier and watched as two nurses loaded him onto another truck that raced off to one of the hospitals. Peter was instructed to drive the car into camp and drop it off at the depot.

As we pulled in beneath one of the entrance watchtowers, a few guards, bows hanging on their shoulders, peered down at us. I shielded my eyes from the sunlight. Peter slowed the truck to a crawl, doing his best to avoid the dozens of soldiers walking around.

"Should we tell Memo?" I asked the others.

"Up to you," said Willie. "If you think we should keep it quiet, I will."

Jenna and Langston nodded in agreement.

Peter turned his head around. "I think we can tell Memo, but we shouldn't tell anyone else. I'll even keep my big mouth shut."

Memo was at the truck depot waiting. Once he saw the blood and dirt on our uniforms, along with squad 1,579 missing, his eyes darted between all of us, counting. He sighed in relief when he realized we were all there.

He didn't need an explanation. "Ambush," he said.

"About twenty Trusselian soldiers knew we were coming," Langston said.

"Our intel said they were two hundred miles west," said Memo.

"Some intel," I said.

Memo nodded. "There may be a few recon squads that slipped through the cracks. I'm glad you're back safe."

Langston gingerly edged his leg over the side of the truck. "There's a lot we need to tell you."

Memo clasped a hand to his cheek. "I'm sure there is," he said, "but first you need to go to the hospital. We don't want that to get infected. And everyone needs some rest. We can discuss things after you're taken care of."

We debriefed with a lieutenant, Peter taking the lead. He recounted every detail of the ambush and our subsequent counter-attack (skipping over the arrows stopping mid-flight), painting a picture that made our victory sound much more impressive than it actually was.

Finally, we were allowed to return to Barrack 19—sore, hungry, and dirty. I took off my blood-stained uniform, removing the Gilded Library note and placing it carefully beneath my pillow.

Willie went straight to sleep, saying he would shower later. Jenna went to the nurse's washroom. I reluctantly gathered my bathroom kit, and, dragging my feet, went to the soldier's washroom close by with Peter. The hot water pelted my body, washing away the dirt, blood, and sweat.

Willie was fast asleep when I returned to the barrack, and neither Peter nor Jenna said anything, though I could tell they were still awake. Back at Uncle Lester and Aunt Helen's, there was rarely a night where Peter and I didn't stay up talking in our room, discussing girls we liked, teachers we hated, stupid things Jexter and Flora had done.

But we'd all just killed for the first time. How did you talk about that? And then, of course, there were the arrows...

I still didn't believe it. I couldn't have stopped them with my mind. It was impossible. But it happened...

Could I do that to everything, or just weapons that were going to kill me? Would I be able to do it again?

I stared at a pile of clothes on the floor. I slowed my breathing, closed my eyes, and dove into my meditation. I tried to visualize the clothes, but I didn't *see* them like the arrows. There was no altered vision, like I was swimming with my eyes open. Still, I reached my hand up in front of me, tried lifting a shirt off the ground and...

Nothing happened. I tried again, and I thought I saw a little vibration of a sleeve, but it was probably just my imagination. I tried once more and this time, there definitely, absolutely, wasn't anything at all.

Langston walked in not long after, hobbling on crutches but smiling.

"Everyone asleep?" he asked.

I nodded.

"I can't believe it," Langston said.

"What?"

"You stopping arrows with your mind!"

"We don't even know for sure it was me."

He sat down in a chair, keeping his leg straight. "I've been thinking a lot, and there's no logical explanation for what happened. I've never read anything about defying gravity. Was that the first time that's happened to you?

"Definitely," I said, although I flashed back to that night we were caught with *Dasher's Revenge*. The baton that the police officer threw at me—it had looked like it was heading straight for me, and then it wasn't.

"We should tell Memo," Langston said. "He'll know what to do. And he might even have heard of something like this before."

"When are we meeting with him? He didn't say."

"Probably in an hour or two."

"You think we can find the Gilded Library before then?" I asked.

"Are you serious?"

"Langston, we've been trying to figure that note out for weeks!"

"It's not gonna be easy to get into," Langston said. "It's for lieutenants and other higher-ups. We're no-names."

"We can't sneak in?"

I'm on crutches. Not gonna be easy for us to pass unnoticed."

There was a knock at the door.

"Can you get that?" I said.

Langston flipped me the middle finger and began scratching underneath his cast.

I got up and opened the door, and in popped Irene. She threw herself at me, running her hand through my hair and kissing me. It was a few seconds before Langston coughed and Irene pulled back. I sure wasn't about to.

She went red. "Oh, hi, Langston. Didn't see you there."

Langston grinned. "By all means, carry on."

Irene pulled up a chair next to him. "I heard there was an ambush. Is your leg alright?"

"It's fine, thanks," he said. "But we were lucky to get out alive, really."

I hoped he wouldn't rehash the ranging, or tell Irene about my stopping the arrows. She'd think I was some kind of freak. *Was* I a freak? Would she want to still date a freak? I needed to change the subject...

"Irene, do you know about the Gilded Library?"

"Sure, my dad used to talk about it all the time."

"Do you want to sneak in?" I showed her the note and explained.

"We can get in no problem," said Irene. She always perked up when it came to breaking the rules, and even more so when books were involved. "Want to go now?"

"I've wanted to for the past twenty-four hours."

"Leo, we just got back from battle," said Langston. "And after you got thrown into the Verdean for stealing a Nefa, do you really want to press your luck? It might be straight to the Pit next time."

"This isn't a Nefa," I said. "It's just a Verdean book."

"That you're not allowed to have," Langston said.

"We won't get caught."

"Leo, your powers won't–"

"Your what?" said Irene.

Langston slapped his forehead, shaking his head.

"Your what?" Irene said again. Her eyes narrowed.

I uh..." I had no choice but to tell her. I did my best to

downplay what happened, but still her face changed slowly from anger to incredulity to what looked like belief.

"We need to get to the Gilded Library," she said.

No questions, no theories. I very nearly kissed her again, but I was in too much of a hurry to get to the Gilded Library.

"Just...be back before Memo comes to debrief," Langston said as I closed the door.

Dusk had settled over Base Camp. All around, soldiers were filing into the Mess Hall. I had trouble keeping up with Irene, who was running, swerving in and out of soldiers as though we were being chased by Trusselians. Finally, in an alley between two old, dusty buildings, she stopped and turned.

"You ready?" she said. Her eyes darted back and forth between my own, like she was reading.

"What d'you mean, ready? Is this it?"

"Just around the corner. I'll distract the guard. There's a side door with a potted plant next to it. Underneath the pot is a key that'll open the door. Just don't forget to let me in afterwards."

"How do you know?"

"Do you have any idea how often I've heard my dad complain about the security in the Verdean? Everyone is always losing their keys, so there's always a spare around. If it isn't underneath the plant, it's somewhere else close by."

She left and started chatting up the guard at the front door. I slipped down a few stairs just in their line of sight, immediately getting down on my hands and knees. Sure enough, there was a small green plant sitting in a large clay pot. I shifted it over a bit, revealing a dirty bronze key.

I opened the door, replaced the key underneath the potted plant, and let myself into a musky, dark room. A few seconds later, there was a gentle rap at the door. Irene.

"You know you're incredible, right?" I said. My heart was beating faster than on the battlefield, but she looked collected, calm.

Irene flashed her giant smile. The way her face lit up gave me goosebumps. "Now, what section are we looking for?"

"342, numbers 2-5."

"This way," Irene said, pointing.

Shelves held stacks upon stacks of thickly bound books. Irene snagged a candle from one of the sconces and used it to light up our way. Every section was packed with hundreds of volumes, each dustier than the last. The rows continued as far as I could see, candles lining the walls. Dust clouded up with each step, so much that I covered my nose and mouth with my shirt. When was the last time someone had been in here? I had to catch myself from sneezing a few times before we finally came upon Section 342.

We turned in and there, on the lowest shelf, were red, leather-bound books with gold lettering on their spine. *1, 2, 3, 4 and 5.* I took out Book 2. The front cover read: *The Whirlwind War: Record 068.*

"The Whirlwind War?" I said. "My dad fought in that one."

"Grab it and let's go," said Irene. "We can come back for the others."

Barely resisting the urge to flip through the pages right then and there, I shoved it into my jacket. We tiptoed our way back through the library, careful to keep an eye out for the guards when exiting, and within ten minutes we were back outside Barrack 19.

"Thank you," I told Irene. "I promise I'll let you read it after me."

She kissed me. "Least I can do," she said. "After all, you're here because of me."

Irene left before I could argue. I walked into Barrack 19 to find everyone awake, sitting in a circle of desks. Smack dab in the middle sat Memo.

"Good evening, Leo," he said. I hugged my jacket, pressing the Whirlwind War closer to my chest.

13. DEBRIEF

"Hi, Memo," I said, trying to keep my voice level.

He motioned to a chair. "Please sit," he said.

Jenna's eyes followed me as I sat down. Langston, whose leg was propped up on a chair, quickly looked away when I met his stare. Memo didn't give me any sideways glances; he didn't even ask where I'd been.

Instead, he took out a large aluminum canister and six cups and poured us each a steaming mug of hot chocolate. I took one sip and instantly was transported back in time.

"Jenna, remember?" I said.

Jenna licked her lips as she lowered her mug. "Mhmm. Yeah, didn't Uncle Lester make it for us our first night at Moulton Street?"

"My dad?" Peter said. "You sure about that?"

"Yeah," Jenna said. "Only time I ever saw him in the kitchen."

Memo smiled and blew softly on his mug. "I hope you're all rested and, in Langston's case, patched up," he said. "I know you debriefed with the lieutenant, but if it's not too much trouble, I'd like you to go through the mission in as much detail as possible. I'd like to hear everything."

Peter immediately launched into the story. Though he told it with much of his usual flair, he tried to tone it down for Memo. That was until we came to the part where I stopped the arrows.

"And then, sir," Peter said. He stopped and looked at me, seeking my approval. I nodded. "Uh…Leo sort of stopped them."

Memo's eyes widened, but just briefly. He turned to me, his face unreadable, his eyes searching, and quickly returned his attention back to Peter. "I understand," he said. "Please continue."

"Sir, I'm not sure you do—"

"I understand, Peter. Please continue."

Peter cocked one eyebrow, shrugged his shoulders, then went on. Though it wasn't his best performance, it was still more dramatic and exciting than anyone else's rendition would have been.

Memo beamed at us. "That was an awful situation to be placed in, particularly on your very first mission. As Arcalaeus mentioned in his speech, the war is going very, very poorly right now. We've lost nearly twice as many soldiers as Trussel has, and it's now apparent that they've started sending guerrilla units closer to City lines than we originally anticipated.

"The Trusselian guerrilla unit you managed to take out was one that has been running rampant over the countryside for months, hitting food envoys like yours and also stealing important documents, sabotaging transport vehicles, and wreaking havoc along the countryside."

"They didn't seem all that scary to me," said Peter.

"Speak for yourself," said Langston, nodding towards his leg.

Peter smiled. "Fair point," he said. "I guess if it weren't for Leo we'd all be dead."

"How are you holding up?" asked Memo, looking around at us.

"Taking a life is no easy thing…"

I looked at the others without saying a word. The real answer, at least for me: badly. The Gilded Library had taken my mind off things for a bit, but the soldiers beside me in the truck getting hit with arrows kept flashing through my head. And the Trusselian soldier all alone at the end, knowing death was coming…what was going through his head?

I stared down at my hands, and for an instant they were covered in blood, but I blinked and they were back to normal.

Live Faithfully. Fight Bravely. That was the motto we lived by. We were here to kill, after all. I kept my mouth shut.

"Jenna," Memo continued. "I assume the head nurses told you to pass out Focus Pills after battle?"

She nodded, rummaging in her bag. "I have them right here."

"Good. Give them to me, please… None of you will be taking them."

"What?" Jenna said. "I mean—are we even allowed to refuse a direct order?"

She handed over the white box all the same. Memo opened the lid, and took out a small white pill—the kind I'd seen Carl swallow before fighting me and Peter. Memo held the pill up to the candlelight before returning it to the case and clasping it shut.

"It'll be our secret," he said. "But you won't be taking these pills as long as you're in my squad." It was the first time I'd seen Memo, or any higher-up for that matter, tell someone else *not* to obey an order. We looked at one another, silently, unsure what to make of it.

Memo broke the silence: "We're done here then," he said. "You won't have another mission for the next few days, so make sure to rest up. You'll still be required to do early morning PT, along with archery and swordsmanship, but there will be a few hours every day for yourselves. Please use them wisely."

Memo stopped beside me on his way out and put a hand on my shoulder. "Do you mind coming outside for a few minutes?"

My stomach dropped. He was going to ask me where I'd been. I was going to have to tell him about the Gilded Library.

"Sure," I said.

I clutched the Whirlwind War book to my chest as we stepped outside. A few straggling soldiers were trudging their way back to the barracks from dinner, but otherwise the grounds were empty. I followed Memo a short way to a fire pit where a few embers still burned gently. Memo sat down on a massive log next to it, and I followed suit.

He scratched his goatee. How obvious did the book look in my jacket?

"What were you doing when you stopped the arrows?" he asked, turning to me.

It took me a second to shift my focus from the book. "Nothing," I said. Memo didn't break eye contact, and he didn't speak. I racked my brain. "I mean, it's all kind of a blur. I might have been meditating? Which is weird, because who meditates when twenty arrows are flying through the air at you? But yeah, I think that's what I was doing."

"There was nothing else that could've stopped them?" Memo

asked. "Just you?"

"I think so. I don't really know. What do you think happened?"

"I've heard about people stopping arrows and even bullets with their minds," Memo said, "but, well...I'd like to do some more research. I don't want to give you incorrect information. Who else knows about this?"

"Just the Sphelix...and Irene."

"Irene?"

"My girlfriend. She's a nurse."

"And no one from the other squad saw you or heard you talking about it?"

"No."

"Let's keep it that way. At least for now."

"I tried doing it again," I said. "Back in the barrack when we got home. And I couldn't."

"That's to be expected," Memo said. "Something must have triggered this...*power* of yours. Was there anything else that happened during battle? Anything that could've sparked them?"

"No, everything was the same. Sir, what do you mean *power*? Can other people do what I did?"

"I'm sure you have a million questions, Leo, and I plan on answering them. But, please, allow me a few days."

I nodded.

"Anything else, sir?"

"That'll be all."

I took one last look at the burning embers before I left and went back to Barrack 19.

"Did you tell him about the Gilded Library?" Langston asked right as I walked in.

"He didn't ask," I said.

"So then it was about the arrows," said Peter. "What did he say?"

"I told him what I thought I'd done," I said, "And he wasn't shocked. He's definitely seen it before, or at least read about the...power. He wouldn't go into detail, though. He wanted to do more research."

"That's smart," said Langston. "Misinformation will only hurt you."

"I guess," I said. "He seemed pretty worried it might leak out."

"We'll keep it a secret," said Willie.

"Did he say anything about the Focus Pills?" Jenna asked. "The head nurses must've told us a dozen times to remember to pass them out, and then Memo just bags it... What am I supposed to say if they ask me?"

"You lie," Willie said.

"But what if I get caught? I don't want more time in the Verdean."

"It comes down to whether we trust Memo," I said. "I don't want you to get a longer sentence either, Jenna, but...I don't know."

"Something feels off," Langston said. "The note about the Gilded Library, stopping those arrows... If Memo is telling us not to take the FPs, he has to have a reason why." Jenna nodded in agreement.

"Can we eat?" Jenna said. "I'm starving, and the Mess Hall is gonna close soon." Before leaving, I snuck the Whirlwind War book beneath my pillow.

The smell of roast chicken reached us before the canopied building even came into view, making me salivate. We were one of the last squads to arrive, though there was a large group surrounding one table.

"Look who it is," said Langston, getting in line behind me for food.

"Huh?"

Langston motioned to the crowded table. "Carl," he said. "I overheard a nurse in the hospital talking about how they'd taken out three Trusselian squads on their ranging. Word must've spread throughout Base Camp."

I gritted my teeth. "I'm so happy for them."

We got our food and sat down. Jenna, who'd gone in front of us, was talking to Willie.

"They're probably going stir-crazy in the house without us," she said. "They never exactly got along as it was."

"Who?" I asked. "Flora and Jexter?"

Jenna nodded. "It wouldn't surprise me if Flora got sent to the Verdean for killing Jexter. I just hope he isn't stupid enough to throw her jacket in the bathtub again."

Langston clumsily set his tray down, nearly knocking over Willie's water glass. "Can you imagine living with the three of you their entire lives?" Langston said. "And now all they have is one sibling left? I'd be ripping my hair out."

"Do you have any siblings?" Peter asked Willie, who was chopping up his chicken like it had betrayed him somehow.

"I had one, but she passed away," said Willie. "A twin actually."

"I'm sorry," I said. "I didn't know."

"Never mentioned him," said Willie, shrugging and continuing to maim his chicken.

"Her," corrected Langston.

"Yeah, sorry," Willie said, forcing a smile. "She was really cool. You guys would've loved her."

"How'd she die?" Langston asked, but before Willie could answer, Irene arrived. She placed her tray next to me, gently squeezing my shoulder before taking her seat. A warmth spread from where she touched me.

She asked Peter about the battle, and he immediately jumped into the same story he'd given Memo—dropping his voice to a whisper when he got to the arrows. But then the conversation steered towards the Gilded Library.

I let Irene take this one. They weren't pleased when they found out I'd gotten the book and had kept it a secret.

"How come you didn't tell us?" Jenna asked.

"Langston knew," I said.

"I didn't know you actually got it," said Langston. "But that's awesome. Why are you here? You should be in there reading."

"Keep your voice down," I said. I glanced around to make sure no one was listening in. There was still a large crowd at Carl's table, where he was no doubt gloating about their successful ranging. "I'll start reading it when we get back. It's about the Whirlwind War."

"The Whirlwind War?" Willie said. "That was the one Memo fought in, right?"

"Yep, with our dads," I said. "I just don't know why someone chose to give *me* the note"

"Maybe they know about your, you know—" Peter said. He did an impersonation of me holding up my hand to stop the arrows.

"How would they?" said Langston. "They gave the note to Leo before he stopped those arrows."

"And the *Whirlwind War* doesn't have anything to do with Leo's powers," said Jenna. "Maybe there's something else in there?"

I wished the others would stop saying the word *powers* to describe what I'd done. It felt off...like I was a mutant or a Supersoldier.

When we arrived back to the barrack, Peter reached up onto my bed and pulled the book down.

"*The Whirlwind War: Record 068,*" Peter read aloud. "Yeesh, that's a lot of records about one war. You wanna read to everyone?" he said, looking at me.

"We shouldn't be reading it all," said Jenna.

"It's going to be lights out soon," Langston said. "Let Leo read it first, and we can pass it around after."

"Fine," Pete said, tossing the book back.

A few minutes later, a lieutenant popped in to blow out the candles. I climbed into bed and cracked open the cover, flipping to the first page, reading by the faint glow of the Orb light.

14. THE WHIRLWIND WAR

The recorded histories of The Whirlwind War, Volume 068.

Lieutenant's Log: November 14, 2132

While on a ranging in Yurton, Squad 490 encountered enemy soldiers hiding out in a four-story building just outside the downtown area. No-name Grise noticed smoke billowing out of the second-story window. Though there were only small wisps, it was enough that it seemed someone might be in there.

After one day of reconnaissance, which included staking out the building, questioning civilians around the town, and scaling a neighboring building for a better vantage point, it was surmised that there was a high likelihood enemy Northron soldiers were hiding out in the building.

I designated No-Names Grise, Body, and Taliaferro to scale the building in the dead of night on November 12th. They successfully entered the building through the third-story window, and proceeded to make their way downstairs to overwhelm and subdue three Northron soldiers. Upon further questioning, it was discovered that the soldiers had been hiding out in the building, living on spare food and water snuck in by civilians, since the Verdean began its occupation of the city two months prior.

The soldiers were questioned and within hours identified the civilians who had aided them. Civilians and soldiers were all executed in town square.

Squad 490 will continue to help with the occupation of Yurton.

Sincerely,

Lt. Clifton Kelemen

It was the first in what looked to be thousands of entries. I paged through, skimming every log and wondering why on Earth anyone would go through all the trouble to put me on a wild goose chase to find it. Sure, the logs were interesting enough, with details about hundreds of missions, but there wasn't anything noteworthy. Nothing that seemed worthy of a covert note, much less risk going to the Pit.

I flipped through page after page, until, in the middle of the book, I saw a name that caught my eye.

My name. Belfin.

Lieutenant's Log: December 8, 2132

While on a ranging in the Northron countryside, Squad 571 was ambushed by enemy soldiers. Unfortunately, one soldier was missing after the battle. No-name Belfin. We spent the next two days searching for any sign of him, but there was no trace. A few enemy soldiers had gotten away during the battle, so it was concluded that no-name Belfin had been taken prisoner.

We were under strict orders to keep our ranging to a maximum of two weeks, and we had already been out for twelve days. However, it was determined by every member of Squad 571 including myself that it was in the best interest of the Verdean to pursue no-name Belfin and try to bring him back safely.

Squad 571 trekked through miles of snow, following various sets of footprints to locate no-name Belfin. On the fifth day, no-name Belfin showed up at our campsite unannounced. When questioned, Belfin said he'd been taken prisoner and had barely managed to sneak away. He had bruises and lacerations in line with typical Northron torture methods. He assured us he hadn't given away any intel, but that he had volunteered fake coordinates for our position.

Rather than pursue his capturers, Squad 571 decided to return from the ranging.

Sincerely,

Lt. Kevin Najera

Belfin—my dad. It was weird seeing his name in print, hearing about his capture secondhand. What had the Northron soldiers done to him exactly? How had he managed to escape? I wanted more details—I was starving for them—but my dad wasn't here to tell the story. Instead I was getting them from Lt. Kevin Najera, whose writing style had about as much flavor as soggy bread.

I couldn't help but be reminded of another time someone gave me something to read, a time I'd failed to pay attention. But this wouldn't be another *Gestalt Diary*. This time I was paying attention.

I flipped through page after page, dust swirling around me, searching for other entries with Squad 571. And then, toward the end of the book, I saw my name—his name—again.

Lieutenant's Log: February 24, 2133

While on a ranging in Prentiss, Squadron 571 successfully infiltrated the city and broke into a safe house that was holding two Verdean soldiers hostage. In the escape out of Prentiss, we encountered a squad of enemy soldiers at the outer gates; we were able to escape, but unfortunately lost no-name Galen Dugan in the battle.

The two rescued hostages provided Squad 571 with detailed information on an attack by Northron planned to occur in early March on the northeast border. We passed this information along to the higher-ups within the Verdean, who were able to plan accordingly and strike a decisive win against the enemy.

No-names Iglesias, Belfin, Michaels, Quaresma, and Herbert awarded Medal of Hardship for their service.

Sincerely,

Lt. Kevin Najera

Belfin—my dad.

Herbert—Uncle Lester.

Iglesias—Memo.

They'd been heroes, given Medals of Hardship.

I couldn't wait to share it with Jenna and Peter so they could see what our dads had done. But why hadn't Uncle Lester ever told us he'd received a medal? Any other soldier would've had it displayed around the house.

I flipped through the rest of the book, but there were no other mentions of Squad 571.

I closed my eyes, telling myself I needed sleep. But I kept pulling the book back out, re-reading all of Squad 571's entries. I traced my dad's name with my finger. He'd been an honored soldier, someone who'd helped Arcton win the Whirlwind War. There were so many things I didn't know about him, that I'd probably never know. But at least this was a start.

Content, I placed the book once more under my pillow and finally fell asleep...

"HELP ME! HELP!"

I jerked awake—someone was screaming in the barrack. I instinctively jumped out of bed. My sword? Where was my sword? I searched for the source of the noise, and in the Orb light I saw someone thrashing in Peter's bed.

"Pete!"

There was no one there. It was just him. He shook uncontrollably in his bed, his screams threatening to wake up every barrack within a mile. Quickly, Jenna went over and put her hand on his arm.

"Shh," she said. "Peter." She shook him gently. "Peter, it's me. Jenna. You're alright. You're safe."

"HELP! HELP ME! SAVE THEM!"

I ran over and knelt beside Jenna. Willie and Langston were sitting up in their beds. Jenna shook Peter vigorously. "Peter," she said, "wake up. You're safe. There's no one here but us."

His eyes opened and he sat bolt upright. His breathing, strained and heavy, started to even out. Sweat poured down his body, his shirt soaked through. He found me through the dark.

"I'm sorry," he said. "I'm so, so sorry."

"You were just having a nightmare," I said. "And after the day you had, no one can blame you."

Jenna put her hand on Peter's forehead. "Willie, pass me the water," she said.

Willie threw her his canteen. She dabbed it on a cloth by Peter's bedside and gently put it to his forehead.

"There's nothing to apologize for," she said. "It happens to everyone. Want a drink?" She handed him the canteen.

He drank deeply from it.

"Maybe a focus pill…" she said. "Why won't Memo let us have them?"

"What do they do?" Peter asked.

"After soldiers enter battle," Jenna said, "They're more prone to nightmares and sudden shocks to the system. It's an occupational hazard"—she used air quotes—" according to some of the head nurses. The focus pills help combat that. They make it easier to relax, easier to have dreamless sleeps."

"Why doesn't Memo want us to take them?" I said.

"I don't know," said Jenna. "Once you start, you're supposed to take them every day. You keep a stash on you at all times."

I remembered the soldier from Squad 1,579. Before he ran into battle, he'd popped a little white pill into his mouth, like Carl. I mentioned this to Jenna, and she nodded.

"Everyone in the Verdean takes them," she said. "Even the higher-ups."

"But they don't even fight in battles anymore," I said.

"You'd think Memo would want to protect us from the nightmares…the anxiety," Langston said. "It doesn't make any sense that he's keeping them from us."

"I could use about ten," said Peter.

"Maybe he'll give them to us later on," said Langston. "I mean, maybe he doesn't want to start us on them too early, like everyone else."

"He's not going to give them to us," said Willie. There was a finality to his voice, and he didn't expand on the point.

Peter eventually lay back down, and Jenna draped a damp cloth over his head, tucking him in. I climbed back into bed and closed my eyes, but sleep didn't come. The images from the mission came flooding back. The arrow in the soldier's rib cage. Blood seeping out. Langston on the ground, his leg ripped through by wood and steel. My hands felt wet with blood again...

And before I knew it, there was a heavy knock on the barrack door, waking us up for another day.

15. LANGSTON'S TALE

The Mess Hall was buzzing. Soldiers squeezed shoulder-to-shoulder, plates and silverware clanging against the rickety tables. Even with how crowded the hall was, green uniforms kept darting back and forth between tables, talking excitedly.

I sat down between Peter and Irene, whose eyes were bloodshot from her first twenty-four-hour shift. She barely had strength to lift her fork up to her mouth. It was one of the few times I felt bad for her working in the hospital rather than being out in the field.

Mashed potatoes topped with peas overflowed my tray, a small burger sitting carefully to the side. The burger was burned black, and I hated mashed potatoes, but I was currently too hungry to care.

"What's going on?" I asked. "Why's everyone running around?"

"Probably decided to start serving cake for dessert," said Willie, who, like usual, took a seat next to Jenna. We'd just gotten back from our second ranging—an uneventful three days protecting more trucks, this time filled with steel and wool. Willie and Jenna had spent most of the ranging off to the side, talking at length and largely ignoring the rest of us. Willie was growing more comfortable with all of us as a result though, and had put together more words over the ranging than during the rest of the time I'd known him.

Langston sat down just then, holding a copy of the *Arcton Gazette*, and slammed it onto the table. "Look at the cover story."

I slid the newspaper closer. A bolded headline read: **Squad 319 Saves the Day**.

"So, what?" I said. "That's good, isn't it?"

"Keep reading," Langston said.

At a time when the war is at its most pivotal point, the soldiers of Squad 319 did their part to help save Arcton.

The squadron, led by 17-year-old Carl Magner, recently returned from a weeks-long ranging where they took out at least two different groups of Trusselians comprising nine soldiers in total. All this, without losing a single soldier of their own.

"You've got to be kidding me," Peter said. "That's not even that impressive. We must have killed at least fifteen Trusselians."

"*They* get the story though," said Langston. "*They're* not Forcies."

"Worth reading the rest?" I asked.

"Not unless you enjoy long-winded descriptions of Carl's bravery and superior fighting abilities" Langston said.

I tossed him the paper. "What do you guys wanna do today?" We'd already done PT, the obstacle course, swordplay, and archery, and we had the afternoon to ourselves. Most of our off afternoons so far had been filled playing cards or going swimming at the beach. It was relaxing, but also made me anxious. Should we be doing more preparation? Should I be working harder at trying to use my powers again?

"I only have half an hour," said Irene sadly. She rested her head on her palm; despite the redness in her eyes, they still had a liveliness about them. "Gotta eat and get back. Forty-two more injured came in last night, and even a couple Trusselians. We're all working doubles at the hospital."

"You're taking care of the Trusselians too?" said Peter. "Why not just, you know, leave them?"

"Orders are orders," Irene said, shrugging.

Jenna turned to me. "Willie and I were gonna go for a hike if you want to come," she said.

"I was thinking about going for a swim," I said. "Pete? Langston?"

"I asked Ulysses if he could do some extra sword work with me," said Pete. "But I'll head over after if there's time."

"I'm in," said Langston. "Just let me grab some shorts."

We finished the meal and cleared our plates, and I gave Irene a kiss on the cheek before heading outside. Willie and Jenna immediately took off towards Mt. Brentwood; Langston jogged off to grab some swim trunks.

"You got a second?" I asked Peter. "We haven't really gotten a chance to talk since the other night…"

"I'm fine," Peter said quickly.

"You sure?"

Soldiers were filing past us in every direction, the dirt road packed tight. Hundreds of new recruits arrived every week, each new squadron forced to live the same hellish two weeks we'd experienced before going to battle, where every minute of every day was accounted for. At least now we got afternoons off.

"I'm positive—it was just a nightmare, Leo. Don't worry about it."

"Alright. You finish the book from the Whirlwind War?" I asked.

"Yeah, crazy. I can't believe our dads received the Medal of Hardship. And my dad never told us. What's up with that?"

"You're sure he never mentioned it to you? You've never seen it?"

"Yeah, hiding an achievement isn't really like him, is it?" Peter said. "He never misses a chance to rub something like that in our noses."

"Probably wanted to save it just in case we came home with some award," I said. "Then he could whip out the Medal of Hardship to take us down a notch or two."

Peter smiled, but his eyes betrayed some sadness. "And if that failed, well, he could always call me stupid and you short."

Peter turned and jogged off to the fighting pit, his green hat bobbing in-between dozens of others. He had the same gait as Uncle Lester, a boisterous, almost cocky walk. I guess you couldn't help but inherit some things from your parents.

The leaves withered and browned, the shorter October days starting to make their presence known. The air had a bit of a bite to it—not quite winter, but not particularly enjoyable when swimming. Langston and I spent nearly an hour jumping off a nearby cliff anyway, swimming to and from the buoys.

Tired, and with my mouth tasting like salt, I spread my towel down on the sand and sat down. Langston swam for a little while, but before long he swam back and sat down next to me. I tossed him a canteen.

"Anywhere to swim in Celwyn?" I asked. "Rivers, lakes?"

"Nah, no lakes or anything. There's a pool, but it's in the Cloud neighborhood, so I never went.

"Cloud neighborhood?"

"Rich people," Langston said. "Never bother looking down at people like me, always with their heads in the clouds."

"Got it. How'd you learn to swim then?" I asked. "I mean, if there's no pool or lake or anything?"

"We lived in the country when I was younger," Langston said. "Only moved to Celwyn a few years back. My dad taught me how when I was younger."

"Where is he now?" I asked.

"A hospital somewhere, I imagine."

"Oh, I'm sorry."

"Don't be. He deserves it."

I was shocked to hear this come from Langston. He'd never said a bad thing about anyone ever, not even a Trusselian.

"He was an asshole," Langston continued, as though that explained it.

"What'd he does?"

"He was a drunk," Langston said. "As long as I knew him, anyway. He'd come home from the bar reeking of liquor and start yelling at my mom. Once I was old enough to step in, I did. But that just made him even more pissed off. And it meant two people getting black eyes instead of one."

"You never told anyone at school? No blackhats?"

Langston scoffed. "They didn't care. My dad was in the Verdean with most of the higher-ups, so there were always strings being pulled. Anytime we talked to the police, they'd just have him walk it off and he'd be back the next day. We were on our own—me, my mom, and my sister."

"That's awful, Langston."

Langston swirled the canteen around. "Just the way life was," he said. "It would've been fine if he had stuck with me and my mom—but one night he started picking on Kim."

"Your sister?"

Langston nodded. "He didn't hit her. He just...you know, screamed at her, called her names. Useless. Lazy. He told her she didn't have any friends. Told her she was going to end up on the street, just like my aunt.

Langston shook his finger, as though touching the point in time. "That's when my mom snapped. She let out a blood-curdling scream, one loud enough for half of Arcton to hear. Neighbors came to our front yard. My mom screamed insults at my dad, ruining what little reputation he had left. She called him a traitor, said he didn't love Arcton...anything she could do to get him out of the house.

"It was a good thing the neighbors came when they did—my dad couldn't do anything to her with all the witnesses. But he wasn't gonna let that go. He tried to calm her down at first, say that she was being dramatic and making a scene. He got really red when she kept yelling, shoving him out of the house."

A shadow crept across Langston's eyes. "That night, I waited. My mom and Kim went to bed. We had a shed out back, and I took a shovel and some of this really thin, strong string we had. I tied the string between two posts on our front porch, about six inches off the ground. And then I waited in a rocking chair that he used to sit in.

"Around two in the morning, he stumbled back, a paper bag in his hand. He was about ten feet from the porch steps when he saw me sitting in the big, wooden rocking chair he loved. The shovel was by my feet, hidden from view. He looked up at me... angrier than I'd ever seen him.

"*Get out,* he said. *You got no right to be in that chair.* I laughed, trying to goad him, infuriate him, tempt him. Finally, I stood up and spat on him."

I leaned back. Langston spitting on his father? I only knew him as a bookworm, someone who not only wouldn't hurt a fly, but also would know exactly what type of fly it was, and probably how to keep it healthy and well-nourished. Yet he'd been ready to kill his own dad.

Langston just kept speaking into his knees. "He still didn't run up the stairs, though," he said. "Not until I called him a coward." He looked up at me, finally. "How come people hate being called a coward more than anything else? Call them a loser, a nerd, a jerk, and they get mad, sure. But whenever you call a man a coward, it's as if you've insulted every atom in his body. And my dad, well, I've never seen him so furious. He came charging up the stairs, but, of course, he didn't see the rope.

He fell flat on his face, and I'd never moved faster than I did then. I grabbed the shovel and slammed the spade down on his back as hard as I could...two, three, four times."

Langston shook his head, blinking at the memory.

"His bones cracked," he continued. "He mumbled a few times, but I kept smashing his back. I couldn't see his face. I only heard the grunts. But I got too close. My foot was right next to his hand, and he reached out and yanked it out from under me. I fell and dropped the shovel and banged my head on one of the stairs. I wasn't dizzy or anything, but he was so quick, even drunk and beaten half to death.

"He had me hog tied before I knew what was happening. He dragged me around back to the shed and threw me inside. He ripped off my shirt and gagged me with it. Then he started kicking my back and stomach, a steel toe in his boot breaking ribs. There's nothing worse than knowing pain is coming and not being able to stop it."

Even now, with Langston's shirt off, I could see an indentation in the side of his chest. The ribs had healed, but incorrectly.

"And then," Langston said, "just as another kick was coming, this one aimed at my face, he just stopped. He was looking at the doorway to the shed..."

Langston paused. It wasn't for dramatic effect, though. At least, not the way Peter would have done it. The memory burned his vision. I felt goosebumps go down my spine, ones that had nothing to do with the cold air.

"My mom," said Langston, "just stood in the doorway, looking at my dad…"

He took a deep breath, and I felt myself take one with him.

"She hit him with the shovel," Langston said. "Knocked him out cold. There was a nasty crunch, and he was bleeding a bit. She was worried, really worried. Ended up sending Kim to go get a blackhat."

"What, why?"

"I told her not to, that the blackhats would side with him."

"And…?"

"How do you think I got here?" Langston said. "I could never have taken care of Kim by myself, so I told my mom to let me take the blame. She cried and cried, but she would've been thrown in the Pit. At least this way I can still earn back my freedom."

"You ever hear from your dad again?"

"No. He could be in Easton or Trussel for all I know."

"How do you know he won't go back to your mom's place once he's out of the hospital?" I said.

"I don't," Langston said. "But I have a feeling he won't. Can't swear to it, but I just think the shovel did the trick."

The sun blazed down. My shorts had nearly dried. I squinted, shielding my eyes from the sun's reflection on the water. Gentle waves rippled against the shore, filling the silence. Sand clung to my feet and legs. Langston's calf wound had all but healed, but a yellow tinge still hovered where the arrow had pierced both sides. Another few days and there would be no trace at all.

16. SCOT-FREE

Book 3.

I got up before the sun rose and carefully dressed while the others slept. Peter murmured in his sleep—something about water, but nothing like the night sweats from before.

Outside, the first amber light crept over the horizon, nipping the tops of the waves and mingling with the Orb light. My breath clouded in front of me; the first snow of the season was close. A few squads rushed by, either heading out on a ranging, or made up of new recruits preparing to go through a torturous day of Basic Training.

There was no guard outside the Gilded Library. I removed the key from beneath the potted plant and again approached Section 342. I knew it was risky, but I took books 3, 4, and 5 this time. They formed a huge bulge beneath my jacket, but it was still early enough that I wouldn't pass by too many soldiers who could notice.

I rushed down the dimly lit hall and out into the morning and closed the door behind me. As I turned to replace the key underneath the potted plant, a voice called out.

"Oi!"

I turned. Carl stood there with the rest of his squad, all fully armed and clearly heading off on another ranging. He smirked at me, and I hastily raised myself up off my knee and stood, trying to keep the books hidden. His hair was primped and combed perfectly, creating a wave over his forehead. Only he and Peter would ever care so much about their hair when heading off on a mission.

"What are you up to, Forcie?" Carl asked.

"Taking a walk," I said. "Got a problem with that?"

"Weird place to stop," he said.

"Had to tie my shoe. Off on another ranging?"

"Someone has to win the war," he said.

"Do any of your friends ever talk?" I asked. "Or are they just there to protect you?" Their faces were shrouded in shadow, but the five bodies moved closer.

"You talk pretty big for someone who's outnumbered six to one," Carl said.

I smiled. "So they're not allowed to talk. Got it. I'd love to stay and chat, but I have a date with a massive pile of eggs and toast in the Mess Hall."

I stepped up onto the ledge, but Carl shoved me back down.

"I saw that girlfriend of yours," he said. "What's she doing with a Forcie like you?"

"I don't know, why don't you ask her?"

"Maybe I will."

Though I didn't like the sound of that, I had more pressing concerns. His friends had formed a semi-circle, surrounding me, and were getting closer.

"Squad 319," a voice called out from behind them, "we're running late. Let's move!"

They parted to let their lieutenant pass. He had a trimmed goatee and wore his hat down low, hiding his eyes.

"Who are you?" he asked me.

"No one. Just trying to get to the Mess Hall."

"Well you'd better get on with it," he said.

I returned to the barrack and hid the books in my trunk. Everyone was still asleep, but they'd be up soon enough.

Except for the kitchen staff and a few other wayward soldiers in need of an early breakfast, the Mess Hall was completely empty. Each time a plate clanged or a knife clattered on the table, the sound rang out through the place. I got in the breakfast line and shoveled some eggs and ham onto my plate, then made my way to an empty table near the entrance where I could watch soldiers come and go.

As a kid, I used to eat a bowl of cereal with my mom before my dad or Jenna woke up. I'd always had trouble sleeping in, just like her. She'd splash milk on my shirt, cracking up, and make faces at me, making me laugh and spit up cereal.

Those memories always sprang up when I ate breakfast alone. After she got sick, my dad started eating breakfast with me so she could sleep in.

He was so deliberate about how he ate, about how he did everything really. He would carefully press down on the bran flakes until he'd added just the right amount of milk. If there was a stray one clinging to the side of the bowl, he'd brush it down to join the rest before taking a bite. Never a stray flake. And then it was back to *Gestalt Diary*.

My mom wasn't one to fuss about the proper milk-to-flake distribution. She always ate with a vengeance, and we'd race to see who could finish first.

Jenna had laughed during both of their funerals, and at the weirdest times. During dad's service I'd been annoyed, even angry that she thought the situation funny, and I'd yelled at her for it. My mom had intervened, saying that sometimes the saddest occasions in life provide the funniest moments.

At my mom's funeral, a few months later, we were at the top of Yellowtree Hill, by our house, where my mom loved to sit in the shade of the tree and read. Peter's whole family was there with me and Jenna. When it came time to spread my mom's ashes, Uncle Lester had trouble with the lid and, next thing I knew, my mom's remains were flying through the air, the wind taking them for a ride out over Arcton City.

I was furious. My mom had specifically requested to have her remains spread at the foot of the Yellowtree, but I heard a giggle from beside me. It was Jenna, her eyes filled with tears, but laughing all the same.

"Mom wouldn't have cared," she said.

I finished my eggs, drained my glass of water, and left the Mess Hall, which was gradually filling up. I hadn't gotten fifty feet outside of the doors when a voice made me turn.

Standing just outside the doorway was a young girl in a Verdean uniform, an apron draped around her waist. Her doe eyes peered around nervously.

"Are you Leo?" she asked.

I nodded. "Who are you?"

She handed me a folded piece of paper. "I was told to give this to you."

At first I thought it might be a message like the one about the *Whirlwind War* books. But it was merely a note from Memo, asking me to go see him in his office.

"Thanks for coming," Memo said, motioning me to take a seat. His office was pristinely organized, with folders and papers stacked in neat piles along his desk and the books on his shelves sorted in alphabetical order. He sat at his desk, straight-backed, reviewing a document that he put on top of one of the piles. His uniform, as usual, was spotless and unwrinkled. But beneath his eyes I saw the hint of a shadow.

. A fireplace raged behind Memo's desk, providing warmth against the morning frost. Flames licked at the logs, charring their coats.

"What did you want to see me about, sir?"

"Your power," Memo said, not beating around the bush. "I feel comfortable now, discussing what I know—and what I've seen."

"So you have seen it before..." I said.

"I witnessed it one other time," Memo said, "and never again. Your power is rare, Leo, but not unique. I've combed every book in the Verdean searching for more information, but sadly, I found nothing." He paused and took a deep breath. "The only other time I saw it—it was your father. He did something almost identical to what you did with those arrows. I asked him about it any chance I got, but he swore it never happened again."

My palms started to sweat. I couldn't believe it.

"Like yours," Memo continued, "his power manifested when his life and his squad's was at stake."

"When?" I asked. "When did he do it?"

"In the Whirlwind War," Memo said. "I was among those he saved."

"The Whirlwind War? How come no one ever told me? Uncle Lester must have been there, too, right?"

I was shaking. I needed to read Books 3 through 5. There must be some mention of his weird power in there. That had to be the real reason that someone had pointed me toward the books.

I still couldn't believe it: my dad had a special power. He'd saved lives with it. Maybe he knew how to control it, too.

"Lester was there," Memo said, "but you need to understand that we didn't tell *anyone* about what we saw Geoff do. Who would have believed us? And if someone *had*, we worried that they would take Geoff from the Sphelix. We were a unit. We were a family."

"How did it happen?" I asked. "Where did he do it?"

"We were fighting Northron, and the war wasn't going well. We were always on the front lines, defending Arcton from wave after wave of attacks. Finally, after making a push into Northron, the Sphelix went on a mission into one of the port cities, Luxxter.

"If you think winter in Arcton is bad, you should see Northron in February. There were twenty-four straight days of snow. After a week of travel, we ended up staying in an abandoned barn one night—or what we thought was an abandoned barn. We woke up to knocks at the door and eventually gunshots, trying to break off the lock. Yes, bullets," Memo said, for I raised my eyebrows. "Guns were more common back then. They blew off the lock within seconds.

"The door flew open and the soldier started shooting, but before the bullets reached us, they simply…stopped. In midair. One was a few inches from me. I even reached out and touched it, wondering what on Earth had happened.

"And then I looked at your dad. He had long hair and a full beard—this was before the Verdean regulated facial hair—and his eyes were closed, his hand held out in front of him. Just as suddenly, he flicked his hand forward and the bullets turned and sprang through the chest of the soldier who'd tried to shoot us."

"He stopped *bullets*?" I said. "He *turned* them?"

Memo nodded. "The other soldiers ran—they probably saw their comrade shot and assumed we had guns, too—and we walked away scot-free. We completed the mission a few days later, and Luxxter surrendered shortly after that. None of it would've been possible without your dad."

So my father had been the one to pass me my power. Did he know, even as a kid, that I had it? Was that why *Gestalt Diary* was so important? Did it discuss this power? Describe how to use it, strengthen it?

"What was he like?" I asked. "I mean—Lester never really talked about my dad, and I was so young when he died…" I felt my cheeks flush. It was a childish question, and not nearly as important as figuring out how to use my power. But still.

Memo smiled. "He had a certain affinity for breaking rules, just like you, Leo. But he was always generous and empathetic, and he was a tremendous leader. I admired him deeply. He was my best friend."

I looked away from Memo, feeling tears growing, and turned my attention to the books in the office. They were all covered in the same, ancient brown leather, the Verdean's green *A* with the whorl circling its head imprinted on the top of each book. No spine had a speck of dust on it. Memo took great care of them, probably read them regularly.

"Leo," Memo said, "Please keep this conversation confidential, and your power even more so. But you can confide in the rest of the Sphelix. You can trust them."

"I do trust them," I said.

"Good," said Memo. He strummed his fingers along the table. "If you don't mind, I'd like to ask you a personal question." No other adult I'd ever met, not just in the Verdean but at school or anywhere in Arcton City, had ever asked for my permission before asking a question.

"Of course, sir."

"Why did you want that book, *Dasher's Revenge*? Why would you risk so much for it?"

"Because of *Gestalt Diary*, sir."

His eyes widened. "*Gestalt Diary?*"

"Yes, sir. It was a Nefa my dad used to read to me as a kid. And, well, I'd never read another one."

"I see."

"It was stupid, I know, but my dad always said it was an important book, and that I needed to remember. But I don't remember it at all.

"It's not stupid," Memo interrupted. "It's natural to be curious. It's a good thing."

"Doesn't feel like a good thing," I said. "My curiosity landed us here."

"Don't beat yourself up too much about that," said Memo. "Some good may still come out of it."

Memo stood and I understood it was time to go. Memo placed a hand on my shoulder as I was walking out the door.

"For what it's worth," he said, "I think your dad accomplished his goal with *Gestalt Diary*."

"How's that?" I asked.

Memo's only answer was a smile.

Peter was the only one still there when I got back to the barrack. Everyone else must have headed out to breakfast. He was struggling to get his shirt on, and when he finally pulled it over his head, his face was pale and white.

"How'd you sleep?" I asked.

"Not well," he said.

"More nightmares?"

He nodded.

"It'll get better."

After he left, I went to my trunk and pulled out Book 3 eager to read more about the Whirlwind War. As I flipped it open, a note fell out of one of the back pages. My heart skipped a beat. It was the same childish scrawl as before.

Loyalty is fickle. Death is final. Neither, for your family, is what it seems.

17. PREPARATION IS PARAMOUNT

"Why can't he just tell it to me straight?" I asked, looking at the others. A few soldiers passed outside the barrack, talking loudly about some pretty nurses that had treated their wounds. I lowered my voice. "Why is it always in a weird, cryptic message?"

Langston held the note. He stared at the handwriting like it was a piece of art, viewing it from different angles, holding it up to the light. It was very Langston of him.

"It's in case it gets in the wrong hands," Langston said. "If someone else comes across this, they won't know who it's for, and they won't know what to make of it."

Willie played his harmonica softly—it was a happy tune he played in the morning when we didn't have the obstacle course to worry about. Jenna sat on his bed, a nurse's textbook on her lap. The cover was peeled and worn, but I could still make out the title: *Common Antidotes and Ointments.*

"And you're sure there were no other letters in any of the books?" Jenna said. "You checked through all the pages?"

"Yes," I said. I hadn't had time to read all the pages, but I'd skimmed them. There were a few more mentions of the old Sphelix—a few where they took out Northron squads, and the one Memo had mentioned where they went into Luxxter and actually captured a Captain in the Northron army. "Look through them yourself."

"And, that's not all," I said. Peter, who was examining a batch of arrows in front of him, turned in his chair. I dropped my voice to barely more than a whisper. "Memo *has* seen my power before. My dad stopped bullets when they were fighting in the Whirlwind War."

Jenna's eyebrows raised. Willie stopped playing the harmonica. Langston and Peter both lit up and smiled.

"So it's hereditary?" Langston said. "Passed down from parent to child. Then, Jenna…" He turned to her. "Have you ever…?"

She shook her head. "Never."

"It wouldn't surprise me if you developed the same power," Langston said. "But there could be a bunch of factors that go into it: gender, age, and of course just pure chance."

"Did Memo say anything else about it?" Peter said.

"It was just the one time," I said. "As far as Memo knows, anyway."

My mind was racing: Who was giving me the letters? Did my dad ever use his power again? Would Jenna be able to develop them too?

Exhausted and overwhelmed, I got into bed.

Before I could fall asleep, though, a loud knock came at our door and Memo walked in. He had deep lines around his eyes and was breathing more heavily than usual. His hair was tied back in a tight ponytail, and his Verdean uniform was, as always, pressed.

"Is everything alright?" Jenna asked, fiddling with a few nurse's vials on her bed. "You look a little tired, Memo."

He gave her a wry smile. "Quite fine, thank you," he said. "I'm a little displeased is all—but no matter. I have news about your next assignment."

It was as if the room instantly received a shot of adrenaline.

"It's nothing like the others," he said. "It's not just a simple transport mission. This time, you're on the offensive, and you're going in outnumbered."

He meticulously detailed the plan. At a strategically crucial tributary—one of the few access routes that didn't require getting through the bay—there were three enemy gunners taking down any Arctonian boats coming in with supplies. Our mission was to get behind enemy lines, sneak up on the gunners, and take them out to allow an armada of supplies we desperately needed to work its way through.

"Gunners?" I said. "You mean like…?"

"Vestiges of previous wars," said Memo. "They're highly powerful, and Arcton had control of them up until a few months ago. But Trussel pushed into our border and secured them."

He rolled out a map and showed us exactly where the gunners were located. "There will be at least four men at each station," he said. "So be as quiet as possible when taking them out—you don't want to tip off the other two stations when you're taking out the first.

"We'll leave early tomorrow to do some recon while it's still light," he continued. "And then you'll go out under cover of night. Oh…and I'll be coming with you on the recon work."

"Great!" said Peter. "Any chance you can fight with us?"

"Unfortunately the Verdean still says no," said Memo. "Perhaps another time."

By the time the truck arrived to drive us to the tributary in the morning, clouds had gathered and a thick mist shrouded the camp. Unlike the last driver, this one was more than willing to talk to us. "Name's Oliver," he said, shaking out his puffy black hair matted down underneath his hat. "I'll be taking care of y'all."

We climbed in, Memo taking the seat closest to the driver.

"Captain," Oliver said with a familiar nod.

"Good to see you, Oliver," said Memo.

We took off through Base Camp, and Oliver wasted no time in putting us at ease.

"You guys see that awful breakfast today?" he complained over his shoulder. "Just beans and rice...what's up with that? We're out here risking our lives and can't even get a bite of meat?"

I didn't know if it was appropriate to complain as well, and it seemed like no one else was sure either, as the Sphelix kept our mouths shut. Oliver was undeterred by our silence.

"This rain is brutal, man. Reminds me I need a haircut. I've got practically two gallons of water stuck in my hair. I'm going to be dripping wet for the next two weeks."

"Your hair looks good," Willie said kindly.

"Yeah, well, anything would look good compared to the mop on your head," Oliver said. "Suppose you let one of these nincompoops shear it off."

"I did it," said Langston, offended. "It's not that bad."

Oliver turned to Langston, barely keeping an eye on the road. "You might want to borrow Memo's glasses next time you're cutting someone's hair."

I was so engrossed in Oliver's banter that I barely noticed the ride and the rain. Mud splashed up with every dip the truck took, a few specks landing on my cheeks. I kept my hood wrapped tightly over my head. About thirty minutes in, when we left the perimeter of the Orb's glow, Oliver ramped up his jokes to even poke fun at Memo. Memo, to his credit, laughed when Oliver gave a short but spot-on impersonation of him tying his ponytail— stiff backed and whistling a song I had never heard from anyone else. A couple of hours later, after passing numerous Verdean camps and outposts, Oliver stopped the truck short of a lookout.

"This is it," Oliver said. "I'm not gonna pull up farther in case Trussel has a watchman. If you guys go up, there should be a good vantage point of the three gunners. Personally, I don't think more than two of you should be in view of the gunners at once."

"Good advice," Memo said, "This shouldn't take us too long. We're going to do most of the planning when we get back to the barracks."

All of us except for Oliver hopped out of the truck and started up the slope to the lookout. We were officially on the edge of Arcton's territory—the front lines. Trussel had pushed miles inward from the old border.

We took it in twos, just like Oliver had said. First Memo and Jenna, then Willie and Langston, and finally Peter and me...

We stayed on our bellies, barely reaching our heads over the top of the hill. At first I only saw the front two gunners—little concrete stations covered in grass and dirt. The third one was back a quarter mile, edging the ocean. I didn't see any soldiers walking around, but that didn't mean there weren't any there.

When it was done, we hopped in Oliver's truck and reversed down a stretch of road before he could turn around and drive forward the rest of the way.

"Three gunners, just like we thought," Memo said. "The one furthest from us—closest to the ocean—is the one you have to start with."

"The one deepest in Trussel territory?" I asked.

"Correct. And you can work your way back towards safety."

"So we won't be able to take a boat across the water," said Langston.

"Too likely that you'd be seen," said Memo. "You're going to have to swim across."

"How strong's the current?" asked Willie. He was clearly nervous.

"Not bad," said Memo. "You should be fine getting there. Getting back though, after you're tired, may be more difficult."

The truck rumbled over a particularly rocky patch, and all of us were thrown two inches up out of our seats.

"Any special medical supplies I should bring?" Jenna asked. "Extra morphine, or even a few FPs...?"

"No focus pills," Memo said. "The typical supplies should do just fine. There's no moon tonight, so they shouldn't even see you coming. Ideally you can get in and out without a single turret going off." He rubbed a hand through his hair. "They should've never..."

"Never what?" I asked.

Memo smiled sheepishly. "Nothing," he said.

"We can do this, Memo," I said. "Don't worry. We'll take care of it and be back before you can cook us a victory dinner."

Memo smiled. "I'll have some hot chocolate ready when you return."

18. A CHANGE IN GAZE

We spent the entire ride back going over strategy for that night's mission. Memo spread out maps on the truck bed, detailing exactly where the outposts were and how best to attack them. His instructions continued until we passed through the gates outside of Base Camp, where a lieutenant stood waiting at the truck depository.

"Captain Iglesias," he said. "I have a letter for you."

The lieutenant handed it over and stalked off, barking orders at a couple of soldiers having a relaxed conversation outside of the inventory shop. The Orb pulsated in the distance, the dull green glow illuminating the road despite the setting sun.

"What is it?" Peter asked.

Memo read quickly before turning to face us. "Willie, would you mind coming back to my office with me?"

Willie stared at him and nodded. Curious, I tracked them as they walked to the Captains' Offices. I looked to Jenna for an answer as to what was going on, but she merely shrugged. The rest of us thanked Oliver for the ride and returned to Barrack 19.

I spent that night cleaning and polishing my sword. Its pommel gleamed in the Orb light while I worked the leather over the blade, back and forth. The dirt and grime slowly dissolved, washing up onto one side of the cloth; I oiled up the other side, applying pressure in small circles over the blade's surface, leaving it spotless. Just as I was sheathing it, the door to Barrack 19 opened and Willie walked in, tossing a pair of keys from hand to hand. He went over to his bed and sat down.

"What are those?" I asked.

"Something Memo gave me," Willie said.

I picked up some arrows and ran my finger over their fletchings, searching for notches or kinks that could mess up their trajectory.

"What's wrong?" Jenna asked

I looked up, expecting her to be talking to me, but she was facing Willie. He was staring blankly up at the top bunk, shaking slightly. His eyes were red.

"Br—Willie," Jenna said again. Langston looked up from his book. Peter set his own sword down. But Willie didn't respond. He just kept staring at the bottom of the mattress above.

"Willie," I said, "What did Memo want?" A deep pit was forming in my stomach. What had Memo needed to tell him in private?

"Nothing," Willie said. "Just wanted to talk about the mission."

Jenna walked over and put her hand on his arm. "Willie, you can tell me. You can trust us. Whatever it is."

Willie didn't meet her eyes. His own started watering, heavy tears coming down his cheeks.

"They died," he said. "There was a raid on my village…my parents were killed."

"Oh," Langston said. "I'm so sorry, man."

Jenna pulled Willie into a tight hug, stroking his trim black hair. Willie didn't audibly cry, but tears continued streaming down his face. It felt like a strong wintery gust had rushed into the barrack.

"Really sorry," said Peter. "I can't even imagine."

"When did it happen?" Jenna asked.

"About a week ago," said Willie. "Just got word now."

I thought back to Willie's twin sister, who had also died. He had no other family. He was alone.

The pit in my stomach started to fill with anger. Trussel was the reason Willie had no family left; this war was the reason. Trussel was endangering Jenna's life every time we stepped outside of Base Camp.

"So, are we still going on the mission?" Peter asked.

"Peter!" said Jenna. "Who cares? We have more important things to worry about now."

"We're going," said Willie, pulling himself out of Jenna's hug. He wiped away his tears. "I told Memo I wanted to do it."

"You can get some revenge," I said.

"Leo!" Jenna said. "We don't need to do this tonight. It can wait. Willie, putting you into a situation like that...after what you've just been through..."

Willie's voice was steel. "I want it," he said. "I want to kill them." He threw the keys up in the air and grabbed at them violently.

From up on his top bunk, Langston raised his eyebrows at me. Willie was always a bit rough around the edges, but now he had murder in his voice.

"Langston, throw me those cookies," I said. "Willie, you want one? You should eat something."

"I'll eat some jerky if you have it," Willie said.

I threw him a piece from my duffel, and he tore into it. With every bite his expression changed further from the scared one he'd worn when he walked in to a cold, dead stare that shot daggers.

I didn't envy the first Trusselian he came across tonight.

19. THE TRIBUTARY

That night, we packed in silence. I didn't want to swim across a river weighed down with books or extra clothes, so all I had was my sword, bow, arrows, a few dehydrated meal packs, and an extra canteen. Willie, who sat on his bed playing a slow, sad tune on his harmonica, carried our only flashlight.

Irene stopped by a little earlier to wish us luck. I wished she wouldn't. Somehow, it made the stakes of war so much higher. Never seeing Irene again was the thing that frightened me most about death.

"Remember to bring an extra pair of socks," said Langston. "Going to be raining hard tonight." He rolled up a pair and stuffed them into his backpack. He was always perfect with his organization—every piece of clothing had its proper spot, each fold left little room for wrinkles. He was like Memo in that way.

"You really think that's going to make a difference?" said Peter. "We have to swim to the outposts. All of our stuff is going to get wet anyway."

"Death starts at the feet," said Langston. "I'm telling you, there's nothing more comfortable than a pair of thick, dry wool socks after being wet for hours."

"I've got a waterproof bag for my medical supplies," said Jenna. "There's more than enough room for everyone to hold an extra pair of socks."

"If Langston says so," I said, tossing her a pair. I couldn't help but laugh at how weird it was. All of us cramming in extra socks on a night when death, if it really came, would be in the form of heavy artillery. But if Langston gave you advice on something, it was usually best to take it.

Jenna sat down next to me. "Leo, have you been able to, you know…"

"No," I said. "I've tried, but I've never been able to make it happen again."

"I hate to ask, I was just curious."

"It's okay," I said. "I'm curious what'll happen too."

"You'll be fine," said Peter from his bunk. His cheeks were already rosy from the dipping temperature. "It's a distress thing, I bet. You need the adrenaline pumping in order for it to happen. You're never going to be able to do it on command."

"Peter's probably right," said Jenna.

"That's a first for you, Pete," I said.

Jenna laughed. "Either way, hopefully we won't need it tonight."

"I wouldn't count on it," said Langston. "I've read about them. They can rip through targets two hundred yards away. We've gotta make sure they don't aim them at us."

"They won't," said Peter. "We'll be careful. Plus, if anything bad happens, we have all these extra socks." Langston flipped him the middle finger. Willie continued playing his harmonica.

Later, as we threw on our coats to leave, I turned to Jenna.

"That power might just be a one-time thing, like it was for Dad," I said. "There's no guarantee I'll be able to do it again. You shouldn't get your hopes up."

Thinking back to my dad, I remembered the note in the *Whirlwind War* book. *Loyalty is fickle. Death is final. Neither, for your family, is what it seems.* What did fickle loyalty have to do with my family? And death—was it my dad's death, or my mom's? Or someone else's?

Jenna brought me back to the present. "It might be a one-time thing, but I'm not worried about tonight regardless. We have the socks, and, even better, we have you. Power or not, it's comforting to know you're next to me."

I gave her a hug, taking in the faint smell of coconut. "Probably not the best time to get all mushy," I said. "You know, right before battle."

Moonlight couldn't breach the storm of clouds and water that rained down upon our hoods in the back of Oliver's truck, but the Orb's glare wasn't blocked by a little water. The dull green followed us for forty-five minutes before we passed beyond its range. For three more hours afterward the only source of light was the truck's headlights. Until we finally came to a stop.

Oliver yelled back to us. "Move quick. Stick together."

The path down to the water was steep, with nothing but slippery grass and mud beneath our feet. I slipped a couple of times before quickly gathering myself. When we were about halfway down, Langston completely lost his footing and knocked into Peter and Jenna, causing all three to go tumbling. Willie and I raced down as fast as we could to check on them, but when we got to the bottom, they were all howling with laughter.

"What took you so long?" Peter asked as I tried to catch my breath. "Didn't you hear about the shortcut?"

"Let's slide down on trash can lids next time," said Langston.

If there was a next time, I wanted to remind him. Yet even Willie, despite himself, gave a reluctant laugh. I couldn't think of a more absurd time to be laughing—especially for Willie—but here we were.

Getting into the freezing cold river wasn't nearly as fun. I immediately went into shock, one giant shiver coursing through my body. I held my weapons in my left arm above the water, frog kicking and using my right arm to paddle. It was slow work, carrying such a heavy load, but we made the journey without too much difficulty, reaching the sand bank on the other side. Willie was last on the shore, as he had feared, but even he wasn't breathing too heavily. The obstacle course had paid off.

Waterlogged boots slowed the trek up the hill. Each time I took a step, my boot gently squished, sinking into the mud and blasting my foot with more water. When we reached the top, we got down on all fours to scope out the landscape.

The front outposts were directly to our right—or, at least I thought they were. Visibility was limited to about twenty yards. Langston of course knew where we were. He pointed and said our first target was to the northeast, so we started off in what I could only trust was the right direction.

CRACK!

I whipped around. The others did the same. I unsheathed my sword and stared into the pitch-black night, hyperaware. Nothing. A twig maybe? Perhaps I'd stepped on something?

But there was a ruffling in the bushes. Someone was in there...

A four-legged creature scurried out, shaking the water out of its fur. My eyes adjusted enough, and the pointy ears of a fox came into view. He sniffed at my leg before realized I didn't have any food and sprinted off back from where he came.

We took a collective deep breath.

"Come on," Jenna said.

Running helped loosen the joints and work out some of the cold that had settled into my bones, but the wind blew me from side to side like Uncle Lester after a night at the bar. Peter quickly opened up a lead on the rest of us, and since I couldn't shout at him to slow down for obvious reasons, I had to sprint to catch up with him and point back to Jenna and Langston far behind us.

Peter stopped, and together we waited for the others to catch up. His eyes were wide, and he gave me a crazed look. "We're gonna do it," he said, giving me a little shove, trying to pump me up too. "They killed Willie's parents. They deserve to die."

"Peter, relax," I said. "We got a long way to go." I didn't point out that the soldiers we were aiming to kill likely didn't have anything to do with Willie's parents' deaths.

The others caught up, and we continued through the waist-high brush, the reeds swaying sharply whichever way the wind blew. After twisting my ankle badly on a root, I had half a mind to ask

Willie for his flashlight, but I knew using it would immediately risk giving up our location.

Just as my ankle was starting to really slow my pace, the outpost came into view. The ceiling was only a few feet above the surface of the ground. The rest was burrowed into the earth, with a few ocean-facing slits and a backdoor, which stood directly in front of us. We ducked down underneath the brush to talk through strategy.

"Should we bull rush them?" Peter asked.

"Let's stick with Memo's plan," said Langston. "We can take a few of them out with arrows and overpower the others."

"If they get even one shot of the turret off, the other two camps will know we're here," Jenna said. "That has to be our number one priority—making sure they don't sound an alarm."

"Willie and Langston, why don't you shoot arrows when we open the back door?" I said. "Peter and I will jump in after."

"I'll fight too," said Jenna. "I'm not just going to stand there and watch."

"Shoot with Willie and Langston," I said. "And then everyone come in after to help."

"You shoot with Willie and Langston," Jenna said. "I'll go to the front with Peter."

"Jenna, now's not the time," I said. "You're shooting with them."

Peter and I crawled our way through the mud and reeds to the edge of the outpost, carefully lowering ourselves into the three-foot-wide trench.

Peter's face was no longer manic with excitement—his eyes

were wide, his breath short. A chilling, unexplainable thought came to me: *Would he freeze up?* I shook it off.

We edged our way to the front door, trying to disturb the deep puddle of water at our feet as little as possible. Muffled voices came from inside.

I drew out my longsword slowly. Peter did the same.

Behind us, Jenna, Willie, and Langston were getting into position kneeling around the door with their bows slung over their shoulders. With the outpost built into the ground, they had to get closer in order to get a good angle on their shot. The seconds crept by like hours.

Finally, all three bows were in hand and pointed directly at the door. Muffled voices still creeped through the concrete walls.

Now was the time…

I held up three fingers and removed one.

I steadied my breath, focusing on the in-flow and out-flow. More muffled noises.

I removed the second finger and reached for the door handle. *Steady your breath*, I told myself. In through the nose, out through the mouth.

My hand clasped the handle, turning slowly.

I threw open the door.

I pulled back in time to see three arrows fly into the outpost. I heard a couple of yells, followed by screams of pain. Without so much as a second in between, another three arrows flew through the door. Peter and I charged after them with a yell, but there was no one to yell at.

There were only three soldiers inside, all sitting at a table. All dead.

Half-full glasses of a burgundy drink were on the table and cards were strewn everywhere. The cards were arranged in a half-circle, with seemingly random ones face up. I didn't recognize the game they'd been playing.

Willie, Langston, and Jenna came in and leaned their backs against the wall and breathed sighs of relief as they looked around. My adrenaline was waning already, leaving me exhausted.

The two turrets were on the other side of the room, looking out at the ocean. Huge magazine clips hung from their cages. The bullets themselves were a foot long, with shiny bronze casings.

"What do we do with the turrets?" I asked. "Destroy them?"

"Better not to," said Langston. "Don't want to make any noise and tip off the others. The Verdean is going to take over these turrets after we clear them out anyway. We should get moving."

Three. Two. One.

I turned the handle and ripped it back as hard as I could. The door didn't budge. Voices from inside rang out, one barking orders at the others.

I turned to Peter. "What do we do?" I said. "Door's locked."

Right as the question left my lips, the earsplitting noise of a turret erupted inside, ripping open the night. Thankfully the massive gun was aimed at the water—where boats came in— but it had served its purpose: the other outpost now knew we'd arrived.

I nearly peed my pants. What little of Peter's face I could see went completely moon-white. My heart thumped in my chest, beating a million times a minute, my mind racing through a thousand possibilities. The Trusselians could attack at any moment.

Think. *Think.*

"How do we open the door?" Peter whispered.

"We don't want to," I said. "They're waiting for it. Follow me."

I motioned for Jenna, Langston, and Willie to stay in position.

Peter and I wrapped around the other side to the turrets, clouds of smoke still hanging over the nozzles. A sliver of light showed from inside, shadows dancing in and out—soldiers moving. I edged up and peered through. Six Trusselians huddled around the door, their swords ready.

I dipped back down and turned to Peter.

"Get your bow," I whispered.

We each knocked an arrow and stuck the head of it inside the sliver.

Thwang!

Our arrows shot through and pierced two soldiers beside the door. They let out guttural yells. Their comrades took this as a signal to rush out into the trench.

I ran around the side, Peter close at my heels. Jenna, Willie, and Langston unloaded arrow after arrow into the others from their high vantage point.

Water splashed everywhere. Or was it blood?

A huge body fell backwards into me. I instinctively tried to catch him, and my blade ripped through his flesh.

Within seconds it was over, the arrows making quick work of

the Trusselians.

As Peter and I made sure each soldier was lifeless, Langston, Willie, and Jenna hopped down into the trench, collecting their arrows from the bodies.

"Let's go inside," I said when we were done.

The sheltered outpost felt like a breath of fresh air. Inside were tables and chairs, but no drinks, and no cards. This group had been more disciplined than the last.

"What happened with the door?" Langston asked. "Did they know we were coming? They got the turret off."

"They didn't know," I said. "The door was locked."

"They shot the turret right after," Peter said. "Wanted to warn the other outpost we were here."

"I think they warned the entire countryside," said Jenna. "That thing nearly burst my eardrums."

"We're lucky it's storming out," Langston said. "Otherwise we might be facing the entire Trusselian army, and not just one more outpost."

"We might be anyway," said Willie.

"Let's blow out these candles and get moving," I said. "They may have already sent a messenger from the last outpost for backup."

"They're going to be waiting for us," Jenna said. "That makes us way more vulnerable."

"I think we just gotta bullrush 'em," Peter said. "Take them by surprise."

"They're not going to be surprised, Pete," Langston said.

"That's the whole point. Our best option is a diversion. Something to draw them away or catch them off guard."

The gears in Langston's head were clearly turning rapidly.

"We tie the flashlight to a tree near the outpost using a rope," Langston said. "The wind is howling right now, blowing branches all over the place. If the Trusselians have a lookout, like they should, he'll see the tree and either go to take it out or fire right from where he is. We should at least be able to draw one or two of them out with the flashlight as a decoy."

Jenna nodded in agreement, and then Willie and Peter did too.

The flashlight blazed to life, and seconds later Jenna's shadow dropped down from the first branch of a pine tree. The wind whipped the light every which way while Jenna sprinted in a low crouch toward where we hid.

Jenna was halfway to us. The base was silent. There was zero movement…

The rain had subsided. Stars were starting to peak through the clouds, twinkling at us from above. The outpost, covered in sandbags, remained dark, stoic.

When Jenna caught up with us and crawled next to me, I exhaled heavily. I hadn't realized I was holding my breath.

"No sign?" she said.

"None," I said. "Looking back on it, a random light in the dark isn't exactly the best trap."

"It's something, though," she said. "And even if it draws out one of them, it's completely worth it."

175

The outpost stayed silent. A few rippling waves reached us, but the whipping wind blocked out everything else.

"When do we revert to Plan B?" Peter asked.

"There isn't a Plan B," Willie said.

"Sure there is," Peter said. "Same thing as last time and the time before that."

The longer we stayed, the more likely it was that Trusselian backups would arrive, at which point we'd either be dead or have to abort the mission. Plus, we needed to get back across the river to get word to the Verdean squads waiting that the outposts were empty and could be taken over. Maybe Pete was right.

Just as I opened my mouth to agree, a shadow appeared right in front of the outpost. It moved like a dog across the path, staying as low to the ground as possible while still maintaining a fast pace. Peter lost an arrow just as he approached our flashlight, and the shadow went down.

"Nice shot, Pete," Langston said.

All at once my vision blurred. A warped darkness took over, and I couldn't see a thing. I shook my head, trying to clear my sight. Blinking did nothing to help it.

"What the…" I gasped.

A lightning rod zipped through the warped darkness, heading right at us—straight for Peter. Faster than I knew what I was doing, I reached out with my hand to catch the light before it could hit him. I did a double take when the light stopped in my hand, pliable and woody.

"Leo!" someone shouted, sounding a mile away. "Leo!"

I struggled to break through the darkness. When I finally did, I had an arrow in my hand.

"Seven o'clock," someone yelled in the distance.

"Over by the outpost," Willie said.

I knocked the arrow I had apparently caught and pointed it at another moving shadow that was retreating to the base, loosing it with a *thwang*. To my surprise, the shaft penetrated the top of the shadow, and it collapsed.

"Let's move," I said.

I didn't know who, if anyone, was following, but I tore off in a dead sprint. Everyone caught up and looked at me expectantly.

"Willie and Pete, go behind and see if you can shoot some arrows in like at the last outpost. We'll wait for some commotion to start before busting open the door."

"You got it," said Willie.

Langston, Jenna, and I posted right outside of the doors, hiding behind the concrete walls. I steadied my breathing. *Short, quick breaths. Long, slow ones. In-flow. Out-flow.*

After a few minutes of waiting, the sound of yelling told us that Willie and Peter had shot their arrows. Nodding at Jenna and Langston, I kicked open the door and led the charge inside. There were five soldiers, but all of them were turned towards the turrets when we crashed in.

I swung my sword violently overhead at a burly soldier with a black eye and long blonde bangs. He blocked me just as my blade was about to make contact with his neck. Letting out a low grunt, he thrust my sword aside and swung quickly for my leg. It barely missed, but I landed a punch to the chin.

He staggered back against the wall, dazed. I advanced quickly, slashing his sword hand. He dropped the sword with a scream of pain, and I lifted my black blade high in the air, ready.

"Leo!" I heard Jenna shout.

I turned, expecting to see her in trouble. Instead, the entire Sphelix stood there, uninjured, with the Trusselians lying on the ground. My opponent was the last of his comrades still standing.

"What are you waiting for?" the man asked. He really was a man—in addition to his black eye and long blonde hair, he had a full beard and a weathered, sandy face with sunken eyes. "Get on with it," he said in his drawly accent. His back was pressed up against the wall, and he slid down a few inches.

"Do it, Leo," said Peter. "Let's get out of here."

"I can't," I said. There was no second thought. I wasn't going to kill this man.

"What?" said Peter. "Leo, we have to. They said take no prisoners."

"Well, we're taking one," I said. "I'm not killing him. He poses no threat to us."

"He just tried to kill you," Peter said.

"And now he can't. His sword is gone. He's completely outnumbered. Besides, we can question him."

"Look, I agree with you," said Pete. "The Verdean won't trust us if we bring this guy back alive. You know how many of our soldiers Trussel has taken back? None. Unless they want to torture them."

"I'm not killing him," I said. "And neither are you."

"Did Memo die and make you captain?" Peter said. He was glaring at me.

"No," I said calmly. "But it doesn't feel right. You know it doesn't."

"We'll get tried for insubordination if we bring him back."

"I'll take the fall for it."

"Leo, I'm not letting you do that."

While we were arguing, something flashed in the corner of my eye. I turned to see the man sprinting towards the door. Willie lunged at him, but missed. As the rest of us gave chase, I thought for a second about shooting an arrow at him, but he was only running away, not posing any threat. Shooting him from behind would be no better than having slain him as he stood before me.

We caught up to him at the cliff. He looked at us like a cornered rat, itching for an escape route. Far below, waves crashed into the cliff's edge. A salty breeze blew the man's hair across his face.

"Stop," I said. "We're not going to kill you."

"I know your type," the Trusselian said, his accent thick with venom. "You cut us up and roast us, laughing while you do it. Then you pick our bones clean. I'm not going down like that."

"Look, we don't do any of that... No!"

He jumped before I could say another word, his body flying down the cliff face and plunging into the icy, raging water of the ocean below.

Jenna covered her mouth with her hand. Next to her, Peter and

Langston shook their heads. Willie alone looked unperturbed, his face stony.

Had the man really thought that we ate the bodies of those we killed? *Ate* them. He'd chosen to die rather than find out if it was true.

I reached a hand to brush some hair out of my eyes and accidentally smeared blood on my forehead. I looked down and realized my uniform was completely covered in it, some my own, some not. My jacket started to press down on me, making it hard to breathe. It was waterlogged, true, but there was another weight constricting my chest. I tried brushing off the blood in the rain, wiping it away. But my lungs felt like they were getting squeezed out...

"Leo," Jenna said, coming over to me. "Short, quick breaths. You're alright. You're hyperventilating."

I tried to open my mouth to say something back, but I couldn't muster the air. I started clawing at the jacket, wanting to rip it off, and finally settled with just throwing it over my head and standing half-naked in the rain. I shortened my breaths, and air started to flow more freely. The constriction eased. My body warmed despite being exposed to the elements.

Then, Langston took off his jacket too. Peter followed suit and put his arm around me.

We looked to see if Willie would take his jacket off as well, but he stayed motionless.

"You're covered in blood," Langston said to him. "Trust me, it feels great to take it off."

"He doesn't have to if he doesn't want to," said Jenna.

"We know," Peter said. "But he should. It feels great."

Willie rubbed his elbow nervously, staring up at the sky. "There's something you should know…"

"Willie, just leave your jacket on," Jenna said. "You don't have to take it off."

"Thanks, Jenna," he said, "It's okay. I'm ready."

"To take your jacket off?" Peter said. "You been thinking about it for a while, Willie?"

"No, Pete," Willie said. "And my name's not Willie. It's Bree…"

Huh?

"What?" Langston said.

"Bree?" I said. "But that's a girl's name."

"That's because I'm a girl."

My airways nearly clogged again. "Oh."

"What?" Langston repeated.

"I'm sorry," Willie said. "I didn't want to lie to you guys, but I had to in order to keep my cover and stay in the Sphelix."

"How…?" Peter asked. "How could we have not known?"

"I'll give you the full story. Just not right now."

"He's—she's right," said Jenna. "We need to send word ahead that we cleared the outposts, and then we need to get back to Base Camp."

We gathered up our jackets and started walking down the path and back to the river. "Just to clarify," I said, "should I call you Bree or Willie? Not really sure how this works."

181

"Call me Bree," she said. *She.* What a weird way to refer to Willie. "Just call me Willie whenever someone else is around."

"Does Memo know?"

"Yes."

Jenna was trying not to smile, but she couldn't help it. Her teeth shone through the night.

"You knew?" I asked. Jenna smiled wider.

Bree gave her short high-pitched laugh. "Of course she knew. Figured it out pretty quick. Girls are good at that type of thing— much more perceptive than boys."

We came upon the area where we had crossed before. No one said anything while we waded through the river, which felt like swimming through a tub of ice now. Willie—well, Bree—struggled to make it across, but I stayed next to her the entire time. Finally we climbed out of the water.

The wind bit at our exposed noses and ears as we made our way to the top of the hill, where Oliver sat waiting for us. He turned the engine into gear. He verbally counted each one of us as we climbed into the back of his truck, disbelief etched all over his face.

"Have to say I'm glad to see y'all back," he said. "I hoped for one or two, but I didn't dare dream of all five."

"Lucky again," I said.

We rumbled back to the Orb's glow, dipping and climbing down the uneven road, trying to brace ourselves against the rain and wind. A small number of vehicles passed us going the other way—other squads going to occupy the outposts we'd just claimed. I didn't care. I just wanted a bed, a cup of hot chocolate, and…

"Socks!" Jenna said. "I can't believe I forgot about them. Here you go."

She handed a pair to each of us. I held them in my hand, dumbfounded.

The others all yanked off their shoes, and I did the same, pulling the clingy wet socks off my feet and throwing them over the railing and onto the road. Once the dry socks were on, all the worry, the hyperventilating from before, slowly evaporated, like a distant memory.

20. JUST ONE

"So, when you said you were going to wait to use the bathroom all those times…"

"I was just waiting until you guys weren't there so I could shower in private."

"And when you kept your underclothes on when putting on pajamas…"

"I'd think that'd be obvious by now."

Back in Barrack 19, I kept trying to think of ways how Bree had been able to keep her gender hidden for so long. In the corner, Memo was listening to our conversation, smiling and stirring a large pot of hot chocolate over a few aluminum burners.

"How didn't the Verdean realize?" Langston said. "They've got birth records of everyone. It's impossible to just impersonate someone else."

"Willie was my brother's name," Bree said. "I enlisted as him. Growing up on a farm, there weren't many people who knew my brother—not like you guys growing up in the city. So they had no way of knowing that the real Willie Greenbelt was about twice the size of me."

"How long has Jenna known?" I asked.

"She found out within the first week," Bree said. Now that I knew she was a girl, her features immediately looked more feminine. Her eyelashes longer, her short hair more stylish. "I just—I don't know, I guess I felt more comfortable with her… I think that helped her sense it."

Jenna didn't meet my gaze. I knew it was because she felt a little ashamed for not telling me, but I didn't blame her. It hadn't been her secret to tell, just like I hadn't told anyone why Langston was in the Verdean.

"How'd you get to be such a good fighter?" Peter asked. Memo handed him a steaming mug of hot chocolate.

"Because of Willie," Bree said. "He was huge, and we fought all the time. I had to figure out how to be scrappy. My dad made us spar all the time, and if he connected on even one blow, I'd have to stop for the rest of the day. I got good at dodging."

"Does anyone else know?" I asked, taking my own cup from Memo. I cupped my hands around its warmth. He finished passing mugs to the others before making one for himself, pulling up a chair, and sitting down.

"Just you guys and Memo," Bree said.

"And we can't tell anyone?"

"Definitely not," Bree said, suddenly serious. "The Verdean wouldn't like it and, best-case scenario, I'll be taken from the Sphelix and made to become a nurse."

"Can't lose our best fighter," said Langston. "We wouldn't stand a chance."

Memo blew into his mug, taking in the conversation as a spectator. He'd hugged each of us as we hopped off the truck, even Oliver. He'd even invited Oliver back, but Oliver said he needed to get home to take care of his son.

"What's gonna happen now that we have the turrets?" Langston asked, turning to Memo. "A lot more cargo is going to be able to get through."

"It'll definitely make life easier," said Memo. "For now, the Verdean will man the outposts. After the war, though, everything will be destroyed."

"What?" said Peter. "Even the turrets? Those things could shoot for miles. Why can't we bring them into battle? Trussel wouldn't stand a chance if we had those in the field."

"The turrets will definitely be destroyed," said Memo. "That's how the Verdean works. It's easy to forget the destruction they can cause. Having those guns, that technology, in the hands of Trussel was a huge hit to us. Easier to just destroy it and not have to worry about that happening again."

"But…but we risked our lives to get it," I said. "We killed them to get it."

"You risked your lives so that it could be destroyed," said Memo.

I was fuming but managed to keep my mouth shut. How could they do that? How could they be so thick-headed? Thousands of soldiers were risking their lives, and they didn't have the courage to use highly deadly weapons?

"I think it's time for a well-earned rest," said Memo. He gathered up our mugs along with the pot he'd used to make the hot chocolate. "Get some sleep and we can discuss more another time. But I hope you know how important the mission you completed was tonight. It could very well change the course of this entire war."

A dark purple tinged the sky, and a few shadowed figures were moving outside. Base Camp was waking up just as we were ready to go to sleep.

None of us even showered, we were so exhausted. Bree started playing her harmonica, and only when the sad, slow tune began did I remember her parents had passed away. She was an orphan now, just like Jenna and me. I wanted to say something, console her, but before I knew it I'd drifted off to sleep…

"LEO, LOOK OUT!"

I jerked awake and squinted against the light filling the room.

"LEO!"

I spun around, expecting an attack, but there was no one there.

"Peter, it's alright." Langston was next to him, trying to shake him awake. "We're not under attack."

Jenna hopped out of bed, bringing a cloth with her. She dabbed it on Peter's head, wiping the sweat off. "Someone bring water," she said.

Peter finally woke up and looked around. His face immediately went red. "Oh, no. I'm sorry. I didn't mean to. I'm so sorry."

"It's fine, Pete," said Jenna. "We understand."

"Doesn't anyone else get nightmares?" he asked.

"I do," said Langston. "I definitely do. I guess I just don't scream out loud, but they're in my head."

"What's wrong with me?" Peter said. "How come I can't control them?"

Jenna continued dabbing the cloth on his head, but he brushed her hand away. "There's nothing wrong with you, Pete," she said.

"Nothing at all. It's just—you're reacting differently."

"I can't see their faces," Peter said. "Of the people I kill, I mean. But I imagine the battles—I see us in danger."

"Me too," said Bree. She was lying in bed, tossing the keys Memo had given her earlier. "Except I see my parents and my brother, too."

"The focus pills are supposed to help with this," said Jenna. "I don't know why Memo doesn't want us to have them. They're supposed to help us cope with battle."

"You don't have any?" I asked. Jenna shook her head. "Right, well, I'm going to get you some, Pete."

"Leo," said Jenna.

"I don't care. He needs one."

Many doors on the fourth floor of the Captains' offices were ajar, revealing captains and lieutenants working at their desks or meeting with other officers. Each had their Verdean uniform buttoned, pressed and clean—just like Memo. My own dirty uniform stuck out like a sore thumb as I walked down the hallway.

Memo's door was closed. I knocked a few times before he said, "Come in, Leo."

"How'd you know it was me?" I asked.

"The security guards. They let me know you were on your way up."

"Do a lot of captains and generals have soldiers come visit?"

"A few, but for the most part I'm in the minority."

"Oh, well thanks."

Memo smiled. "Of course," he said. "My door is always open. What's on your mind?"

I didn't want to ask him for the pills anymore. I was nervous now, and maybe I was overstepping my boundaries. He was my superior. Who was I to question him?

"On second thought, sir," I said, "Maybe I should come back another time."

He peered at me through his glasses, which slid down his nose a bit. He pushed them up gently with his index finger. "You can tell me," Memo said. "I won't judge or be angry."

I couldn't figure out what it was, but Memo could disarm instantly, like I had no choice but to trust him. Maybe it was the glasses.

"I was wondering if there was any chance I could get a focus pill," I said. "Peter's been having really bad dreams—night sweats. It would only be one pill, and I don't think it would hurt him."

"I'm sorry, Leo," Memo said, "But I can't give you one."

My heart sank. "Can I ask why?"

"Of course. But I must first ask you to close the door. "

I did so and sat back down.

Memo clasped his hands together above the desk. He tilted his head back and forth, like he was changing his mind about something, then changing it back. The fireplace was again aflame behind him, though it looked to be on its last legs. Memo turned abruptly and threw another log in. When he turned back to me, he wasted no time.

"The reason I don't let you have focus pills—well, there are a couple reasons," Memo said. "For starters, you and the rest of the Sphelix are going through an awful experience. Taking a life is no easy thing. Thankfully, you haven't had a friend lose his or her life.

"That time after the initial shock," he continued, "the initial deaths, is almost worse. You're left sitting with the emptiness, believing that you will never be whole again. But that's not true; you just will never be the same."

He paused, picking up a pen and twirling it in his fingers.

"FPs allow you to take your mind off the bad that's happened so you can focus on the future and what's to come. Sounds good, right?"

"Yeah," I said. "That sounds like exactly what Peter needs. To stay in the moment—isn't that what you always say?"

"I do, but Peter needs to do so on his own. All of you do. These traumatic experiences aren't things that can be forgotten. They will surface one way or another. You need to spend time with the events, try to make sense of them or at the very least expose yourselves to the pain, and work through it, so you can become a stronger person."

"But isn't it easier to just take the pills and move on?" I asked. "That way he can get some sleep?"

Memo took off his glasses and massaged right between his eyes. Had I questioned him too much?

He put his glasses back on. "The pills dull the pain," he said. "But they also make you unquestioning, and ever loyal. You follow orders without thinking for yourself. Anything you're told to do, you do. No questions asked."

"What's wrong with that?" I said.

"Taking every order you're ever given is a slippery slope, Leo. The pills also do more than that—they make you happy, content. When the effects wear off, you crave more because otherwise you'd be exposed to pain again."

"They sound like mind control pills," I said.

"More insidious," said Memo. "Because you become dependent, addicted to them."

I nodded. "And all the soldiers are taking them?" I asked.

"Most of the lieutenants, generals, captains...everyone," said Memo. "You and I are in the minority."

"Did you ever take them?" I asked. I suddenly realized how personal a question that was. "Sorry, I'm just..."

"I did," Memo said. "Focus pills weren't introduced until I was a lieutenant, and I was reticent at first. I questioned everything, like I try to instill in the Sphelix, but eventually I relented and began taking them. And then I couldn't understand why I'd ever refused. Life was great, I was happy."

Memo's face darkened and he looked up at the ceiling.

"But then, over time, I started making worse decisions, things I never would've done had I not been on the FPs...

"When I went off them for good, it was the toughest period of my life. It was like a tidal wave came crashing down on me, making me relive every painful decision I'd ever made—not just when I was on the pills, but any time ever."

"I'm sorry, Memo, I didn't mean to—"

"No need to apologize," he said. "I needed to go through that pain."

I had so many questions: What was the worst thing he'd ever done? How had he gotten off the FPs? Had any other squads tried to refuse them? But before I could work up the courage to ask any of them, Memo said, "I'm sorry, Leo, but I think that's enough for today. Thank you for coming to me with your concerns about Peter."

"Thank you, sir."

He stood up and walked me to the door, but before he opened it, he turned to me once again.

"Please tell Peter I'm sorry. I just don't want him to experience what I went through."

"Yes, sir."

As I stood in the cold hallway and closed the door behind me, I saw Memo dabbing at his eyes with a handkerchief.

21. GENERAL MAGNER

"What do you think Memo did?" Peter asked.

"I don't know, but it really messed him up," I said. "I've never seen him that emotional."

"Yeah, but you know Memo—he'd probably cry if one of his buttons went missing," Peter said. "Come to think of it, that's probably what happened. He forgot to clean his glasses for a few weeks, and when he finally stopped taking the FPs, he was overcome with guilt."

Peter and I slipped and slid our way on the icy ground to the Mess Hall, the rest of the Sphelix lagging behind. It had been a couple weeks since we'd taken over the three strongholds—and since my conversation with Memo about the focus pills—but we could still talk about little else.

I now noticed soldiers popping the tiny white pills in their mouth everywhere I looked: in the Mess Hall, walking to a Tactics and Strategy class, out in the fighting pit.

"I wonder what it's like to take an FP," I said. "Think it's like being drunk?"

"If it was, my dad would be taking them constantly," said Peter.

I gave a reluctant laugh. It was nice that despite Peter's night terrors, his sense of humor hadn't changed. I worried about him constantly but kept my concern to myself. He didn't need to be asked every day how he was doing. And with the way the war was going, after another few weeks, he might never have to see battle again.

The *Gazette* published a number of articles detailing the Verdean's push into Trusselian territory. Memo told us to temper our expectations, but I couldn't help but envision living back in Arcton City, seeing Irene whenever I wanted, and not having to worry about anyone in the Sphelix getting hurt.

A welcome warmth greeted us in the Mess Hall. We filled our plates and found a table where Irene and a few other nurses were sitting. Irene smiled as I sat down.

"You hear?" she said.

"Hear what?" I asked. Jenna and Bree sat down across from us.

"Came out in the *Gazette* today—we just occupied Denth."

"That's great!" said Jenna. "Hopefully the war will be over soon."

Langston plopped his tray down, a few green beans rolling down a mountain of mashed potatoes. "Means longer rangings for us until then," he said. "If we're going that deep into Trussel, we could be gone for weeks or months."

Just then the front door opened and in walked Carl and the rest of his squad. A number of heads turned their way—a common occurrence now that they'd been mentioned in the *Gazette* every other week. They were the poster squad for the Verdean, having successfully taken out twelve Trusselian units without losing a single soldier. There had still been no mention of the Sphelix in the *Gazette*, but, as Langston reminded me, that was to be expected for a Forcie squad.

A few nurses stared as they walked in. Irene turned her head in disgust. "They're so full of themselves," she said. "It's repulsive."

"Your friends don't think so," I whispered. None of them noticed I'd said anything—they all had the same dazed look on their faces as they watched Carl's squad get into the food line.

Irene shook her head. "If it wasn't for Carl's dad, I doubt they'd be getting so much attention in the *Gazette*."

"What d'you mean?" Peter asked. He picked lightly at his food. He wasn't eating nearly as much as he used to.

"Carl's dad is a general," Irene said. "He's probably the fourth most powerful person in Arcton. I thought everyone knew that? Why do you think his squad is filled with guys that look like Supersoldiers?"

"Why'd he volunteer?" I said. "If his dad is so high up, it's not like his family needs the extra food stipend."

"A lot of parents force their kids to," said Irene. "It reflects well on the family if their son or daughter chooses to volunteer for the Verdean. All my parents' friends pretty much forced their kids to do it. I always told my parents I wouldn't, but then, of course, my dad found a way around that. It shows that the whole family is loyal and whatnot. You know, that they believe in Arcton, that they're willing to risk their lives…"

"I'd risk my life for you." Carl was standing right behind her, carrying a tray of food, his friends behind him in an orderly line. "You don't have to sit with these losers—we have a table over there. Where real men sit."

He put his hand on the small of her back. She squirmed away, sitting up straight, revolted. I stood up and shoved his hand away.

As one, the rest of the Sphelix rose up behind me.

"Touch her again, and I'll knock you out," I said.

"Come on, buddy," Carl said. "I was just being friendly. Nothing wrong with that, is there?"

"Touch her again, and I'll knock you out," I repeated, more slowly.

Carl's smile faltered. "What—trying to impress your girlfriend? I'll touch whoever I damn well please."

"Why are you even here?" Jenna said. "Go eat your dinner and hit on a girl that actually likes you."

"I wasn't asking you," Carl spat. "No one's interested in a bitch like you."

SMASH!

A tray collided with Carl's face and he hit the ground. Bree dropped the tray and jumped on top of him.

One of Carl's friends ran up as Bree started to throw punches. I flung my chair at him to catch, which he did, and I tackled him into the rest of his group, grabbing his neck and arm and twisting them back.

A yell erupted from the surrounding tables, everyone clambering close to watch.

Out of the corner of my eye, I saw Jenna deliver a kick to the chest of another one of Carl's lackeys. Peter and Langston were squaring up with three others, their fists clenched, each side waiting for the other to make the first move.

I continued my arm-lock, delivering blows to his body with my free hand, but a strong arm yanked me up by the back of my shirt.

"What do you think you're doing?" a cool voice said in my ear. I turned and saw a grown-up version of Carl, complete with the cleft chin, sandy-blonde hair, and furrowed brow. Five silver stars adorned his left breast in a perfect star. Next to me, Bree had her fist frozen mid-punch and was looking up at him.

"I repeat: what do you think you're doing?" There was venom in his voice.

"Noth—Nothing... sir," I added.

General Magner turned to Bree. "Remove your hands from my son," he said. Bree had no choice but to obey. He grasped my shirt tightly, twisting it. "Captain Iglesias will be hearing about this, as will Arcalaeus himself. Do I make myself clear?"

I nodded.

"I'm afraid I couldn't quite hear that." His breath reeked of coffee.

"Yes, *sir*," I said.

"As for that bitch of a sister, you might do well to give her the same warning." He turned to leave.

I reached back and cocked a punch, but before I could throw it at General Magner, a soft, strong hand grabbed my wrist. "Don't," Irene hissed. She grabbed me around the waist and pulled me back. "Don't."

She continued her pincer hold on me, and half-walked, half-shoved me out of the Mess Hall. I crunched through the freshly fallen snow, flakes continuing to fall gently around us. She didn't loosen her grip, and before long the others caught up with us.

"Br—Willie that was awesome!" said Peter. "Carl had no idea

what hit him."

"And Jenna!" said Langston. "That was something else. I've never seen a jump-kick before."

Jenna looked away sheepishly, but clearly pleased.

I was still fuming. "If it wasn't for his prissy dad, we would've kicked the crap out of him," I said. "Just 'cause a general walked in…"

Irene loosened her grip on me and settled on holding my hand. The others continued bashing Carl, his dad, and the rest of squad 319. As we neared Barrack 19, Irene, her olive skin reflecting the green Orb light, squeezed my hand and nodded in the other direction. We said goodbye to the others (Peter gave us a wolf whistle) and walked through the other barracks, passing the armory, and eventually sitting down on a large stump near the obstacle course.

The ropes swayed lazily against the walls. The mud crawl was lifeless and glassy. Irene rested her head on my shoulder. I kissed her, taking in the lemony scent.

"You can't lose your cool like that," she said. "I need you."

"He doesn't get to talk to Jenna like that," I said. "Not Carl, not his dad."

"Carl's dad gets to do whatever he wants. That's the way it works. If you'd hit him, you'd have never been able to leave the Verdean. Or worse—you would've been sent to the Pit and I never would've seen you again."

"So, what?"

"*So what?*" Irene pulled her head off my shoulder and stared at me, her brown eyes darting back and forth between my own. "Leo, you can't just think about yourself. What would Jenna say if she never saw you again? Or Peter? Or me? I need you, Leo, we all do. It was selfish to try and hit General Magner."

A wave of embarrassment spread through me. She was right, of course. Irene had always been one of the few to call me out when I was in the wrong. She was never mean, but she was straight and to the point.

"I'm sorry," I said. "You're completely right."

"It's fine," she said. "Please just don't let it happen again."

Snowflakes continued to swirl, blanketing her hair, a few falling on her eyelashes. I cupped her flushed cheeks in my hands.

"I really am sorry," I said, kissing her.

22. ONE LAST MISSION

"Get up!"

Someone was shaking me out of bed. My breath rolled out in fog in front of me as I opened my eyes. I turned to see Memo's glasses and lined forehead.

"Time to get up," Memo said, before leaving to wake up the others.

I reluctantly kicked off my covers, January bringing with it the frigid air, and sat down in one of the desks still in my pajamas. Memo's eyes were bloodshot, and there were deep bags beneath them. His typically impeccable uniform was wrinkled. He rubbed his hands together for warmth, waiting for us to bunch the desks together and sit down.

"The war is coming to a close," Memo said. "We have Trussel on their heels, giving ground quickly. The Verdean has decided that it is time to deliver the death blow, and they've chosen the Sphelix to deal it."

Us? Why not Carl's squad? They were the ones getting all the publicity.

"As we speak, the Verdean is launching an all-out offensive on the eastern border of Trussel, pushing in towards the river city Brill. This offensive is in part to dismantle their strongholds, but also to serve as a decoy, drawing most of Trussel's attention towards the east, and away from the west coast. That's where the Sphelix will enter."

"We're going to Trussel?" said Langston. "How are we getting there?"

"By boat," said Memo. "Bree, you'll be in charge of captaining it."

"You know how to drive a boat?" Peter asked.

Bree nodded.

Memo continued. "Bree will be able to get you to the west coast of Trussel. From there, it's a two-week hike to Brill, where the forces from the east should be knocking on their door. Your mission is to infiltrate Brill and abduct one of their generals – his last name is Nygaard."

"How will we know how to find him?" Langston asked.

"We know where his office is located," said Memo. "It's heavily guarded, but the attack on Brill should take away some of their soldiers.

Jenna didn't try to hide her skepticism. "So we're supposed to enter Brill sight-unseen, kidnap a general, and then waltz out of there?"

"I know how it sounds," said Memo.

"It sounds like a suicide mission," I said. "Couldn't we just kill the general?"

"The Verdean wants General Nygaard alive so they can interrogate him," said Memo.

"Are there any other squads coming with us?" Langston asked.

Memo shook his head. "It's not an easy mission, and I think the higher-ups probably intended for that to be the case. They want the war over quickly, and a mission this dangerous...it would raise morale around Arcton to extreme heights. It might end the war right then and there. And I've been assured that when you complete the mission you'll be released from the Verdean with honors."

His last words hung in the air like a mist, taking a moment to settle over us.

I shivered.

We could make it out alive. Peter, Jenna, Langston, and Bree could be back home in a matter of months—safe.

"And if we die?" Bree asked.

"You won't," said Memo. "I wouldn't let you go on this mission were I not certain you'd all make it back alive." The promise was less inspiring given how Memo looked. Stray hairs poked out from his ponytail, and his cheeks were pale and hollow.

"We trust you, Memo," I said. "We'll be ready. When do we leave?"

"One week. That'll give us enough time to prepare."

Memo said goodbye and walked out, leaving us in a stunned silence after the door closed behind him.

"I can't believe we're going into Trussel," Langston finally said.

"Did anyone else think Memo seemed angry?" Jenna asked, yanking on a sweatshirt and blowing into her frozen hands. "Or was it just me?"

"Why do you think that?" Langston said.

"His fingers," Jenna said. "He was strumming them on the table the entire time. Normally, he keeps them folded in his lap. He was also talking faster than normal, stumbling over his words."

"Maybe he was drunk," Langston said.

Bree shook her head. "I don't think Memo's had a drop his entire life," she said.

"You think it's something we did that made him angry?" Peter asked.

"He just hates seeing us go on missions," I said. "He's not like the other captains. He doesn't want to see us hurt."

Bree pulled on a black beanie, prepping for the flurry outside. "Agreed," she said. Her voice seemed to have become more high-pitched over the past few weeks. How had she ever convinced me she was a boy? "He might even want to come with us on this one. Can you imagine? We'd be invincible."

"Fat chance," said Peter. "I can't believe the war is coming to an end, though. We'll be home soon."

"Assuming we make it through this mission," I said. "Seems ridiculous we're the ones going into Brill alone while the rest get to stick together and be a diversion."

Langston gave a reluctant smile. "It's the Verdean's world. We're just fighting in it.

"We'll all be fine," said Bree. "And then Leo can go play house with Irene."

I threw a stray pillow at her while the others whistled and cat-called. It was the first joke I'd ever heard Bree make.

Irene threw a rock across the water. It skipped as though jumping on ice before finally being lapped up by a wave. "I can't believe you're getting out!" she said.

"There's a big *if* in there," I said. "It's not going to be an easy mission."

"But Leo, this is incredible news! And you'll be fine. You've already gotten through so much."

I tried to act more excited, but I couldn't fake it. Obviously I was excited at the prospect of returning home, but there were so many things still on my mind. The last note from the *Whirlwind War* books—*Loyalty is fickle. Death is final. Neither, for your family, is what it seems*. I still had no idea what it meant. And the focus pills...it didn't sit right that the Verdean was taking away its soldiers' decision-making. And then my power—I would've never known I had the ability if I hadn't gone to war. Would I ever use it again?

Irene was bundled tight in a large puffy jacket, a blanket draped over both our shoulders. She skipped another rock along the bay. We had the beach to ourselves, the cold keeping all the other soldiers away.

"I'll be relieved when it's all over," Irene said. "I hate seeing all those mangled limbs, the blood everywhere. I have half a mind to jump into the bay right now to try and get myself at least *feeling* clean."

It was hard to sympathize with Irene. I felt bad for her, sure, but at the same time she wasn't risking her life out in the field. She didn't have to worry about her sister or best friends dying...

"What's up?" she said. My face must have betrayed some of what I was feeling.

"Huh? Oh, nothing."

"You sure? You don't maybe think my job isn't as important?" she said. "Not *manly* enough for you?"

I glanced away at a few rocks. "I didn't say that."

"Let me tell you something," Irene said, "While you're out there fighting the war and getting all the glory, I'm in the hospital working sixteen-hour shifts. And, contrary to what you might think, it's not just a walk in the park. I've cleaned out wounds from every body part imaginable—some of which you've probably never even heard of. I've comforted countless soldiers who've just watched their friend or brother die. I've cleaned enough puke and blood to fill half the bay. I've changed diapers—yeah, diapers—for full grown men. I fix IVs for soldiers, resuscitate others, and I've done everything else that's needed of me—without the chance of getting my name in the paper. It may not be the most glamorous job, but don't you dare roll your eyes when I talk about how much I want this war to end."

Her cheeks were splotched red with emotion. She might as well have slapped me.

She turned towards the water. How was she always right? Every single time.

"I'm sorry," I said.

She turned to me, and then looked away again.

"I mean it," I said. "You're right. Seeing the dead bodies in the field is the toughest part of battle for me—I can't imagine what it's like to see dozens of them every day, and also have to save their lives."

Irene nodded. "Did you ever find out the meaning of that last message?" she said softly. "The one about loyalty and death?"

"I've been so focused on our missions and getting back home, I haven't had time to figure it out."

"Keep thinking about it," she said. "Someone clearly cared enough to get you two messages. The first one proved your dad was a war hero. The second…well, just make sure Langston keeps trying to solve it."

"You don't think I can do it on my own?"

She smiled and shrugged. "Doesn't hurt to have Langston."

"We'll be together soon," I said. "Just you and me. No rangings to go on, no sixteen-hour shifts in the hospital. We can get married and read *Dasher's Revenge* and go swimming and not worry about a thing."

"You want to know what happens in *Dasher's Revenge?*" Irene asked.

"I'm not sure," I said. "Do you think there's another copy somewhere out there? I wanna read it for myself without spoilers."

"As far as I know it's the only one, and it got taken by the Propa Department. We'll never find another copy."

"I'll hold out a little longer. Gotta stay optimistic. I'll read it someday."

23. TO THE SEA

Memo stood beside the truck depot waiting to see us off. His dark-green slacks were once again neatly pressed and clean, but his eyes gave away his lack of sleep. The dark bags remained, and he looked like he was having trouble focusing. He forced his face into a smile. "Got everything you need?"

"Yes, sir."

"Spare clothes, canteens full, swords and arrowheads sharpened?"

"Yes, sir."

"Month's worth of rations?"

I nodded. "Yes, sir."

"Good," Memo said. "Be careful. Complete the mission, but remember that your lives are more important than General Nygaard's. You're no use to us dead, and you certainly won't be able to deliver him if you get yourselves killed."

Then he hugged each one of us. His grasp was strong, and I realized how much muscle he had underneath his perfectly pressed uniform. He might be old, but he wasn't over the hill. He could probably take Peter in one-on-one combat.

If only he could come with us.

When we arrived at the loading zone a few minutes later, we saw Oliver sitting in his truck, smoking a cigarette and humming to himself.

"Got any more of those?" Langston asked, climbing into the

back.

Oliver skillfully ashed the butt over the window. "They'll screw up your aim with an arrow," he said. "Make your hands all shaky. Why do you think they only let a simple old driver smoke 'em?"

"You're telling me the higher-ups know you're smoking?" Jenna said.

"Not a chance," said Oliver. "Gotta roll these babies myself. They will kill you, though."

"Yeah, so will this war," said Langston.

Oliver shrugged. He put the car into gear and eased out. The morning light just peaked out over the horizon. We headed away from the water, towards the Orb and its never-ending green whorls. Minutes later we were out of the gates and climbing Mt. Brentwood.

No one spoke. A combination of exhaustion at the early hour and excitement at the prospect of going home after this mission kept my mind busy.

A little after mid-day, we came upon a razed farming village. The whole area had been occupied by Trussel just a few short months ago, but now, the homes and buildings had all been ransacked and destroyed. Crows sifted through the piles of wreckage. I didn't want to think what lay beneath them.

Bree's mouth was open as she took in the scene. She'd grown up on a farm, likely in a village similar to this one.

Without a word, Jenna got up and sat next to Bree, who leaned on her.

The road soon turned away from the ocean and into a valley.

There were a few more farming villages—some razed, some intact—and we even came upon an oil field. A couple huge, giraffe-like machines screeched loudly while they worked, sucking up the black substance from the ground and depositing it into massive metal containers. This was the power for this truck, the fuel. And there wasn't much left.

Our truck continued burning oil. The cloudless day slowly yielded its blue sky to the fiery sunset, painting a burned horizon. Oliver drove until we came to a small dock off the coast, the waves crashing and the salty air filling our lungs.

Oliver hopped out and unlocked the padlock to help us get our backpacks out.

"Be careful," Oliver said, throwing my own heavy pack to me. "I want to be sure I can drive you on your next mission." He shook each of our hands in turn, grasping mine last. I made to pull away, but he held my hand, bringing it into his chest, and me along with it, grasping me in a one-armed hug. "Do good, brother," he said, patting me on the back with his free hand. "See you later."

"See you later," I said, unsure of what had just happened.

"What was that?" Langston asked me when I joined the others on the trail down to the water.

"I have no idea," I said. "He just decided to give me an awkward hug."

"You played it off really well," Langston said.

"Really?"

"Not at all."

The boat we were given was, to put it bluntly, a piece of crap. Molded wood with one ripped sail hanging from a pole. If there had ever been a coat of paint, it had long since faded.

Langston shook his head. "It'd be ironic if we drowned on our way to a suicide mission."

"I can steer this, no problem," said Bree. "We have a *motor.*"

Sure enough, at the back of the boat (the stern, Bree informed me) was a pitch-black engine filled with precious oil.

"They actually trust us with it?" Peter said. "We've got to be the youngest squad ever to get control of this much oil."

Langston and Jenna pushed the boat out from the dock. Waves lapped overboard, soaking my pants. Bree pulled hard on a handle, revving the engine before it finally caught. We moved slowly at first, easing our way over the waves, before Bree stepped on the throttle and took us to another speed altogether.

When night fell, Bree consulted with Langston and one of his textbooks about where we were heading using the stars, which had just begun to poke through the night, as guides.

Everyone was preoccupied—either steering the ship or sleeping—and I nervously glanced around to make sure no one was looking. I didn't want an audience when I tried again.

I inhaled through my nose and exhaled out through my mouth. I stood up straight and arced my shoulders back. After a few breaths, I focused my mind inward, examining myself.

Visions from my life ran like logs down a river. I followed the stream, jumping from memory to memory, log to log—Aunt Helen telling me my dad had passed, watching Jenna's smile after she ate cake for the first time. Holding onto a memory was like trying to hold water in your hands. My mother's death. Shooting targets in the backyard. Bree hitting Carl with the tray of food in the Mess Hall. Jenna running around in the yard with only a diaper on, then promptly falling into some mud and looking like she'd pooped herself.

Further and further my memories took me down the river, curving this way and that.

The night after my dad died. A couple months later getting the news about my mom. I was the oldest. I was responsible for taking care of Jenna, or at least so I'd thought.

Helen took responsibility for both of us, though. Unconditional love for two that weren't her own. Where would we be without her?

And just as easily I withdrew back upriver. Like a tidal wave hurtling over land, the river crashed towards the rest of the Sphelix, where everyone was a source of light. With varying degrees of intensity and color, Peter, Jenna, Bree, and Langston all issued some type of heat from their bodies.

The inanimate objects on the boat didn't give off heat. Instead, just as when I'd seen the arrows—had really *seen* them—it was like I was viewing everything underwater. The wood boards of the boat, the DMP's in my backpack, the herbs in Jenna's aid kit— everything was suddenly in this warped vision.

I reached out my hand and focused my conscious on my backpack, trying to move it. Slowly, I moved my hand upward, and, much to my surprise, my backpack lifted several inches off the ground. Amazed, I lost my focus, and it fell back down with a soft thud.

I'd done it.

I took a deep breath, my heart pounding.

On my second attempt, the backpack got up to eye level before I freaked out with excitement and it fell back to the boat.

This was nuts. I could control this power. No one else had noticed what was happening—Langston and Peter had dozed off and Jenna was talking quietly to Bree, who was guiding the ship. They had absolutely no idea.

I needed to let them know. I focused in on Peter's jacket, my vision warping. I steadied my breathing and slowly started to lift the cotton closest to his armpits. His shoulders rose up, and soon after the rest of his body followed until no part of him was touching the deck. I lifted him higher and higher in the air until he was a good five feet off the boat.

Jenna and Bree were deep in conversation, unaware that Peter was floating, like a scarecrow, just a few feet away. As for Peter, he was still sleeping. I had to keep propelling him forward at the pace of the boat to keep him with us. Feeling my energy start to drain, I guided Peter towards the girls. When he was just a few feet away, his eyes flickered open.

He yawned as he looked around, completely oblivious to the fact that he was floating five feet in the air. Hearing his yawn, Jenna and Bree both turned around at exactly the same time.

"AHHHH!!!" All three shrieked at the same time, Jenna and Bree falling backward.

I cracked up so hard that I completely forgot I was responsible for keeping Peter suspended in midair. He came crashing down to the wood deck with a loud thunk. Jenna and Bree stood up and looked down on Peter's disheveled body.

"Peter!" Jenna said. "You have a power too?"

"Do I?" Peter said, slowly getting to his feet. "I just woke up and there I was—floating."

But then it dawned on him. On all three of them. They turned and saw my grin.

"You snock," Peter said, reaching down and throwing a spare canteen at me. "You get a weird power, and then use it to play a prank on me?"

"You nearly gave us a heart attack," said Jenna.

No matter what I tried, I couldn't wipe the smile off my face. This, of course, continued to piss off the others.

"Quit laughing," Jenna said. "Leo, that wasn't funny."

But I couldn't stop. The angrier they got the funnier it was, and I was well past the point of self-control. Eventually, my funny bone struck Peter as well, and we both keeled over, holding our stomachs.

Langston slept through the entire episode. But when he woke up and heard the story, he was the first person to realize the real significance behind it.

"You can control your power?" he said. A button had left an imprint on his cheek.

"I think so," I said. "Not sure how reliable it'll be."

"Leo, that's amazing," Langston said. "Really impressive. Nice to know you can control this when we're heading into the belly of the beast."

Before I could respond, Jenna interrupted. "Speaking of which," she said, "How long until we get to shore?"

Currently there wasn't a single land mass in sight. We could've been in the middle of the ocean, halfway to The Forgotten Isles, without even knowing it. Or at least I wouldn't know.

"We've got a few more days," said Bree. "We're lucky the waters have been so calm, otherwise this trip would really be miserable."

Even with the calm waters, it was miserable enough. Sitting out on a deck with no real shade while the sun beat down on our exposed bodies for hours on end was draining. Even though it was winter, my skin still burned red, wind biting at my face.

On our fifth night out at sea, clouds threatened what had previously been a smooth ride. Bree kept glancing up nervously at the sail, to which she'd switched as soon as we'd gotten a decent distance from shore. Would it hold up if a storm hit?

The clouds shone white in front of us, illuminated by the recently waning moon.

Looking for a distraction, I challenged Jenna to a game of "Frying Pan," which we used to always play as kids.

"Would you rather break your arm or your leg?" she asked.

"Arm, no question," I said. "Would you rather eat just plain rice for the rest of your life, or Uncle Lester's cookies?"

"Rice, without a doubt. Uncle Lester can barely make cereal let alone…"

She broke off.

"Jenna, we playing or what?"

Jenna pointed to a spot behind me. "Look," she said.

Just in front of the clouds, an array of colors—orange, purple, blue—formed an arch like a rainbow. Each color ran in a perfect line from one end of the arc to the other, glistening in the moon's silver-white light.

Bree, Langston, and Peter all stared up, their eyes softening at the sight. It looked like a gateway to bliss.

"What is that?" I asked.

Not even Langston knew.

Bree guided us straight towards the arc in the sky, and within hours we spotted land off the port side of the boat.

Trussel.

24. TO THE SHORE

We dragged the boat into a nook on the beach just as the sun began to rise again. We gathered fallen branches and leaves to cover and camouflage it. Crows flew overhead, crying out. A bed of small gray rocks covered the shore, extending up in a gentle grade until it hit a lip where dirt took over. I licked my lips, trying to get rid of the briny tang left over from the ocean.

Langston consulted the map to figure out where we were. We strapped on our backpacks and took off up the trail. The further we walked along the dirt path, the more snow we encountered, a gentle crunch accompanying each step. Thankfully, there were no other footprints.

By the end of the day, with the sun a deep, blood-orange and my legs and tailbone both whining, I was more than ready to break for camp. We cleared snow from an even patch of ground and Langston started instructing Jenna and Peter on how to properly set it up.

Never one to be handy, I offered to get some firewood. When I returned, arms full of dead branches, Langston, Jenna, and Peter were still working on the tent. A little way off, I found Bree digging a pit for the fire, her hands working like a dog going after a bone.

I set my branches down and watched as she arranged them in a pyramid atop an orderly base. She smashed flint and rock together, until a spark caught onto some dry brush. She blew softly, encouraging the small flame, growing it higher and higher. Bree placed the flaming brush into the pyramid, continuing to blow the fire higher until the whole structure was ablaze.

I held up my hands to the warmth, stretching them out.

"Is there anything you don't know how to do?" I asked, impressed.

"It's not my fault you city boys have never been out in the wilderness," she said. "My brother and I used to do this all the time when we went camping. This was one of the more fun chores."

"I'm sorry about your parents," I said, before I could stop myself. It was the first time I'd mentioned them.

"Don't be. There are people way worse off."

"It still sucks."

"You've lost your parents too," said Bree. "You and Jenna are doing fine. I'll be okay."

"After this, you can come live with us in Arcton City," I said. "If you want."

"Thanks, Leo."

I could tell she wanted the conversation to end. Normally I would've let it pass, but I pressed on.

"I don't know what I'd do without Jenna," I said.

Bree continued blowing gently on the fire. The flames licked the wood, charring the bark.

"Mind if I ask what happened to your brother?"

"He died," she said, matter-of-fact.

I fell silent. She kept spinning the stick between her hands, her beanie preventing me from seeing her face. I shouldn't have asked. It was none of my business. Not something you want to talk about when you're off on a mission. I wouldn't want her prodding about my mom and dad either.

She looked up at me, her eyes watery. "Sorry," she said. "I shouldn't be short with you. It's just—I'm not one hundred percent sure he is dead. We never saw a body or anything. I just know that the blackhats took him one night and he never came home. I kept telling myself for the first few weeks that he'd come back, appear at the door one morning. I couldn't give up hope. But that just made it worse."

"Well, he might still be alive. You never know."

"There are times to have hope, Leo, and this isn't one of them."

She didn't want any sympathy, no condolences. I didn't know what to do with that.

"You guys must have been close."

"We were twins. Didn't really have a choice. We were nothing alike, though. He was a little on the slow side. Had trouble picking up simple things like math and writing. Even in conversation he could never quite communicate exactly what he wanted to say."

"I know how that feels—"

"Not like Willie, you don't," she said. "He got into trouble a ton at school because he was way bigger than everyone else, and whenever there was any type of physical activity, he'd get too rough and run into someone, or not understand the rules fully and accidentally cheat.

"But you would've loved him. He could take a joke better than anyone. We used to make homemade popsicles in our ice trays during the winter. Just put a stick in an orange juice concoction and watch it freeze. One day I made a batch with mud. I told him it was chocolate flavored. He got through about half a dozen before realizing what I'd done—and then he couldn't stop cracking up."

She smiled at the memory. Her hair showed beneath her beanie, long enough now to look like a boy's bad haircut.

"He wasn't good with blackhats," she said. "Always asking too many questions, not understanding that he should just shut up and do as they told him. One blackhat around our block knew my dad and usually did what he could to look out for Willie. Told other hats in the area about his situation, told them not to be offended if he didn't do exactly as they said.

"But then, a visiting blackhat was in from the city one week, and Willie was out in the middle of the road, bouncing a ball, minding his own business. Willie had finished his chores on the farm for the day, and he loved bouncing a ball as much as Peter likes telling stories.

"This blackhat told him to get off the road. I wasn't there—I was still doing my chores—but a neighbor said that Willie looked at the out-of-town blackhat just completely confused. Like he didn't know what the heck this guy was talking about. And the hat, not knowing Willie, stepped up to him and whacked him in the head with his baton."

Bree paused. She took a deep breath, trying to maintain her composure. I wasn't sure whether she wanted to scream or cry.

"When I say Willie was huge, I mean, like, he was enormous. He would be the biggest soldier in the Verdean, hands down. And this idiot hat goes up and smacks him on the head. Willie couldn't really control himself, and he never understood the authority a blackhat has—so he wound up and knocked the guy to the ground. The hat went unconscious and broke his arm on the way down.

"My dad knew what was coming. He tried his best to use his contacts to keep Willie safe. But his ties didn't run that deep, I guess. Next thing I knew, there was a knock at the door and a group of blackhats stormed in and took him away. I begged and pleaded with them to stop. My dad did what he could, but there's nothing you can do once the hats decide to take you. We were fighting a losing battle. Took me a while to realize that."

She looked down at the burning fire. There was no need to blow on it anymore. The flames had caught.

"And you never heard from him again?"

"Not once."

"We could've used him in the Sphelix," I said. "Guy that big— Trussel wouldn't know what hit 'em."

Langston finished up his tent and came over to get warm by the fire. Jenna and Peter followed not long after.

We all ate a dehydrated meal pack by the fire before turning in. Exhausted, I was asleep before my head hit the backpack. Unfortunately, sleep didn't last long. I had nightmares and woke up every other hour, shivering and drenched in cold sweat.

The furious wind slipped through the tent. The night dragged on.

A blizzard hit on our tenth day in Trussel. Each step required a heave of strength. Flurries of snow flew at my face, blinding me.

Ice filled every crevice of my jacket.

"What's that?" Peter said.

I squinted in the direction he was pointing and could barely make out the outline of a small, red cabin. As we got closer, I saw smoke billowing from the chimney. It must have been the only home for miles.

"Think they have food?" Peter asked.

"Got to at least be warm," Langston said. "Should we risk it?"

"I'm freezing my butt off," I said. "I don't care if there's an army in there. I'd do anything to get out of this cold for a few minutes."

"There'll be people in there," said Jenna. "You know what we'll have to do to them afterward. We should find shelter instead and wait out the storm, not in there."

I realized she was probably right, but it was so cold. "We can tie them up afterward," I said. "It's secluded, too. Who are they going to tell?"

We took a circuitous route to get to the home, staying out of sight in case anyone happened to be looking out a window. When we were close enough, I could see a family of four sitting around a dining table, the mother shoveling eggs onto her son's and daughter's plates.

We all crept up to the front door, our swords and bows ready, and on the count of three, Peter kicked it open and we stormed in. The mother and father immediately grabbed their kids and shielded them from us, their hands outstretched as though flesh could stop our swords and bows. The children screamed and started crying.

I lowered my sword. "We're not going to hurt you," I said. "We just want shelter for a bit, and maybe some food if you have extra."

"Why are you here?" the man asked. His young boy looked terrified behind him, barely sticking his head out from around his dad's torso. The little girl mirrored the pose behind her mom.

"That's not important," I said. "All you need to know is that we don't want to hurt you or your children. We've had a long trip and just want food and shelter. Can you give us that?"

"Yes," the woman said, in the drawling Trusselian accent. "Please lower your weapons. You're scaring my children." Her husband glared first at her and then at us. But the woman was already bustling around the kitchen, taking out plates and cutlery, cracking eggs in the pan, and boiling water beside it, into which she eventually threw peas.

I sheathed my sword. The others followed, yet still the husband and children looked at us with a combination of loathing and terror. I motioned for them to sit back down, and they did so, albeit slowly. The boy, who looked no older than seven, started eating again. The little girl soon followed suit. First, tiny bites that they slipped in when their dad wasn't looking, but then they were practically shoving the food hand over fist into their mouths.

The mom brought a new batch of eggs, divvied out onto plates, and set them before each of us around the table. We ate greedily, and before she even put the peas on our plates, the eggs were gone.

She dropped a steaming pile of peas on my plate. "Thank you," I said. "The eggs were delicious."

She nodded.

Everyone else also said thank you or complimented her cooking, and one by one her acknowledgement became more and more pronounced, until finally, after Peter shared his gratitude, she replied, "Of course, dear."

Dear. She called him, *dear.* The husband looked like he wanted to throw his plate at Peter's head. Or maybe his wife's. She was back in the kitchen, pouring glasses of milk for her new guests. He got up to help her bring more glasses.

The woman set a glass of milk down in front of Jenna. "Where's the nearest town?" Jenna asked.

"About ten miles east," the woman said. "There are a couple villages—suburbs of Brill—and then five miles further is the city itself."

"And the next closest house?" Langston asked.

"Not for a few miles. We're secluded out here on purpose. We thought it would keep us away from the war." She shook her head.

"Well I'm glad you're out here," Jenna said. "We were freezing to death, and I can't tell you how good your cooking is. Practically as good as my Aunt Helen's."

As the woman thanked her, the man made a sudden movement with his right hand. I launched myself across the table onto him, sending dishes crashing to the ground, and a metal object went sliding away on the carpet. Bree quickly helped me pin down the man, each of us putting a knee into his back.

The object came to rest very close to where the youngest boy sat.

"Grab it," I told Jenna. Jenna scooped up a small revolver and handed it to me. It felt lighter than I expected, but the steel was warm from where the man had hidden it close to his body. And for an instant I envisioned pulling the trigger and putting three bullets into his belly.

I handed it back to Jenna. "I don't want it," I said. "You hold onto it."

The mother turned to me, her eyes tearing up and her face bright red. "I'm sorry, I didn't know he was going to try that. Please don't hurt him. Please not my children."

Beneath my knee, the man kept jerking violently, trying to break free. Langston handed me a rope, and we tied his hands to his legs, leaving him hogtied in the middle of the floor. The mother was hysterical, begging me on her knees not to do anything to her husband.

I ignored her.

"How'd you get that gun?" I asked.

"Screw you, scum," he said. His drawl was less pronounced. Perhaps he'd moved here? "We were dead the moment you came bursting in. You can give up the act now."

"We have to kill him," Peter said. "He tried to shoot Jenna."

"We can't," Jenna said. "Not in front of his children."

"Not at all!" his wife said. "Please, he wasn't thinking straight. We'll do whatever we can. Food? Water? More information on the villages? Please don't kill him. Oh, please."

"Kill him," Bree said. Her face darkened. "We don't have any way of knowing he won't try to do something else if we let him go. He might track us and kill us in our sleep. He definitely knows the woods better than we do."

"We can tie him up and take his gun," Langston said. "We should have a watch out whenever we sleep anyway. He's not a real threat without the gun."

"Where did you get it?" I asked the man again. He spat at me. His wife kicked him.

"He got it from his dad, who got it from his own dad," she said. "It's been passed down in his family for generations. Please, take it with you."

"Very generous," Langston said. "But we were gonna do that anyway."

"There's no way we should leave him here," Peter said. "Not unattended. He'll make us pay. Mark my words. Leo?" He looked at me. The others were waiting for my opinion as well.

I felt a certain sense of appreciation for the power I'd apparently been given—decider of this man's fate. The actor for the Sphelix. It meant a lot to me that they sought my approval for what they wanted to do. I looked at the young boy and girl who had remained silent during this exchange, tears running down their faces. The boy hugged his little sister, trying to reassure her.

"Jenna, you were the one he was going for," I said. "You should make the decision."

"I say we take him with us and dispose of him on the way to Brill," Peter said.

Jenna shook her head. "We'd be taking their father away from them. And taking this woman's husband, which means even more work for her."

"They're gonna grow up to be Trusselian soldiers," said Bree. The young boy and girl were looking up at Jenna, tears streaming down their cheeks.

"They might," Jenna said. "But for now, they're just kids. As old as Jexter. And they've played no part in this war. He was doing what he thought was right. Just like us."

Jenna looked again at the children. She saw herself—she saw me—in the faces of those kids. She couldn't take their father away.

We stayed in the cabin overnight, the man tied up, taking turns keeping watch over him. The snow continued to fall outside.

The next morning, the man was still hogtied. His revolver, along with the three bullets, were stowed in Jenna's backpack. We told the mother not to untie him for a full twenty-four hours. She agreed, and thanked us over and over again for sparing his life. The boy and girl just watched.

Whipping wind and swirling snow greeted us outside, the snow filling the collar of my jacket no matter how hard I pressed it against my body. On we marched, down into gulches and over hills, until finally, on the second night after leaving the cabin, a city came into view. Brill.

Built against the base of a mountain, a river curved along Brill's walled perimeter. A blue glow illuminated the city—did Brill have its very own Orb? But as we got closer it turned out that the blue light was a combination of hundreds, maybe thousands, of little street lights, shaded azure, that kept Trussel lit up day and night. How much electricity did they have? Or were they powered by something similar to what powered the Orbs?

"It's beautiful," Langston said.

We climbed up and over a rocky hill nearby, eager to stay out of sight and get some shelter from the wind.

My muscles and bones practically squealed with delight once the tent was set up and we retreated inside, but I couldn't fall asleep.

I unzipped the entryway to the tent, and the immediate change in temperature was enough to almost blow me back inside—but I yanked down my beanie a little more and went out to relieve Langston, who had taken the first watch.

"You sure, man?" Langston said. "I've only been out here for like twenty minutes."

"Yeah, get some rest. I'm gonna need to tire out a bit more before I can sleep."

The freshly fallen snow provided an excruciating silence—especially compared to Arcton City, where there was always a man yelling or a raccoon rustling around, no matter the time of day.

The blue lights from Brill reflected upon the night sky, casting an eerie glow. But the familiarity was comforting. I'd never liked the Orb's pulsations, the dominance it cast, but being reminded of something from home put my mind at ease. At least for a little while. Morning was coming, though, and with it, our final mission.

25. BRILLIANT BLUE

"We can't get through that way," Langston said, slapping my hand away from the map. "There's too many guards, and we'd be out in the open for too long. Brill's a semi-military base. We'd be dead before we scaled the wall."

"What's your idea then?" I asked. We'd spent the previous couple days doing recon around Brill, gathering information for our mission. And today, finally, we spotted a sentry sent ahead by the other Verdean forces. He told us they'd launch the attack tonight around midnight.

All day we debated the best way to infiltrate Brill, and my eyes were now starting to droop. So far, all we'd decided was which way to leave our camp. So, not the most progress.

"Leo, you should get some rest," Jenna said. "You look awful— no offense. But you're going to be no use to us tonight if you're sleep-deprived and irritable."

"Irritable? Maybe it's because of your snoring that I can't—"

"Leo, when's the last time you ever yelled at any of us?" Bree said. "You're irritable. You can't help it. "

"Get some rest, man," Peter said, patting me on the back. "We can take over the plan. You've got to trust us."

I knew they were right, but if anything, that made me even more eager to help.

"What about digging underneath the outer wall?" I suggested.

Langston sighed. "First off," he said, "the map clearly states that their wall goes ten feet underground. And we have about six hours before the attack starts tonight. You're going to have a hard time digging two feet down in that time, let alone ten down and another ten feet back up."

"Go to bed, Leo," said Peter.

I swallowed my pride. I fell asleep almost as soon as my head hit the pillow. A dreamless, restful sleep overtook me, and I would've slept all day and all night had Jenna not poked her head in, her cheeks red from the cold, to wake me up.

"Come on," she said. "We're having dinner before we take off."

No one said much while we ate the DMPs. The wrapping paper crinkled loudly. Everyone stared at their food. There was no effort at conversation.

Normally the silence would make me uncomfortable, but in the presence of these guys, it was different. I didn't need to fill the silence. No one did. We just sat there, all of us, working the tough food over in our mouths, hoping it wasn't our last meal.

I fingered my sword, inspecting the perfect groove right down the blade's center. My bow was strung and my arrowheads sharpened.

I was cautiously optimistic about the whole thing. We could survive. We might make it back alive! And who knew what perks that would have... discharge from the Verdean for one, but maybe Peter would get an introduction to someone at the Arcton City Theater so he could write plays. Jenna would go study to be a full-time nurse, or maybe get promoted within the Verdean's ranks. At the very least she'd be safe...

We climbed up and over the hill, ants on a dull-gray hill. Brill's blue street lamps glowed heavenly in front of us.

When we got to the bottom, we draped our white bed sheets over us to blend in with the snow, and moved slowly to avoid detection from sentries on top of the outer wall.

The sewage drain, a circular stone passage that emptied out onto an icy lake, was easy enough to find. Thankfully, it wasn't currently in use, although some brown leftovers sat atop the ice. Jenna was first to climb up into the grate. We all followed, tiptoeing carefully on the muck and sludge, pinching our noses at the awful smell.

"Leo," Peter whispered, "Remember when we snuck into Arcton's sewers and you fell face first?"

"Don't remind me," I said.

"And then you met up with Irene and still smelled like—"

"Yeah, not my finest moment."

I was afraid to feel the walls around me for support (for obvious reasons), so instead I chose to put one arm out in front to prevent me from crashing into anyone. Still, I walked slowly, stepping gingerly on the sludge below.

Not even five minutes into the passageway, I bumped into Bree, who had apparently run right into Jenna in front of her.

Langston walked straight into me from behind. "What happened?" he said.

"The passage is barricaded," Jenna said. "Iron slabs covering the entire thing."

Langston pushed ahead, grabbing the metal bars. "If only I had a jib," he said, "I could break these open."

"We only have an hour left until the attack starts," Peter said, arriving from behind. "There's no way through them?"

"Not unless we have a jib, according to Langston," I said.

"Leo, why don't you try?" said Jenna.

"What d'you mean?" I said.

"Leo…"

"Oh. Yeah."

I closed my eyes and focused on my breath. In through the nose. Out through my mouth. But the disgusting sewer made me want to puke with each breath. I covered my mouth, trying to focus inward and get the warped vision…

"I can't do it," I finally said. "I'm sorry, I just— I don't know why I can't."

"I have an alternative," said Bree. In the darkness, I sensed her turning to me. "But you're definitely not going to like it."

"What is it?" I said.

"Jenna and I can get in," Bree said.

"No way!" I said.

"We can pretend to be Brillian civilians," Bree said. "If we're just two unarmed girls wearing white t-shirts and some of those jackets we brought where the Arcton *A* is on the inside, they'll never suspect it."

"There's no way," I said.

"You don't think we can do it?" Jenna asked.

"I *know* you can't do it." I said. "None of us can with just two people. And why do you think just wearing t-shirts instead of your uniforms is going to help you blend in at all?"

"Langston isn't the only one who reads," Bree said. "White shirts and civilian jackets are what women wear, and it's not like they know Arcton is about to attack them. Brill probably hasn't even experienced war yet. It's only been outer villages and cities. The guards won't be expecting it at all."

"She's right," Langston said. "It's our best chance. And we don't have a better option now that the sewer is out of the question."

"So you're just going to walk right up to the front gate and ask to be let in?" I said.

"Pretty much, yeah," said Bree. "We'll say we went looking for Jenna's cat or something."

"What about the accents?" Peter said.

"You mean like this?" Jenna said, in a perfect imitation of the low drawl.

"This is absurd," I said.

"It'll work," said Bree. "They'll never expect two skinny girls to be the ones to infiltrate their city."

"What happens if you get caught?" I asked.

"There should only be a few guards on duty in the Northern gate," Langston said. "They shouldn't be too suspicious. But then you'll have to find a way to let all of us in."

How were Langston and Peter not backing me up on this?

"Should we kill the guards?" Jenna asked.

"Too risky," Langston said. Jenna gave him a suspicious look. "Not because you can't physically do it, but because then we have a few bodies lying around. See if you can get to the top of the wall instead and throw down a rope or something."

There was nothing else to do but wish Jenna and Bree luck. We exchanged hugs and said goodbye. I held Jenna a split-second longer than normal.

"I'm going to be okay, Leo," Jenna said, releasing me. "I've got Bree."

Langston, Pete, and I dug ourselves a foxhole in the snow, hoping to be camouflaged from any sentries.

Jenna and Bree were going face-to-face with the enemy, unarmed and unprotected. If anything went wrong, I should be there.

In the foxhole, we didn't talk. We huddled together for warmth, spreading Jenna and Bree's jackets over us, keeping a watch for anyone approaching or a rope being slung down from the wall. Now and then we'd hear the clanging of a gate or faint voices in the night.

Heavy snowfall buried us.

A short while later—it was impossible to tell just how long—a dark figure stalked by. I readied my bow, aiming an arrow right at its chest. It halted, turning its head this way and that, searching for something through the falling snowflakes.

"Leo," Bree's voice whispered. "Langston, Peter. You guys there?"

I lowered my arrow, and we rushed towards her. "Where's Jenna?" I quickly asked.

"She's on the wall, waiting to help pull us up."

"You pulled it off?" Peter said. "How'd you get that coat?"

"We had one soldier interfere, but we took care of him," Bree said. She picked her own coat up off the ground. "When we walked up to the guards outside they said we weren't the first ones to go beyond the wall, and wouldn't be the last. They were actually surprisingly friendly about it. For Trusselians, I mean."

Bree took us to a spot about fifty yards further north, where a rope hung down. It was impossible to see the top, but somewhere up there was Jenna. Bree gave two quick tugs on the rope. It dangled motionless for a few seconds before being pulled up a few inches three separate times.

"Good to go," Bree said. "Who wants to go first?"

"You, you're the lightest," Langston said. "Then you can help Jenna bring up the rest of us one by one. Should speed things up. We don't have long before the attack starts."

Bree dropped her backpack against the wall, and we all did the same, tucking the packs under the sheets. They wouldn't be much use to us inside.

I scanned the area for Brillian sentries or actual civilians taking a walk outside the protective walls, but all was quiet.

Bree finished securing the rope around her waist and began to climb. She was quick up the rope, using her legs to grip the nylon and help propel herself up. One by one, Langston, Peter, and I tied the rope around our waists and began the climb.

When I reached the top, I thanked the others and straightened up, brushing some snow off my uniform. I walked to the opposite edge and nearly lost my breath.

Hundreds of tiny blue street lamps sparkled out at us like stationary fireflies. Unlike Arcton City's perfectly coordinated and gridded streets, Brill's were a complete mess. Not a single road was straight, each curving this way and that, intersecting with others without any semblance of a plan. Taller buildings were intermixed with smaller ones, ponds strewn about everywhere. The entire city was chaos.

A river snaked its way underneath bridges and along snow-covered streets. In the summer Brillian kids must've swam constantly. I would've. The water exited through the outer walls on the south side, where, Langston said, it eventually flowed back into the ocean.

"Do you guys hear that?" Bree asked.

"Hear what?"

"Shh… Listen."

A dull rumble grew louder and louder. And then, coming from the lake and out of the woodwork of the forest came soldier after soldier after Verdean soldier. Hundreds streamed toward the southeast wall of the city, launching arrows as they ran. Others carried massive ladders that could reach the top of the outer wall.

Down below, Brill's own soldiers ran to that side of the wall, caught completely off-guard, yelling instructions at one another.

We stood atop the wall, completely transfixed.

WHOOOOP! WHOOOOP! WHOOOOP!

Ear-splitting sirens sounded. Now it wasn't just soldiers running below. Civilians were rushing into their own homes, tiny ants scrambling to find shelter. It was pure madness.

"Let's go," Peter said.

We took off down a flight of stone steps, trying desperately not to slip on the ice. The first street sign said Essex. According to Langston, who had done his best to commit a map of Brill to memory, it ran parallel to the street where General Nygaard would be.

There were a few civilians still out, and those few were too preoccupied to notice the Arctonian soldiers walking directly in front of them. A few men stepped out of a broken glass door in front of us, carrying armfuls of jewels.

"Thieves," I said, wanting to chase them down. But this wasn't my city. What did I care if the Trusselians were stealing from each other?

Ignoring them, we continued our light jog. Soon we were at Longberry Street. It was wide enough for five trucks to pass through easily and lined with large, ten-story buildings. There were smaller homes dispersed throughout that more closely resembled the shanties put up near the Pennyway. It was weird having poor with rich, side-by-side. That would never happen in Arcton City.

"Is this the right cross street?" Bree asked Langston, searching around for some other sign.

"It's on Longberry, but we're still a few streets away," Langston said.

"You don't think he's in one of these homes, do you?" Peter asked.

"If he is, I hope it's in one of the smaller ones," I said. "The mansions probably have all sorts of security placed around them."

"It's an office building, remember?" Jenna said.

Voices rang out from up ahead. A loud, high-pitched hum accompanied them, like ten trucks all driving simultaneously.

"More soldiers," Langston said.

"Quick, behind here," Jenna said. We rushed into a small alleyway nestled between two homes and waited as the voices and the hum got louder.

Finally, just within eyesight, no fewer than thirty soldiers and a tank—a real-life tank—rumbled down the street, apparently oblivious to the full-on attack going on at the outer wall.

Motioning to the others, I retreated behind a house on the corner with an outstretched awning. The blue lights from above stopped just short, and I hid in the shadows. As the rest of the Sphelix followed, one of the Trusselian soldiers yelled out.

"Did you see how many there were?" Langston asked, panting against the wall. "This is suicide."

"We should retreat," I said. "Leave Brill, take the boat back to Arcton. We can make up an excuse for why we didn't kidnap General Nygaard."

"No way!" Peter yelled. A thunderous crash rang above our heads. Smoke billowed from a house just twenty yards away.

"What was that?" I asked.

Langston's face went pale. "The tank is shooting," he said. "They must've seen us."

"Let's get out of here," Jenna yelled.

"We traveled too far to be scared," Peter said. "We're the Sphelix! The higher-ups would never give us a mission they didn't think we could finish."

Another explosion went off, this time in the building next to us. The entire side of the house was ripped apart and the nearby blue streetlights were flattened. Rubble fell at my feet, my ears ringing loudly. A cloud of dust billowed, submerging us.

"We're outnumbered at least five to one," I said, coughing. "We can't take them out."

"You can, Leo," Bree said. Her eyes darted around warily. The tank's rumbling grew louder. The drone of its engine crept closer. "You can take most of them out, and we don't have to risk anything."

"I can't use my power on command," I said. "Let alone take out an entire squad of soldiers."

"If you try and fail, we're right back where we started," Langston said. "If you do it, we can continue on."

They were right. Of course they were. But my hands still trembled as I turned from behind the side paneling of a wall and saw the ridged slats of a fully-armored, fully-manned tank rolling one on top of the other directly towards me, soldiers fanned out on either side.

And then I saw him. Just behind the tank, wearing a fur-lined jacket, and frantically searching around, was General Nygaard. There was a sword at his hilt, and he barked orders at the other soldiers, urging them to keep a look out. He jogged to keep up with the tank. But why wasn't he in it?

"Oh no, are those…" Jenna said.

General Nygaard's rear-guard came into view just then, and I understood why he chose to be outside the tank.

Walking right behind were five of the biggest men I'd ever seen. Despite the freezing temperatures, they wore only thin, long-sleeved shirts, around which two straps crisscrossed. Each had a shield at their back.

Supersoldiers.

They'd always been a joke, a hypothetical, a tale kids in the neighborhood told each other, but these soldiers were frighteningly close to those descriptions.

The five Supersoldiers didn't so much walk as strut, their massive upper bodies swaying like bulldogs.

Two of the Supersoldiers carried a mahogany chest between them. The others peered around, searching the streets for any potential danger. Despite the assault on their city, they showed no emotion. They looked like they'd been given steroids so they could grow bigger, and I didn't want to think about the training they probably underwent.

Smoke climbed out of the rubble from the tank's second explosion. The tank wheels were turning now, coming around the bend...Behind me, I heard the others knock arrows in their bows, ready to fight...

I tried to calm my mind and focus. I concentrated on my breath, but it was like a fly kept buzzing around, distracting me. Closer and closer the tank rolled towards us, the soldiers beside it. The odds of our being killed were increasing by the second.

"Leo," Peter said, "you've got to do it now. Those are Supersoldiers."

What did he mean by "it"? Blow up the tank? Strangle the soldiers? The only thing I'd ever done with "it" was stop arrows and make Peter float.

The tank continued on its slow, unstoppable path toward us. Soldiers jogged up ahead to check any blind spots, looking around buildings and down side streets. Three of them checked behind a building directly next to us.

Bree put a hand on my shoulder. "Leo," she said in my ear. "Take a breath. Concentrate." I did as she said. "Good, now again. You have plenty of time. One last breath."

It was just the trick. The warm touch on my shoulder trickled throughout my body. The friendly touch connected me to my breath. I inhaled and focused on the air rushing through my nostrils and filling up my lungs…

My vision warped. An extravagant building made of cement and steel poles took shape in my mind. The steel formed the base that held the nearly fifty-foot building intact.

As the tank passed underneath that building, I snapped and broke the steel wickerwork at its base as well as the walls and supports.

To my surprise, the side gave out, and the rest of the building teetered over on its edge. Like a hole in a dam, the rest of the structure toppled over—right on top of the tank, pancaking half the soldiers in the process with a loud crash.

A storm of dust rose in the street, and the remaining soldiers that weren't buried under cement cinder blocks staggered through it. A huge blockade now encumbered the road,

Bree jumped out from behind me and loosed arrows as quickly as she could; the rest of us did the same. The Trusselians yelled amongst themselves, searching for the shooters, but they were covered in dust. I charged, raising my sword.

A Trusselian soldier came out of the dust cloud swinging two swords violently. I retreated a few steps and blocked a couple of his blows. After a few more swings, I saw an opening. With a quick stab, I pierced him right above his hip. He let out a guttural yell, but kept swinging, unknowingly opening up his wound more and more until, finally, his swings slowed.

Remaining patient, I retreated further while he continued his frantic movements, until I saw another opening. This time, my blade pierced flesh and bone in the middle of his sternum. He exhaled a grunt and collapsed.

Langston was fighting another soldier; Jenna went over to help him, and the two of them overpowered the Trusselian. Peter and Bree both made their way toward me, covered in dust. My throat started to tingle, and I gave a huge cough, trying to clear it out.

"Here," Jenna said, handing me water. "That'll help."

"Did anyone see General Nygaard?" Peter asked.

"I think he's on the other side of the rubble," Langston said. "With a few more soldiers."

"I think he might be in the rubble," said Jenna.

"Damnit," Bree said.

"We have to check the other side," I said. I hoped I hadn't compromised the mission. Why didn't I take down a different building?

I led the way up the stones and rubble that stood nearly a story high. A few inches from the top, I stopped climbing and strained my ears, but still there was relative silence. Maybe the building had crushed everyone else, including the Supersoldiers? If so, General Nygaard was buried underneath a few tons of brick and cement.

I inched my head over the top of the rubble and saw four of the five Supersoldiers standing around the chest they'd been carrying before as though waiting further instruction. The fifth wasn't with them, either crushed beneath the rubble or off to get help.

I waved at the others to come up. "I don't see Nygaard," I said. "But there are four Supersoldiers. Langston and Willie—I mean Bree, sorry—you go over there," I said, pointing. "And get ready to fire arrows. You guys shoot first and then duck. We'll follow with a second round."

Langston's eyes were wide with terror. "Leo, are you sure," he said. "If there's no Nygaard, maybe we should get out of here."

"We can take them," I said. "Especially from long range. And they're protecting that chest for a reason."

Langston and Bree got into position quickly and signaled that they were ready to fire on command. I gave them the okay and turned back to look at the soldiers.

A couple *twangs* came from my left, and two arrows shot out. One was true, lodging itself in a Supersoldier's collarbone. The other sailed three feet over their heads.

Peter, Jenna and I each shot off a round of arrows right afterward. Jenna's lodged into one soldier, mine missed, and one Supersoldier—stunningly—caught Peter's arrow with one hand

and snapped it over his knee.

The Supersoldiers took out their shields and blocked the next two arrows that Langston and Bree loosed, then ours right afterward. They stood close together, forming a wall that our arrows wouldn't be able to penetrate.

"We've got to move in," Peter yelled. "We're never going to get the chest by just shooting arrows."

"Agreed," Jenna said.

Without another word, Jenna climbed over the top and ran down. Peter and I both scrambled after her, launching arrow after arrow at the two hulking soldiers, more to keep them in their defensive position than in any real hope of making contact.

Out of the corner of my eye I saw Langston and Bree charging and loosing arrows simultaneously. The Supersoldiers didn't dare drop their shields to shoot back. We kept running and shooting, getting closer, but our arrows still glancing off the shields.

But then the Supersoldiers rose up simultaneously, and started charging at us.

Suddenly we were on the defensive. I tried to backtrack, but it was too late. Both shields slammed into Jenna and Peter. I managed to duck out of the way but dropped my bow.

I reached in my scabbard and yanked out my sword just in time to deflect one of the behemoth's heavy blows. It stung both my hands, and I felt my wrist give a pop. I kicked the Supersoldier off and retreated.

Both of them were side by side again, brandishing their own swords dangerously. Peter and Jenna backed into me…

As one, each Supersoldier threw his shield at us, charging again.

I charged back, trying to cut off their momentum, and slid at the legs of the Supersoldier on the left. I slashed at his thigh as he dove over, but missed.

I rolled a few times and sprang to my feet, expecting another onslaught, but the soldier was now fighting with Peter. Despite Peter's strength, he could barely block the massive blows. A clap of thunder rang out every time their blades met.

I sprinted as fast as I could and thrust my blade up through the Supersoldier's lower back just as Peter ran out of space into which he could retreat.

The Supersoldier gave an involuntary twitch as the blade ripped through his chest, pulling back in agony before he fell lifeless onto Peter.

A scream rang out from behind me, and for a wild second I imagined Jenna alone against the other giant, but I turned to see Langston and Bree standing there with her. The Trusselian Supersoldier writhed in pain on the ground beside them, blood soaking the snow.

"Get him off me!" Peter shouted. "Please! Get him off!"

"Sorry, Pete," I said. I tried to find a grip for my feet so I could shove the Supersoldier off.

Peter was now screaming at the top of his lungs: "Get him off! Get him off!"

I pushed over the Supersoldier with one final shove, and Peter emerged, drenched in the man's blood. Peter's face was as pale as the sidewalk. I helped him to his feet. He stood for a second before collapsing back down, resting his head on the wall.

"You okay?" I asked. "Was he that heavy?"

"It wasn't the weight," Peter said. "It—It..." He was shivering like crazy. I took off my jacket and wrapped it around him.

"Pete, what's wrong?"

"It was his eyes," Peter said. "They were staring right through me when you killed him. And...and I saw the life go out of them. Oh, why did we do that?"

"Peter, you alright?" Jenna said, walking up to us. "Is he alright?" she asked me when he didn't respond.

"He'll be fine. Let's get out of here," I said. "Quickly." Langston and I each slung one of Peter's arms over our shoulders while Jenna and Bree carried the chest—made of old, burnished mahogany—each holding a silver handle.

After a little while, Peter could walk under his own strength.

"Back to the gate," said Langston.

We got out of the city without seeing another soul. The guards who had been stationed at the north entrance had apparently left their posts—a stroke of good fortune, it seemed, and our first in a long time.

Right as we got out of the gate, though, distant screams made me turn.

Boats and homes just outside the city walls were on fire. Brillian troops stood atop the ramparts, unleashing volleys of arrows into our forces, which seemed to have doubled from the initial attack.

A horn rang out, and the southern gates opened. Brillian soldiers were marching out to meet our forces.

The blue street lights lit up Peter's face as he watched the battle. His eyes were wide, his breaths coming in quick bursts.

"Looks like our night isn't over yet," Langston said.

"Far from it," Bree said.

26. THE COWARD'S TOES

Screams and shouts echoed in the distance. The clanging of steel rang out. We agreed to hide the chest, which Jenna and Bree were still lugging, before returning to join the battle.

"Are we sure we have to join the fight?" Jenna said. "We did our part."

"If there are other squads fighting, we have to help," said Bree. "You know that's how it works."

The Verdean fleet was downriver about a half-mile from the northern gate. We hid the chest underneath the bow of a boat far from the battle currently raging, throwing some dirty clothes and our backpacks over it. I turned to jump off and head back into battle, but stopped short when I saw Peter, sitting, staring down between his legs. He kept shaking his head back and forth.

"Pete?" I said. He didn't respond. "It's not your fault—what happened. You were doing your job. There's nothing wrong with that."

Silence again.

Jenna joined in, putting a hand on Peter's shoulder that he didn't seem to feel. "Peter," she said, "you can't blame yourself for what happened. If Leo hadn't killed him, he would've killed you."

Peter didn't look up.

"Peter," Langston said, "I know this is tough, but we've got to get back in there."

"Can you keep going?" I asked. "Or do you want to stay here

with the chest?"

"He can't stay," Bree said. "If the Verdean finds out he didn't join the battle, he'll be thrown in the Pit for cowardice."

"Well, he's in no shape to go fight," I said. "I'd rather have him here than in battle. We can make up an excuse. Tell them we wanted extra protection for the chest."

"Bree's right," said Langston. "We should bring him, but have him stay in the back. He doesn't have to actually fight, but he does have to come with us. We already failed to capture General Nygaard."

I turned to Jenna, hoping for some backup. Tears were in her eyes, but she nodded. Peter had to come.

For his part, Peter didn't seem to really care one way or another. Like a puppet, he slowly got up and followed us off the boat, heading towards the distant screams.

Why was he so petrified? Peter had killed and seen others die right in front of him before. *What had changed?*

Up ahead, a field of bodies stretched between Brill's outer wall and the river. Hundreds of soldiers stood on each side, all just shadows running into one another from this distance. It was impossible to tell the two sides apart.

But then the shadows started running towards us—all the Verdean soldiers. My initial instinct was that I had mixed up which army was which, but then I realized that they were sounding the horns for retreat. Calls of, "Back to the boats!" rang out. The fighting was over.

Peter would be okay.

I turned to the Sphelix. "Let's go," I said. "Let's get out of here." There were only four of us... Peter was gone.

"Where did he go?" I asked.

"Maybe he went back to the boat," Jenna said. "We should go before anyone sees us without him."

The retreat was in full flight now, and out in front of everyone was — who else? — Carl, his sandy-blonde hair bouncing in the wind, a good fifty yards ahead of the next closest Verdean soldier.

"RUN!" he screamed. "In the boats. Oh..." He stopped in his tracks, recognizing us. "Leading the retreat, I see. Classic Forcies. Why don't you go do a bit of fighting for a change?"

"Eat it," Langston said. "We've done more fighting tonight than you."

"Is that why Peter's not with you?" Carl asked. "Is he...*dead?*" His voice was grotesquely hopeful.

"He's still in there," I lied, "but he'll be back shortly. You can go ahead and continue being the actual leader of the retreat."

Carl looked like he'd been hit by another tray from Bree. His cheeks flushed a deep red, but he was so far ahead of everyone else in his squad that he didn't dare pick a fight.

Other soldiers rushed past us, various injuries among them. One man had his arm bent backwards and, hunched over, was carrying it with his other. A skinny boy with a gash across his cheek held up a bloody stump where his hand should have been. He had a shirt wrapped around it, fear in his eyes.

We didn't wait around. Peter was sitting in the boat when we returned. We pushed off quickly, Bree revving the engine. Jenna and Langston kicked out from the riverbed. We were one of the first boats to set sail, but the rest of the fleet soon followed.

No one said a word to Pete. He was clearly in shock—at the war, at what he could do to a human being. I just hoped that shock would be the worst of it.

Trusselian archers raced out along the shore and fired volleys of arrows at the Verdean boats. We'd been one of the first to push off, but there was still a mad rush in the water. Boats collided with one another. Soldiers sprinted along the dirt and leapt into boats at random, water splashing up in huge waves. All the while arrows came hurtling in the dark, thumping into the wood.

Bree kept us to the bank of the river under cover of overhanging trees and away from the other boats heading back home. After an hour, the yells gave way to silence.

Jenna bundled Peter up in two warm coats and wrapped three scarves around him. I didn't try to make conversation. Now wasn't the time. His blank stare said more than his voice ever could.

We sailed through the night. The following day was a constant battle to stay hydrated and cool while the sun beat down on the tops of our heads.

I busied myself with checking on Peter and fiddling with the wooden chest, trying to pick the metal lock clasped to its side. I had about as much luck with the chest as I did with cheering Peter up. He stayed mostly unresponsive, asking to be left alone or feigning sleep.

Thankfully, we made great time, and on the fifth morning after leaving Brill we were one of the first boats in the armada to make it back to Arcton. We pulled into the same stretch of beach we had left a few weeks ago, and Oliver was again there to meet us. Langston and Bree yanked out the chest from underneath the ship's deck and brought it into the back of the truck. Peter climbed the steeply sloped hill easily. When he saw Oliver's beaming face outside the truck, he even cracked a small smile and allowed Oliver to hug him.

I pulled Jenna aside right before we got in the truck. "Is there any way we can get some focus pills?"

"You shouldn't be taking those," Jenna said, "You know what Memo said."

"Not for me. For Peter. If this isn't a time for a focus pill—"

"I'll ask Memo when I see him," Jenna said.

Oliver had brought along a huge supply of DMPs of every variety imaginable. We devoured chicken sandwiches and cut-up apples, and we even dug into a can of soup that Oliver managed to keep warm for us.

Langston munched on a peanut butter and jelly sandwich. "Oliver, have I ever said I love you? Like, not pretend love. I'm straight up in love with you."

Oliver gave a huge laugh. "Food out there that bad, huh?"

"It's nice to see a friendly face, too," said Jenna. "You get used to running from anything that moves."

Oliver brushed back some sweat running down his brow. "I can't believe you guys did it again," he said.

"Is there any way we can open the chest?" Peter looked around at us. It was the first time he'd spoken a full sentence since leaving

Brill.

Langston once again fumbled with the padlocks, but, like before, they resisted being opened. "Maybe it needs a woman's touch," said Jenna, brushing Langston aside and trying to finger open the lock.

Again, no luck.

Bree and Peter both struck it with their swords, but the lock still wouldn't budge.

Langston turned to me. "You might be able to do it," he said.

"I'm not gonna be any better with a sword than Pete," I said.

He glanced at Oliver, who was focused on the road. "Not your sword," he said. "Something else."

"Oh."

I slid the chest between my legs, closed my eyes, and began to reach outward with my mind. The warped vision was instantaneous. I found the truck and saw its insides: the engine, filled with its pistons and rods working feverishly; the oil that powered the engine; the welding on the doors, holding them in place.

Eventually I focused on the chest itself, which appeared dark— like it was covered in soot. I opened my eyes to take a look under the sunlight; its burnished mahogany glinted. The handles, a little older, still shone brilliantly.

But it was the lock I needed. I refocused and closed my eyes. My breath slowed, air flowing in my nose and out through my mouth…

The lock.

Through my warped vision, the dark soot covered it, acting like an extra protection, preventing me from being able to tell what it was made of, where it came from… I couldn't *see* it.

I kept prodding with my mind, nudging at it like a pick axe scraping away dirt. At first it was unchanged, but then, slowly, the soot started to fall away—revealing a shiny lock in my mind's eye.

And then, all at once, I *saw* the lock—the inner machinations, a tiny steel maze with miniature bolts.

With a twist of my conscious, I unhinged it. The lock sprang open.

I opened my eyes, the warped vision receding. The others had their jaws open, shifting their gaze back and forth between the chest and me.

"Don't just stand there," I said. "Open it."

Langston was closest. He pulled back the top, revealing a similar mahogany interior. I stood up to get a better look. Langston reached down and took from a corner of the chest a small stack of documents—no more than fifty pages in total.

"What are those?" Bree said, unable to hide her disappointment. "We did all that for some paper?"

Langston sifted through the pages carefully. He shook his head.

"This isn't just paper."

27. THE HIDDEN PAPERS

"They're diagrams," Langston said.

"Diagrams?"

"Hold on."

"Langston, come on."

"I'm reading. Here, take a look."

He handed me an envelope he'd finished scanning. On the front page was a sketched diagram of what appeared to be a Supersoldier. The following pages were filled with formulas and complex directions; it may as well have been written in a different language. I handed it off to Jenna.

The second envelope was less cryptic. They were letters. The first was written by Carl's dad, General Magner.

General Nygaard,

Thank you for your last correspondence.

Thirty-two Verdean guerilla units will arrive at southeast border of Trussel, by Restoration Forest, on January 11th as part of counterattack.

Sincerely,

General Magner

Minister Nygaard,

Verdean forces delayed two weeks. They will now reach Bluerock on January 24th and will occupy for a scheduled two weeks.

I also received confirmation that the last of the Trusselian forces have cleared out of Arcton.

Sincerely,

General Magner

There were dozens of letters, all addressed from General Magner to General Nygaard.

"Why was Carl's dad writing to General Nygaard?" I asked.

Before anyone could answer it dawned on me. Blood rushed to my head, and I started to sway. This couldn't be.

"Langston..."

Langston was shaking his head, reading some of the other letters. I hadn't noticed the gash across his cheek, the dried blood on his neck.

"General Magner's been feeding inside info to Trussel," Langston said.

"What?" said Oliver. "General Magner?"

Bree was reading through the letters now, her face darkening with every page.

"It's treason," continued Langston. "Oliver, we need to get these letters straight to the higher-ups. General Magner's been communicating with one of Trussel's generals since the beginning of the war it looks like."

"Let me see those," said Oliver. Bree handed them over. Keeping one eye on the road, he skimmed through them quickly. "We need to get these to Memo," he said. "Keep that chest hidden behind your backpacks when we get to Base Camp. Memo will know what to do."

"What about the envelope with the Supersoldier on the first page?" Jenna asked. "Why did he have that?"

"Instructions on how to make a Supersoldier," said Langston. "Maybe Carl's dad gave Nygaard that too. Maybe that's why he had those Supersoldiers protecting him."

"So then does Arcton know how to create Supersoldiers too?" I asked.

"At the very least Carl's dad might have known how," said Jenna.

"Will Carl's dad be executed?" asked Bree.

"Without a doubt," said Langston. "Those letters are really bad. No wonder Arcton wanted to capture General Nygaard; they probably knew he'd been involved with something. We're lucky he had that chest."

We arrived at Base Camp after lights out. A few office windows were lit up when we drove down the winding slope of Mt. Brentwood, but even those would soon be extinguished. I wanted to eat. I wanted to sleep. Above all I wanted to see Irene, but before any of that we had to visit Memo.

At the security checkpoint, we kept the chest hidden underneath our backpacks, Bree sitting on top of the pile. The guards, nearing the end of their shift, didn't even ask for our ID papers as they waved us through.

Even though he'd driven the entire day, Oliver was still quick to help us unload.

He tossed me my backpack. "You guys going to carry the chest, or want me to bring it to Memo?"

"We'll carry it," Bree said.

"Thanks for everything, Oliver," Jenna said. "Meant a lot having you drive us."

"Luckiest job in the world," Oliver smiled, giving me a hug. "Make sure you go straight to Memo with that. No detours."

The guards that usually sat outside the Captains' Offices to check in visitors were off their shift. But we weren't surprised to see Memo walking down the hall shortly after our arrival.

Memo smiled genially, hugging each of us. "You arrived quicker than I expected!" he said. "And what's this?" he said, looking at the chest.

Before anyone could answer he put a finger to his mouth and beckoned us to follow him.

No one spoke until we reached Memo's office, a warm fire raging behind his desk, the tiled floor clean and squeaky. Langston and I hoisted the chest beside his desk, set the revolver down on top of it. We hadn't even thought to use it in Brill. Stupid. Finally, Langston placed the papers on the desk and returned to his seat.

Massive bags still sat under Memo's eyes; tufts of hair stuck up on the back of his head. He smiled at us warmly, but it was straining him. He needed sleep. Also a shower.

"Are you okay?" Jenna asked.

Memo smiled weakly. "I should be asking you that," he said. "It's so good to see your faces."

"Memo, there's something you should know," I said. "Those documents..."

I told him what we found, what it meant. Memo listened intently, flipping through the letters and Supersoldier diagrams, shaking his head in disbelief.

"We fought Supersoldiers in Brill," said Jenna. "And those diagrams, those documents…do you think Arcton has Supersoldiers as well?"

Memo shook his head. "I don't know."

"We need to report General Magner," I said. "Carl's dad should be tried for treason because of this!"

Memo paused. He stacked the documents neatly in front of him.

"We can't," he said.

"What?"

"We can't report these to the higher-ups," said Memo again. "Not yet, anyway."

"Memo, Carl's dad is a traitor!" Bree was beside herself. "We have to expose him! He could've killed us by telling Trussel we were going to attack Brill."

Memo forced his voice to be calm. "I understand that, Bree. I promise you I do. But I need time to dig around and see what this means before we start accusing one of the highest-ranking Verdean officials of treason. It's a serious offense with dire consequences. Do you—"

There was a knock at the door. Memo pulled the chest behind his desk and slid the papers off into a drawer. Jenna got up to answer it. Without being invited in, two lieutenants pushed past her and asked Memo for a private word.

"Of course," Memo said politely. He turned to us. "This'll only take a minute. You may wait outside."

We pressed our ears to the door, trying to get a bit of their conversation. The voices were muffled, but Memo's got increasingly louder as the discussion went on.

Around me was a circle of blank faces. No one spoke, all of us too tired and too confused. Why were the two officers here so early in the morning? Couldn't it wait? Why was Memo so scared to report General Magner?

Ten minutes later, the door finally opened and Memo stood before us. The energy in his eyes had all but vanished.

"Peter," he said, clearing his throat. "These two men are going to escort you to the Pit. Please do not resist, and please do not say a word to them or anyone else. I'll send a letter to your parents as soon as I get an opportunity."

"What? Why?" I asked. "Peter didn't do anything. Why's he going to the Pit?"

Memo gave me a warning look. "There have been accusations made against him," he said. "And the Verdean has deemed them legitimate enough that there needs to be a trial.

Memo lowered his voice. "Pete," he said, "everything will be fine. But you need to be on your best behavior the next couple of days. Do not say anything to anyone about the accusations—not a guard, not a prisoner, not a worm crawling in the dirt. You need to promise me you'll keep your mouth shut."

Peter didn't say anything. He looked terrified. More scared, even, than when the Supersoldier had fallen on top of him. "What accusations?" Peter asked.

"We don't know all the details right now," Memo said. "Peter, look at me." He put his hands-on Peter's shoulders. "You'll be fine. You need to promise me you'll keep quiet while you're away."

Peter just stared at him, tears starting to roll down his eyes.

"Peter, you need to promise—"

"I promise," Pete said.

"Thank you. Please walk with these gentlemen." The lieutenants advanced toward Peter and grabbed his arms.

"Let him go!" Jenna shouted, and she went after one of the guards, murder in her eyes. Langston managed to restrain her.

"Memo, you can't let them do this," I pleaded. "He didn't do anything!" I rounded on the guards. "You're scum! What have you done, huh? Peter just—"

"Leo, quiet!" Memo hissed.

Peter looked back as they led him away, and our eyes met for a brief second. He was breathing heavily, terror etched across his face, but, even worse, I saw resignation. He turned away from me, putting his head down, and walked out the door.

I slammed my fist into the wall. "You can't do this!" I screamed. "No! Let him go!"

Memo grabbed my shoulders from behind and spun me around to face him. I wanted to fight back, wanted to see Peter, but Memo's massive hands held me in place.

"Yelling won't do you any good," Memo said. He strode across the room, preventing anyone from going after Peter and the guards.

I felt my cheeks running wet, but I brushed the tears away angrily.

"This will be tough for you to hear," Memo said. "But what's done is done. Peter's been accused of cowardice. I didn't want to tell him because I didn't want him to react to the charges and possibly give away any incriminating information."

"Memo, this is ridiculous. They can't do that!" Bree said.

"Leo was yelling the exact same thing at those guards," Memo said. "You'll notice that it didn't change anything. The Verdean has made their decision. There will be a trial in a couple days to determine his fate. His accuser will have to come forward and when he does—"

"It's Carl," I said. "Carl's the one who accused him of cowardice."

"That helps," Memo said. "But we need to prepare for everything. What happened in Brill?"

"Who cares about Brill?" Jenna said. "We found out General Magner is a traitor—and now Carl's accusing Peter of cowardice?"

"Why can't we report General Magner?" Langston asked.

"For starters, we don't know if these letters are real," said Memo. "We don't know if they actually came from General Magner. I can't go around accusing officials that outrank me of treason without concrete evidence. I understand you're all upset, Langston, I really do. But we can't afford any mistakes right now. Not one. We need to tread carefully. Now, please, tell me what happened in Brill."

Memo took a deep breath, exhausted.

"Please," he said, "I need you all to trust me on this."

And for the first time my trust wavered. What if Memo had known about the communication? What if he'd known about the treason and had done nothing about it?

But the moment passed. Memo had never led us wrong before. So I told him everything – General Nygaard's death, Peter freaking out after we killed the Supersoldiers, how he'd then left us in battle. I left no detail out.

"We'll fight this," Memo said, "but it won't be easy."

"What if we can prove General Magner was a spy?" said Bree. "Shouldn't that help Pete?"

"It will, but there's no guarantee with that either."

Memo looked at Jenna and me. "You two need to head back home. I'll send a message to Helen and Lester, but I'm sure they'll want to see both of you."

A lump suddenly lodged in my throat. Neither of us spoke. How do you tell a mom and dad that their son is on trial for his life?

28. TWO RESPONSES

The ride back to Arcton City was quiet and lonely.

No Oliver joking from the driver's seat.

No Langston reading a textbook.

No Bree sitting quietly, looking angry.

No Peter...

Just Jenna and me, probably sharing the same thoughts: How were we going to tell Helen and Lester? Every scenario I envisioned had them blaming me for what happened to Peter. And honestly, they'd be right. He wouldn't be in the Verdean if it weren't for me; we never would've been in Brill. We'd still be in school, coming home every night to Aunt Helen's cooking.

Dasher's Revenge. Who cared why it was banned? Who cared what *Gestalt Diary* was about? I wished my dad had never read it to me, had never made me so curious about Nefas in the first place.

Peter was stuck in the Pit, getting picked at by fire ants and who knew what other cruel punishments they'd thought up. He was alone and scared, and could possibly spend the rest of his life there. Or be killed.

"Leo," Jenna said. "It's not your fault. None of this is on you."

"I should've never let you two come with me to get *Dasher's Revenge*," I said. "It was selfish."

"We were coming no matter what you said. It's been like that since we moved in with Helen and Lester. The three of us have stuck together. Remember last year when that girl—what was her name—Lindsay? Remember when she kissed Peter and her brother found out and wanted to kill him? You stepped in and tried to fight him."

"Yeah and then he knocked me out with one punch," I said.

"Point being, you had his back."

"I vaguely remember you jumping onto Lindsay's brother and yanking out his hair," I said.

"Well, someone has to be the enforcer." She got up and sat next to me. "It's weird, but I'm glad we went through this."

"Jenna…"

"I'm serious," she said. She pulled out the blue emerald necklace mom had left her and stared at it. "You trust me now. I'm not just your little sister. I'm not tagging along everywhere. You know who I am and what I can do."

"I knew that before," I said, offended. "I've always stuck up for you."

"It's not the same thing," Jenna said. "But this isn't your fault. The letters from the chest, the letters snuck into your bed, the focus pills…"

She glanced nervously at the driver, but the window separating us from the front seats were closed. A few birds flew overhead. The sun glared down at us.

"It's Arcton that's to blame," she said. "Arcton—not you."

Her blue eyes stared into me. I'd never seen her this serious before.

"Thank you," I said. "But the fact is if I hadn't wanted to get that book, Peter wouldn't be in the Pit right now."

Jenna rolled her eyes but, thankfully, dropped the conversation. I was too exhausted to continue. We hadn't slept in well over twenty-four hours. I let the sun's rays beat down on my face, and dozed off.

I woke up to the wheels rolling through the snowmelt of Arcton City. We got off at the truck depot and made the walk back to Lester and Helen's.

Happy waves and stunned looks greeted us on the street. Lucinda gave me a big hug, seeming to forget that Peter and I had stolen a couple oranges from her years ago. Zakary, the butcher, didn't bother taking off his blood-splattered apron before giving Jenna and me bear hugs. His beard bristled against my face. I screwed my mouth up into a smile as he slapped my cheek, his hands dirty, and let it deflate again once he finally walked away.

The sidewalks were crowded. People were out enjoying the sunshine, walking in and around mounds of snow that still hadn't been cleared away. It would've lifted my heart, seeing friends and neighbors for the first time in months—but it was almost as if they were from another life. And I couldn't forget why Jenna and I were here.

The closed shutters and billowing chimney of 64 Moulton was soon visible. I dragged my feet, in no rush. Jenna led the way inside. Uncle Lester sat reading the *Gazette* in his armchair, drinking a cup of coffee no doubt spiked with whiskey. Aunt Helen clanged away in the kitchen, the smell of roasting onions warmly greeting us.

In his stupor, Lester didn't even notice the door open, so we went directly to the kitchen.

Aunt Helen.

She was the first and last person I wanted to see. There was such comfort in seeing her finally, yet knowing what I'd have to tell her spoiled it. She looked up as we walked in and, with a yelp, immediately dropped the ladle in the pot. She reached us in a few quick steps and threw her arms around both of us.

"Oh, thank Heavens," she said with delight. "Are you staying through the night? Can I fix you some lunch? Where's Peter?"

Jenna and I exchanged looks of confusion. Helen didn't know. How could she not know? Memo said his message would reach them before us.

"Um…" Jenna said, searching, but she hesitated too long.

Aunt Helen clutched at her elbows, suddenly shivering. "What's wrong?" she asked. "Where's Peter?"

"We thought a message had been sent," I said. "A message was supposed to—Peter's alive," I added, seeing Helen's legs start to sway. "Come here," I said, taking her arm and guiding her onto the living room couch. She sat down gingerly. Uncle Lester barely raised his eyes from his paper.

"Uncle Lester," I said, "It's best if you hear this too."

"I heard," he said curtly.

"What do you mean you heard?" Helen said. "Heard what?"

"Peter's a coward," Lester said. "Trial's in a few days."

"What? Why didn't you tell me?"

"Messenger came to the door. Handed me a letter from Memo.

Explained everything. Didn't see the point."

Aunt Helen stood up. She grabbed the mug from which he was drinking and smashed it against the wall.

"Peter's going on trial, and you didn't think to let me know!"

"Forgot, I suppose."

"Lester!" she yelled, throwing her hands to her head and turning her back on him. She was shaking, her face reddening. "Lester! It's Peter!"

"What's the point?" he asked. "From the sounds of that letter, he isn't going to be cleared. When have you ever heard of someone the Verdean brought charges against getting off?"

Helen didn't say anything. Tears welled in her eyes. She looked up, her face red, her eyes flowing.

Uncle Lester continued. "Always been a disappointment, and now he's gone and made it official."

"Are you kidding?" Jenna said. "A *disappointment?* Do you know what we were doing on that mission? Do you have any idea what Peter did over the past six months—he saved my life at least once, and killed dozens of Trusselians. And you're calling him a disappointment?" Jenna spat at his feet.

Lester, too, got to his feet, although he was a bit wobbly. "Excuse me?" he said. "You don't speak like that to the man who raised you, girl. I taught you better than that."

"You didn't teach me anything!" Jenna said. "That was Aunt Helen—and she taught me not to listen to a lazy, fat drunk."

Uncle Lester's face reddened and he clenched his fists. I stepped between him and Jenna.

"He's not convicted yet," I said. Helen grasped Jenna and stood next to me while I continued. "Peter should get off. Memo at least thinks so."

"What happened to him?" Aunt Helen asked. "Please."

Jenna told her. She was straightforward, describing the night exactly as it felt: the exhaustion from the war and the long journey, the fear when we saw the Supersoldiers, the isolation of being the only squad inside Brill. After she was done, I think Aunt Helen, and even Uncle Lester if he was paying attention, understood why Peter acted as he did.

Aunt Helen shook her head. "Supersoldiers," she whispered.

"What he did wasn't cowardice," I said. "If anything it was…it was… It was brave."

"Brave?" Uncle Lester laughed. "That was weakness. You have to be ruthless to make it in war. Clearly he's not. Your story confirms it."

Aunt Helen and Jenna both looked like they wanted to slap him. This was his son—my brother—we were talking about. Lester had government connections he could rely on to help support Peter, yet he was going to give up without a fight.

I cocked my fist back and punched Uncle Lester square in the jaw.

Lester's head whipped back and he fell in his chair. He rubbed his chin, trying to open his mouth, but unable to do so fully. A satisfying sting settled into my hand. He glared up at me, his beady brown eyes narrowing.

"You'll go down just like your deadbeat dad," he said.

"At a bar?" I said. I motioned to the mug shards. "That's what you're heading for. Not me."

"Oh, you think your dad died in a bar?" Lester said.

"Lester, stop," said Helen. "You promised…"

"Who cares what I promised," Lester said. "Your dad didn't die in a bar fight, you ungrateful snock. He was executed. He was a traitor, and Arcalaeus ordered him dead. And I was left to raise the runts."

The air escaped my lungs. I looked at Helen. "Is that true?"

Helen had tears in her eyes, but slowly nodded.

"I'm sorry, Leo, Jenna," Helen said. "We were going to tell you after you got back. We never wanted to hurt you—"

I was stunned. All this time…

Jenna stood up straight. "Doesn't matter," she said. "Peter's what's important now."

"When's his trial?" Helen asked.

"Wait," I said. "You can't just lay that on us and then change the—"

"Drop it, Leo," Jenna said. "We'll worry about it later." She turned to Helen. "The trial's in a couple days. We might have to testify. And we have our story figured out so it doesn't look like Peter left the battlefield."

"You don't have to lie —"

"Aunt Helen, stop," Jenna said. "It's not up for discussion."

Tears streamed down Helen's cheeks. She smiled and pulled Jenna into an embrace. "I would do anything to be there," she said.

"We'll let you know as soon as it's over," Jenna said. "At the very least we'll write, but we'll try and come home as well."

"Thank you," Helen said, kissing Jenna. "Now let's get you two some food. You look as though you've eaten nothing but celery since you left. Don't they feed you out there?"

It was a somber meal. Helen served freshly made onion soup with a few generous chunks of bread. We'd never gone hungry while living with Lester and Helen, but so many kids definitely made the rations smaller. Whenever a dish was passed to you, it was wise to take as much as possible because odds were you wouldn't see it a second time.

Now, though, with me, Jenna, and Peter gone, it seemed like Helen had enough for leftovers. Lester didn't eat, instead choosing to pour himself another drink and sulk in the living room.

Jexter and Flora were at school and wouldn't be coming home until well after Jenna and I had to leave, which we did shortly after lunch, my belly swollen with soup and chocolate chip cookies.

Helen nearly strangled me with her goodbye hug.

"Don't do anything stupid," she told me, holding my face in her hands and staring hard. Helen's blue eyes were the mirror image of Peter's. "Whether the verdict is good or bad, don't you do anything to get yourself into trouble. Peter wouldn't want that."

"Yes, ma'am," I said. "Say hi to Jex and Flora for me. Wish we could've seen them."

For a while neither Jenna or I said a word after leaving Moulton Street, though Jenna looked back a couple times.

She finally spoke once we'd reached the hardware store on the Pennyway. "Lester thinks he's a goner," she said. "He wouldn't go to the trial even if he could."

"Screw Lester," I said. "Just...screw him."

"I can't believe Dad was...you know."

"I wonder what he did," I said. He'd fought in the Verdean, been a hero from what the Gilded Library books said. How could he have become a traitor?

"We never saw his body," Jenna said. "We saw Mom's, remember? Do you think they don't let traitors get a proper funeral?"

"Hopefully Carl's dad doesn't get a funeral, selling us out to the Trusselians like that."

"He won't," Jenna said. "Memo will make sure of that. Hey, that second letter you got..."

"What?"

"*Loyalty is fickle...*" she said. "Do you still have it?"

I reached inside my backpack and pulled it out, handing it to her.

"Leo," she said. "*Loyalty is fickle. Death is final. Neither, for your family, is what they seem.*"

"Dad!" I said.

"It's the only explanation," Jenna said.

"So, the person who's giving me those letters knew about Dad," I said. "Who could it be?"

"I don't know—Memo?"

"Why wouldn't he just hand me them?" I asked. "Rather than go through the trouble of hiding it in my pillow?"

"Lieutenant Yawkey?" she said.

I laughed. "Don't think he has the brains to do it."

But another person had crept into my mind. After all, we'd never seen his body. I didn't tell Jenna what I was thinking, though. It was childish. Stupid.

"Helen thinks we're going to try and break Peter out," Jenna said.

It was the first time it'd crossed my mind. The Pit held prisoners deep in the mountainside, with heavy security. No one had ever escaped once they went inside. Besides, even if we did manage to bust Peter out, we would have nowhere to go. We couldn't very well bring him back to Base Camp or Arcton City.

The trial was his best and only hope.

"It shouldn't even come to that," I said. "If we can prove Carl's dad is a traitor, Peter will get out no problem."

Jenna nodded. There were too many questions, and we had no answers. My head overflowed with thoughts and theories. My dad a traitor. Someone sending me secret messages. General Magner a traitor. My power...

We passed Lucinda's market, and I went inside to snag a bag of oranges. The shelves were only half-full with goods. The oranges were five bits, and I gave the cashier a ten note, telling the girl working to keep the change. I tossed one to Jenna and dug my finger into the skin of another, peeling it back.

I didn't know what waited for us in Base Camp, and I wasn't eager to find out. If I could've, I would've walked right back to Helen and Lester's, curled up in bed with a book, and stayed there for a week.

But Jenna kept dragging her feet through the snowmelt, one step at a time, and so did I.

29. THE TRIAL

Bree and Langston were in Barrack 19 when Jenna and I got back the next day. It still felt empty, foreign, without Peter there. I hopped straight into bed, exhausted. I wanted to sleep and forget about the trial.

"Leo?"

I rolled over. Langston was standing there, holding a copy of the *Gazette*. Jenna and Bree were sitting together, playing cards and deep in their own conversation.

"There's something you should see."

"What?"

He held out the *Gazette*.

"I'm not really in the mood to read, Langston. What's up?"

"Arcton and Trussel are engaging in peace talks," Langston said. There wasn't any happiness in his voice. Who cared if the war was ending if Peter wouldn't be allowed to enjoy it?

"Oh," I said. "When's the trial?"

"This afternoon," he said.

"D'you know where?"

"Memo said the Captains' Offices. I'll wake you up when it's time. How'd it go with your aunt and uncle?"

"As well as we could've expected."

"Sorry, man." He rolled up the newspaper. "Get some sleep. I'll make sure you're up."

Sleep never came. After an hour of just lying there, I tried meditating, focusing on my breath, but Peter's screams kept filling my brain. And then, of course, there was Carl...

Carl would be there today to formally accuse Peter of cowardice. His dad, General Magner, would be there, too, with his smug face and perfectly manicured dirty-blonde hair. Irene should've let me punch him when I had the chance...

There was a buzz around Base Camp—the *Gazette* article had spread like wildfire, and news of peace talks lifted everyone's moods. Squads were no longer rushing to the obstacle course. Many were given mornings off and only vaguely encouraged to stay in shape.

The Mess Hall was filled with smiling faces; a few soldiers tossed peas to one another, trying to catch them in their mouths. Soldiers swam in the mud at the obstacle course, others in the bay.

It was sickening. All of it.

Peter had done more than any of them to win the war, and he was locked away in the Pit while they got to enjoy all the benefits. None of them had taken out the outposts on the Tributary, none had fought off Supersoldiers.

The Captains' Offices came into view. We checked in with the guards and were sent up to Memo's office. The hallway was practically deserted. Apparently even the higher-ups were celebrating the end of the war.

Memo was sitting behind his desk when we walked in, reading some papers with a furrowed brow. He managed a weak smile.

"Good to see you," Memo said. "Let's head over."

He got up and led us further down the hallway to the very end, where there was a set of double-doors. A couple of lieutenants standing guard opened them.

A dozen curved benches, split in the middle for a walkway, stretched from wall to wall. They faced an elevated platform at the front with three separate chairs. A raggedy one for the accused. A dull but solidly constructed one for the witness. A high-backed one of polished mahogany with a couple steps leading up to it for the judge.

"Who's the judge?" I asked Memo.

"Every trial is different," said Memo. "It's whoever the Verdean feels is appropriate."

"Were you able to see if the papers were real or—"

"Not now, Leo," Memo whispered.

Verdean soldiers with various numbers of stars emblazoned on their chests packed the benches. We were the only no-names—that is, other than Carl and his squad.

Carl's hair had grown longer over winter, now nearly reaching his shoulders. General Magner, five traitorous stars across his breast, smiled when he spotted us walking in.

We sat directly across the aisle. Memo took a seat next to me, his face unreadable. Bree and Jenna held hands, neither saying a word. Langston kept his head down.

A door closed with a clang in the back, and there he was— Peter, between two lieutenants, being marched down one of the side pathways. A black-and-blue bruise covered the right side of his face, and scratches marred the left.

Hisses rang out from the audience, some yelling that he was a traitor before the trial had even started.

Peter didn't look at us while walking to the stand. One of the guards shackled his hands to the chair on the right. Eventually, Peter scanned the vast hall and his eyes met mine. I nodded and gave an encouraging smile. He blinked back.

A door opened behind the platform and, to my surprise, Arcalaeus walked out. He was fitted in the Verdean uniform, the only difference being the sixth star – directly between the five others – plastered onto his breast pocket.

I'd never been this close to the President or seen him in so much detail: he was shorter than I'd imagined; wisps of white hair sat weakly on top of his head, as though they could be blown off by a well-aimed sneeze. Brown splotches, double the size of freckles, covered his face.

"Wow, he's old," Langston whispered. Jenna elbowed him.

Everyone stood immediately, and Arcalaeus moved nimbly to the chair. When he sat, the rest of us resumed our seats, but there was a tension in the room now. Everyone sat up straight; there were no more whispers.

"Did you know Arcalaeus was going to be the judge?" I asked Memo.

He shook his head.

"Today," Arcalaeus said, "we will hear the case against Peter Herbert, who has been accused of cowardice." His voice was high-pitched, but not in a funny way. The hair on the back of my neck stood up.

"We shall first hear from the accuser," said Arcalaeus, "Mr. Carl

Magner."

Carl stood and strode to the witness stand. He walked up with purpose, and I realized he had no second thoughts about his allegations. Though Carl had been leading the retreat, he believed Peter to be inherently guilty and didn't see a trace of hypocrisy in his accusations—just hatred for Peter.

Carl positioned himself comfortably in the chair and smiled up at Arcalaeus.

"Please go into detail about the events in question," Arcalaeus said.

"Gladly, sir," said Carl. "The attack on Brill was in full effect. We'd engaged them outside their southern gates, and my squadron was right in the middle of the battle when I spotted a couple stray Trusselian soldiers who looked like they were trying to outflank our forces. Naturally, I went after them."

Oh, how brave.

"As I did so," Carl continued, "I saw Peter's squad heading toward the battle—I don't know where they were before that, probably hiding from the fight, but at least they were finally heading into it."

I stood up to call him a liar, but Memo grabbed my arm, yanking me back down. His eyes were wide with terror. Carl saw me from his seat and paused, but he went on.

"I didn't see Peter with them and at first thought he might have been killed, but then, after I'd killed the Trusselians who were trying to outflank us and the horns for the retreat sounded, I saw Peter in their boat, just sitting there. I knew immediately that he had refused to join the fight because he was scared."

He'd obviously practiced a lot—probably with his dad—but even then it was clear that he had a natural ability to perform. His story, where he, Carl, was the hero, and Peter was the cowardly deserter *sounded* true. After all, why on Earth would he lie? He was the hero speaking out against the immoral and despicable acts that threatened Arcton's oneness.

Whispers of admiration swirled from the audience, but Arcalaeus silenced them by clearing his throat. For such a physically small man, he could command a room.

"Thank you," Arcalaeus said. "It takes a courageous young man to speak out against cowardice, especially from one of his fellow comrades. The importance of accountability—this immutable commitment to the oneness that gives Arcton its strength—can't be overstated."

It was as if Arcalaeus had already made up his mind. Why even bother going on with the trial if he was already congratulating Carl?

Carl stepped down from the witness chair, beaming, and sat next to his father, who clapped him on the back and tousled his hair.

Arcalaeus called up the rest of the members of Carl's squad. In turn, each hulking soldier reiterated Carl's claim that he'd gone after the Trusselians while they continued fighting.

Did they actually believe Carl had gone after the other Trusselians alone? The last soldier popped a focus pill into his mouth as he climbed off the stand.

Of course. They were following orders. Every last one of them.

They didn't care if Peter was innocent or guilty, so long as they were doing what they were told. I ground my teeth.

After the final member from Carl's squad stepped down, Arcalaeus addressed the room again.

"I now call the accused, Peter Herbert, to the stand."

Peter limped over like a wounded animal. I couldn't believe Arcalaeus had allowed him to be treated so poorly before a conviction. Either way, Peter didn't exactly inspire confidence— maybe pity, at best, assuming those watching could feel such a thing.

Arcalaeus spoke right as Peter sat down. "You have been accused of cowardice," Arcalaeus said. "This type of behavior is not only detrimental to the longstanding ideals of Arcton, but it also jeopardized the lives of your fellow soldiers, many of whom sit in this courtroom today. How do you plead in this case?"

Peter paused and looked at us. Guilt fell across his face, and his eyes began to water. *Don't listen to Arcalaeus,* I wanted to tell him. *You didn't jeopardize our lives at all. None of us are mad at you. Please just say not guilty...*

"I plead not guilty," Peter said. "And I wish to testify."

I sighed in relief.

"Very well," said Arcalaeus. "You may begin."

"I suppose I'd better start off with what went on inside Brill," Peter said. "We were on a mission, as you might know, to kidnap —"

"Ahem, Mr. Herbert," Arcalaeus interrupted. "I'm afraid I'm going to have to cut you off. You see, that mission was classified.

Kindly skip that part and proceed to where you are outside the city. *That* is where the alleged cowardice occurred."

"Yes, but in order to understand—" Peter said.

"The facts will do, Mr. Herbert," Arcalaeus said. His voice stung the air. "I do not wish to condemn you without hearing your side of the story, but unfortunately I must unless you adhere to the rules of this courtroom."

Peter shook nervously. He had no choice but to continue from where we'd left Brill.

"Sorry," he said. "Um, yeah... So we left Brill with our objective completed—and we went back to the boat... So we had seen the fighting—and we wanted to make sure we still had the chest, I guess. You know, we wanted to keep it safe."

My heart fell further into my stomach with each word. How could his storytelling suddenly desert him at such a crucial time?

Peter continued. "So we were all gathered at the boat, and I didn't want to stay behind. I love to fight. But someone had to, so I did. And, yeah, that's why I wasn't in the fighting outside of Brill..."

There was stunned silence. Langston dropped his head into his hands.

It was a disaster—worse than listening to Jexter tell a joke.

Under the best of circumstances the story was awful, but following Carl's masterful testimony, it was a downright disaster.

Awful whispers circulated around the audience. Arcalaeus let them continue, and didn't say anything. He wanted Peter to stew on that chair, to break him. I clenched my fists.

Finally, Arcalaeus broke the silence, and the whispers died, like a window slamming shut.

"You may sit down, Mr. Herbert," he said.

Peter limped back uneasily, tears rolling down his face, his fate sealed.

"Is there anything we can do?" I said, turning to Memo. "He's going to get convicted."

"Just wait," he said.

"We should tell everyone about General Magner," I said.

Memo peered around to see if anyone had heard before silencing me with a look. "Not a word about that," he said.

"Does Mr. Herbert's commanding officer wish to testify?" Arcalaeus asked.

"I do, sir," said Memo. He gave me another serious look before standing up and taking the witness chair. He nodded at Peter reassuringly.

"Captain Iglesias," Arcalaeus nodded. "I take it that you have testimony you'd like to present on behalf of Mr. Herbert?"

"That's correct, sir."

"By all means proceed."

"First," said Memo, "I think it important to understand that Peter and the rest of his squadron were at the tail end of a mission which the Verdean deemed of the highest priority. They single-handedly infiltrated Brill when they were met by five Trusselian Supersoldiers—the sight of whom would have caused the accuser, Mr. Magner, to wet his own pants."

A few people laughed behind us. Memo continued before

Arcalaeus could reprimand him.

"Yet despite facing off against five Supersoldiers, a tank, and plenty of reinforcements, Mr. Herbert and the other members of Squad 19 fought valiantly and killed the five Supersoldiers before returning to the boats just outside of Brill."

"Captain Iglesias," Arcalaeus interrupted, "Squad 19's mission is classified. I have already warned once against giving testimony regarding it. I will not do so again."

"Apologies, sir." But Memo was not the least bit thrown off. "In an effort to conserve the little food they had left, in addition to the many stores of healing potions and significant weaponry, including a gun they recovered, Mr. Herbert and his squad left all of these supplies in their designated boat. Yet rather than leave these valuables unattended, the squad decided to leave a sentry in the boat to guard them should a Trusselian break free from the fight. There was no cowardice in this decision, only prudence.

"So they drew straws, and the short straw, which happened to be Mr. Herbert, had to stay behind and watch over the precious cargo."

Mention the chest. Why isn't he mentioning the chest?

"I'm told by his squad mates," Memo continued, "and you may call them up one-by-one and ask them yourselves, that Mr. Herbert threw a tantrum when he was forced to be left behind. He asked each of them if they'd take his place—he didn't want his friends going into battle without him," Memo said.

The audience was silent. Memo's words absorbed the room, impossible not to believe. Carl slouched in his seat, nervously glancing around like a wounded animal. General Magner folded his arms in front of him and glared at Memo.

"I would also like to point out," Memo said, "that the rest of Squad 19 was heading to join the battle when they saw Mr. Magner leading the retreat back. There was no one else out in front—just him. Additionally, Mr. Magner never even so much as *saw* Mr. Herbert on the night in question, and thus came to this heinous conclusion with no concrete evidence."

Carl sunk all the way down in his seat. A collective hush rippled throughout the audience.

Memo had captured their attention in a way that not even Carl had managed to do. Conversations broke out now amongst the crowd, everyone speaking with their neighbor about the accusations.

Arcalaeus banged his gavel to restore order and quiet the crowd.

"Captain Iglesias," Arcalaeus said. "I'll remind you that Mr. Magner is not on trial here, and there has been no evidence that he acted in anything less than a manner befitting a soldier of the Verdean Guard. Thank you for your testimony. You are dismissed."

Arcalaeus eyed Memo as he got down from the witness stand and took his seat beside us. He then peered into the audience, as though daring anyone else to speak out in his court room. No one did.

"Next on the stand," Arcalaeus said, "will be Langston Rhodes."

Langston stood up and walked to the stand. Arcalaeus questioned him about the night in Brill, and Langston reiterated everything Memo had said: We'd completed our stated mission and decided to pull straws to see who would guard the valuables and the gun. Just like Memo, he didn't mention the chest. Jenna followed, and then Bree. Both of them were just as composed as Langston, and the collective story was perfect.

Finally, Arcalaeus peered down at me. "Leo Belfin," he said. "Please take the stand."

As I walked to the stage, I gave Peter a half smile, which he returned. He looked like he was feeling better about his chances now that Memo and the rest of the Sphelix had testified.

I didn't meet Arcalaeus's sunken eyes as I slid onto the surprisingly comfortable, beautifully polished chair to his right. Arcalaeus's arms were skinny, practically just bone, and there was a faint stubble of white hair on his chin. His head was disproportionately larger than the rest of his body.

Hundreds of pairs of eyes from the audience focused on me. I took a deep breath.

"Mr. Belfin," Arcalaeus said. "Am I to understand that you stand by what the other members of your squad have stated?"

"Yes, sir," I said.

"Very well. You may sit back down."

"Sir?"

"There's no need to waste any more time," said Arcalaeus. "I shall assume it is the same story."

I found Memo in the audience. He had a cocked eyebrow,

clearly unsure what to make of this. I stood up and walked back to my seat but before I'd even sat down Arcalaeus was speaking again.

"I feel I have enough evidence from which to make a decision," he said. "I will retire and ponder before announcing my verdict."

With that, he popped a focus pill into his mouth and walked out the door.

"They have to let him off," Langston said. We were back in Memo's office, waiting for the verdict. "Memo, you were incredible."

"Why didn't I get to testify?" I asked.

"Probably didn't want our case getting any stronger," Bree said. "Didn't want yet another person saying Carl was the real coward."

"Bree, be quiet," Jenna said.

"Why? It's the truth."

"We don't need anyone else going on trial," Jenna said. "What do you think, Memo?"

"You never know," he said. "We did everything we could. Peter's fate is in the hands of Arcalaeus."

"But there's no solid evidence," I said. "Peter didn't do anything wrong. There's no way he gets convicted. We killed five Supersoldiers—"

"Memo, can we tell Arcalaeus about the letters from General Magner?" Langston asked.

"I don't think it's a good idea," Memo said. "Not yet."

"Why?" Langston asked. "Those letters prove the he's a traitor. Arcalaeus needs to know that. I'm sure he'd be willing to give Peter a pass."

"The act of cowardice is separate from the mission you completed," Memo said. "Retrieving a gun and fighting Supersoldiers is an exceptional feat in its own right."

"Memo—" I said, but a loud bell rang out through the hallway before I could continue.

Jenna went white. "The decision," she said.

When everyone was seated on the rows of benches, Arcalaeus walked back out and took his seat on the podium. The witness chair remained empty. Peter gave me a small smile when I walked in this time.

My insides were turning. I knew—I absolutely *knew*—he was going to be declared innocent, but what if I was wrong? Memo had been convincing, but this was the Magner's and the verdict had been quick…I put my head between my knees, unable to watch.

Arcalaeus cleared his throat a few times before finally speaking.

"There have been numerous testimonies," said Arcalaeus. I couldn't help but notice the profound silence that reverberated through the room. "I've been able to reconcile everything that's taken place, and, after careful deliberation, I have reached the verdict…"

Jenna grabbed my hand, squeezing tightly. I looked up, trying to stay composed for Peter.

Arcalaeus continued, his hand still holding the gavel.

"I find Peter Herbert…guilty of cowardice detrimental to the stability of the Verdean Guard."

All the air went out of me. I collapsed in my chair. Peter, who had just seemed so hopeful, sank as well. Tears welled in Jenna's eyes. Bree put a reassuring hand on her shoulder. Langston squeezed his Verdean cap tightly between his hands.

Memo alone didn't move, his face unreadable.

"As punishment for your cowardice, Mr. Herbert," Arcalaeus said, "you are sentenced to life in the Pit."

"What?" I yelled. "That's ridiculous. He didn't do anything wrong."

Arcalaeus turned his head towards me slowly. I glared at him, wanting to charge and punch his withered face. Why wasn't anyone else in the courtroom angry? Everyone had heard the testimonies.

"Please escort Mr. Belfin out of the hall," Arcalaeus told two lieutenants.

I wasn't going quietly. "Carl didn't even see anything!" I screamed. "This is bullshit!"

Memo stood up and grabbed me by the arm.

"Shut up," Memo said in my ear. When I didn't stop yelling, he said "Leo! Keep your mouth shut." I was stunned into silence— not by his anger, but by his fear. He used a pincer grip to keep my arms in place and rushed me out of the hall. He kicked open the front doors, shoving me through them.

I caught one last glimpse of the hall, a sea of heads turned towards me. I only had eyes for one person, though: Peter, handcuffed to the stand, his mouth slightly open.

Arcalaeus continued speaking as though nothing had happened. "Mr. Herbert will be transferred—" I heard, but then the doors closed, drowning out his voice.

"Memo, how?" I asked, tears streaming down my face. "How? Peter didn't do anything wrong. He's done more for the Verdean than anyone else in there."

"Not here," Memo said, looking over his shoulder. "Barrack 19."

30. BAIT & SWITCH

Memo still had a hand on my shoulder when we reached Barrack 19, as though he were afraid I might make a break for the Captains' Offices to finish my screaming match. He only removed it once we were inside.

A few shirts and socks were still strewn on top of Peter's bureau, and a pant leg poked out from a closed drawer. Peter's bed sheets were tucked in, but there was still an outline where he used to sit on the bed.

"Please sit down," Memo said. His voice had returned to its usual calmness. But for once, I disobeyed him. "Leo, I know how painful this is," he said. "It's heartbreaking to see Peter up there, and that was a sorry excuse for a trial. He deserves better."

I turned away, unable to face him. I was scared my voice would crack with pain if I tried responding.

"But, Leo," Memo said. "You have to keep your temper."

The door opened, and Langston, Bree, and Jenna walked in.

"What was that?" Jenna yelled, coming right for me. "You can't go around acting like a child, Leo. There are lives at stake here. You're lucky they didn't drag you away to the Pit too."

"I'd like to see them try," I said.

Jenna was shaking. "Leo, come on!" she said. "I need you here. This is hard on all of us."

"What am I supposed to tell her?" I said. "I can't look at Helen and tell her that Peter is going to rot in that place. I can't deliver that news to Flora, and I can't do it to Jexter. I know there are lives at stake here, Jenna."

Jenna's cheeks flushed and her eyes glistened.

"Why did Arcalaeus punish him so harshly?" Bree asked.

"It's the second time in six months something like this has happened," Memo said. "There was another case a few months ago, and the judge—not Arcalaeus—was more lenient. He only gave the soldier a few years in the Pit. Arcalaeus feels he has to punish anything other than absolute obedience. Fleeing in the face of war is one of the most criminal offenses in their eyes."

"So his life is over," I said. "Just so they can make a point."

I couldn't take it. Memo's submissiveness, his acceptance. Peter would've been fine if Memo had just given him a focus pill like every other commanding officer. Or if Memo had just told Arcalaeus about General Magner...

There was a knock at the door. Without waiting for an answer, it opened, and in walked Arcalaeus. The temperature dropped ten degrees. He stopped just over the entry and considered us all for a moment.

"I'm sorry to barge in," Arcalaeus said. "I hope I wasn't interrupting anything."

"Not at all, sir," said Memo. He went over and shook the President's hand. Beads of sweat dripped down the back of Memo's neck. "Would you like to take a seat?"

"I'm fine standing, thank you, Captain Iglesias. I wanted to address the rest of your squadron for a moment, if that's alright."

"Of course, sir."

Jenna edged closer to me.

"That was terrible business back there," Arcalaeus said. "I take no joy in trials like that, especially for a young man whose future was so bright.

"But I hope you understand my reasoning for punishing Mr. Herbert. To maintain order in the Verdean, rules need to be followed, directives adhered to. This contributes to the *oneness* that holds Arcton together. We are only as strong as our weakest link, and failing to punish your friend would've led others down the same slippery slope."

I glared at him. Why was he here? He'd just ruined our best friend's life. And he didn't even know that one of his generals was communicating regularly with Trussel.

"You're angry still," Arcalaeus said. "And I understand that. I'd expect nothing less from a squadron so accomplished—that fire and passion is undoubtedly what served you well in battle. Which is why I'm so pleased, and yet sorry, to say that your time of service in the Verdean Guard has come to a close. Unless, of course, you wish to stay on as lieutenants."

None of us said a word. I shook my head slightly.

Arcalaeus stood, expecting an answer, maybe even a thank you. After all, it was what we'd been hoping for since we became soldiers in the Verdean: to go home, resume our normal lives, live happily ever after…

I debated the possibility of grabbing my sword and jamming it through his chest.

"And might I add," Arcalaeus said, "that, upon completion of your schooling, your names will all be shortlisted for jobs at any department you so choose. Arcton rewards its heroes."

Jenna, Langston, and Bree all had the same reaction: stony faces, no words.

Did Arcalaeus really think he could bribe us into being loyal? I gritted my teeth, doing everything I could to prevent myself from charging the president.

"Thank you very much," Memo said. "That is most generous of you, and I'm sure they're in shock being offered that honor. Mr. President, would you mind giving them a couple of days before they make a decision whether to go home or rise in the ranks of the Verdean?"

"Of course, Captain Iglesias. I realize it's been a long couple of days for them. Just inform one of the generals of their decision when it's final."

Arcalaeus made to leave, but right before he got to the door, Langston broke the silence.

"Sir, why did you take down the gunners? The ones at the tributary?"

I saw, again, fear in Memo's eyes. He gave a slight, imperceptible shake of his head at Langston.

But Arcalaeus wasn't angry. He paused, looked at Memo and then back to Langston.

"An interesting question," Arcalaeus said. "I wasn't aware that we had, but then again, those decisions are typically made by generals, and not by me. Although I am surprised Captain Iglesias told you."

"My apologies, sir, I merely —"

"No explanation is needed," Arcalaeus said curtly. "The reason, Mr. Rhodes, for our destruction of those weapons is that they threatened the safety of our soldiers. In particular, yours and the rest of Squad 19's. The reason that Arcton—along with Trussel, Vacson, Easton, and Northron—pledged to enact the Devolution is to preserve lives. Plain and simple. We humans, again and again, have proven ourselves incapable of wielding great power."

Langston nodded but didn't respond. Arcalaeus, taking his silence as understanding, continued.

"Imagine, Mr. Rhodes, that every citizen in the world had access to a truck or to a gun. Think of all the death that would occur. People would accidentally ram their trucks into one another, endangering innocent lives, or they might rob each other at gunpoint.

"By limiting these technologies, rolling them back, we ensure the safety of our people. That was the bedrock on which Arcton was built: stability and safety. And we had to think not just of weapons but of information, too. There was a time many, many years ago, when newspapers weren't controlled by the government, but by individual citizens. There were hundreds of newspapers around the world. All this information was supposed to bring everyone in the world closer together. To connect the entire world. Sounds pretty great, right?"

I nodded along with Langston.

"What we didn't realize, however, is that we also allowed the spread of misinformation. Lies could be told more easily than the truth, and with all this information flying about, no one had any idea which was true and which was not. The spread of misinformation led people to hate one another, turn against one another. Again, putting lives at stake. Jeopardizing stability. Jeopardizing safety. Jeopardizing our *oneness*.

"That is why we had to stay true to the Devolution, why we had to tear down those gunners. For our own safety.

"Now, if you'll excuse me, I have another meeting I must attend. I look forward to hearing your decisions."

Arcalaeus waved goodbye and left. Memo went to the window and made sure he was out of sight before turning back to us.

"You'd all make terrible politicians," Memo said. He went to the fireplace, pulled a few logs to him, and began striking flint onto a dead brush. He was almost as skilled as Bree, and the flames rose high into the chimney within a couple minutes. "Arcalaeus offered you prestigious jobs, and none of you could say anything to at least convince him you weren't angry?"

"I couldn't care less what he thinks," Bree said.

"That's not the point," said Memo. "Arcalaeus is the most powerful man in the country. He could have all of us, me included, thrown in the Pit without a second thought."

I turned away from the conversation and warmed my hands by the fire. The flames crackled, and orange embers glowed below.

"Memo, why didn't we tell him about General Magner?" Jenna asked. "You must have had enough time to determine if the letters were real; the diagram of the Supersoldier definitely looked real. That information would've shown Arcalaeus all that Peter did for

Arcton. It would've saved him."

"No, it wouldn't have," Memo said.

"How do you know that?" said Jenna.

"Because Arcalaeus knew about those letters when they were written," Memo said. "He knew General Magner was communicating with General Nygaard because *he* was the one who ordered it."

My head was spinning. Why would the Verdean intentionally tell Trussel where and when we were going to attack? I turned to Langston, who looked just as puzzled.

"The war was fake," Memo said. "Or, fake in the sense that the presidents of both Arcton and Trussel knew how it would play out. Trussel would advance into our territory, and then we'd push back into theirs. After the attack on Brill, there was always going to be another peace treaty signed."

"You mean..." Langston said. "That—that we fought and killed for nothing?"

Memo ran his hands through his hair. "Yes, Langston. You risked your lives for a war that was never going to change anything. Peter is in the Pit for the same reason."

"Are you kidding?" I asked "How long have you known? How long has this been going on?"

I didn't know until I saw the documents inside the chest," said Memo, "but I had my suspicions before that. General Magner wasn't going rogue; he was acting on Arcalaeus's orders. And the diagrams on how to create Supersoldiers...Trussel and Arcton must've been sharing that information on purpose."

"But why?" Bree asked. "Why go through a fake war?"

"War is the best way to get people to rally behind a government," Memo said. "Think back to when Trussel first attacked us..."

The day after the attacks, we were let off school to attend a rally down on the Pennyway. I waved an Arcton flag at the passing soldiers, along with everyone else. The streets were so jammed with bodies that there was barely room to move. Everyone kept whooping and screaming at the soldiers like they were celebrities, as if Arcalaeus himself was walking down the Pennyway.

"So Arcton and Trussel both knew?" Langston said. "And they let thousands of soldiers die so that they could, what, have more power?"

Memo nodded. The sky in the window behind him was beginning to fade to a burnt orange.

Where were we living? What had we done? I went over to the trash can, breathing heavily, retching.

Almost immediately, there was a hand on my back, patting me. I turned, expecting Jenna, but it was Bree.

"How does it give them more power, though?" asked Jenna. She sat cross-legged, her hands jammed into her pockets. Her eyes were curious, searching for answers.

To my surprise, Langston answered. "It's part of the Devolution process, isn't it?" he said. Langston's brain seemed to be working faster than the rest of ours combined.

Memo nodded.

"How is war a part of Devolution?" I asked, still bent over the trash can.

"It's like a bait and switch," said Langston. "Remember, at the Tributary, when we used that flashlight to attract the Trusselians' attention when really we were attacking from somewhere else?"

I nodded.

"It's the same thing," said Langston. "Arcton distracts everyone with the war—they get everyone focused on the enemy, throw rallies to keep us happy, and have a reason, meanwhile, to take away trucks and guns and make electricity in shorter supply. This consolidates the government's power."

"And focus pills," said Bree. "They do the same thing. Numb everyone, make them follow orders."

"Is every country in the Combination in on it?" Langston asked.

Memo nodded. "It looks that way," he said.

"What are we supposed to do?" I asked. "We just fought a fake war, and now we're supposed to return to our normal lives like nothing's changed? What about Peter?"

"You have to give it time," urged Memo. "We just got this information—anything we do now will be hurried, irrational." No one responded. The lines on Memo's face were more pronounced than I'd ever remembered. "Give me time, please. I'll figure something out. Now, I have a Captains' meeting I need to attend, but we'll talk tomorrow."

Memo walked to the door, looked back at us briefly, and left without another word.

Jenna wrapped a blanket around her shoulders. Langston pulled up a chair and took a seat. Bree went and grabbed the keys Memo had given her on the night her parents died, along with her sword and whetstone. I knew we were all thinking the same thing.

"I need to see Irene first," I said.

31. IRENE

I found Irene at the Mess Hall at a table crammed with nurses, all talking happily. The end of the war meant the end of their long shifts, the end of seeing soldiers injured or dead. Irene's eyes met mine when I walked in. They were steely and astonishingly blue.

She didn't smile; she must have heard about Peter.

After a hurried goodbye to her friends, she stood up and strode out of the hall with me, wrapping her hand around my own.

"I'm sorry, Leo," she said once we were outside. "I'm so sorry."

I nodded, fighting back tears. We walked until we were at the beach, out of range of anyone else. Night had fallen, but the Orb light provided enough visibility. We sat down on a bench, the waves lapping in. She didn't take her eyes off me.

"I can't believe they sentenced him to life," she said. "After all you guys did."

"I can," I said. "I can now, anyway."

"What do you—"

I explained everything to her: what we'd found in the chest, what the documents proved, and why Arcton had been communicating with Trussel. I went through everything down to the last detail. I needed her to understand. I needed to convince her. It took more than thirty minutes to lay it all out.

"Leo, I—why would they make up a war?"

"It's not about oil or water or food or anything like that," I said. "They create war because they think it makes us more loyal to them."

"How does war do that?"

"It keeps us focused on something other than our lives. It gives us a common enemy that isn't the government. Think about it: we were ready to do anything for Arcton. I hated Trussel more than anything. I wanted them to suffer, to die for threatening us. Think about everyone now. They all believe they helped win a war, that they helped save Arcton."

Irene was silent. She wrapped her arm around me, pulling me close. Out on the water, clouds were starting to roll in—not rain or snow, but fog. Wind whipped at our faces.

"We're going to break him out," I told her. "We're getting Peter out of the Pit tonight."

"Leo, wait a second."

"He can't spend the rest of his life in there," I said.

"Give me a minute to process this," she said. "You're saying the war was a hoax created by the Arctonian government, and now you're going to break Peter out of a fortress that has never once been broken out of?"

"Yes. Do you want to come?"

Her eyes widened. "You're throwing a lot at me."

"I know, and I'm sorry. But I want you to come."

"Leo, it's...it's a lot. You're sure about the documents you found? You couldn't have just misread them?"

I shook my head. "Langston, Memo...everyone agrees. I promise. The war was a sham. You were treating injured soldiers over a war that meant nothing. There was always going to be a peace treaty."

Irene nodded. She believed me.

"Where are you gonna go?" she asked.

"Away—we have a plan. There are islands we're going to escape to, and from there we'll figure it out. Bree has the keys to a boat she stole a while back. Please come with us."

"Leo...I can't."

It was as if a hot poker had been shoved into my heart. She had to come. I couldn't leave her.

"Why not?"

"I can't leave my family behind. My mom, my dad—"

"Your dad who sold you out?"

"He's still my dad. And my little brother. Leo, I love them. I can't never see them again."

"But you'll be living in a country that lies to you," I said. "A country that sends us out to war to die just so they can continue to control us."

"Maybe we can fight it from the inside? I mean, what are you going to be able to do if you run?"

"I don't know. But I'm not letting Peter rot his life away."

"I know you won't. I just...I can't leave my family, Leo."

What could I say to convince her? She loved her family just like I loved mine, but no one in her family was going to be in the Pit for the rest of their lives. Irene had always been levelheaded, thoughtful. She never just let her emotions steer her; it was one of the things I respected most about her. It was a big ask to have her come on this mission.

"I love you," was all I could say.

Tears streamed down Irene's cheeks. She shook her head and kissed me, placing our foreheads together. She cupped my cheeks.

"I love you too."

I turned and got up, but she grabbed my hand and pulled me back to her body. Her arms wrapped around my waist, and she pressed her lips to mine, hard.

An hour later we were still together on the bench. The fog had nearly reached us, but for now the stars were barely visible through the Orb light. Irene's head rested on my chest, rising and falling with my breath.

"I think someone else knew what Arcton was doing," Irene said, not lifting her head.

"Who?"

"Those letters you got. I've been trying to think why someone would give them to you. I keep thinking about that last one: '*Loyalty is fickle. Death is final. Neither, for your family, is what it seems.*' Clearly someone wanted you to know about your dad with those books on his old squadron. And we know his loyalty changed—he was called a traitor and killed. Why else would someone send you those messages?"

"But who could've sent them?"

"Must be high up in the Verdean to know all that," she said.

I nodded. It was getting late, and my night hadn't even started yet. I ran my fingers through Irene's hair; it was smooth and sleek. She looked up at me, her eyes no longer full of tears.

"I have to go," I said.

"I know."

"You're sure you don't—"

"I'm sure, Leo."

"I do love you. I wasn't just saying that so you'd come with me."

"I know."

There was so much still left to say to her: *I love you. I want to spend the rest of my life with you. I'm scared of what I'm about to do. I'll never see you again, and I won't ever be happy without you. Please, don't let me go. Make me stay. Kiss me again. Tell me everything is going to be alright, even if it's a lie.*

"Thank you," I said.

"For what?"

"For everything." I let my lips graze against hers one last time but then pulled away quickly, knowing that if it lasted too long they would become glued together. A few tears were gliding down my cheeks, but she managed to hold hers within her crystal-blue eyes.

I left her on the bench and walked the lonely path back to Base Camp. I promised myself I wouldn't turn for one last look, a promise I nearly kept. When I reached the obstacle course, though, I couldn't help but turn back. Irene was still on the bench, her head bent, a silhouette against the fog. The clouds of mist crept further along, eventually swallowing her.

Just a dream. If only this were just a dream.

32. THE PIT

Barrack 19 was all nerves. Jenna, Langston, and Bree had shed the Verdean uniform and instead were dressed in dark sweatshirts and pants. Swords hung from their hips and bows poked out above their backs.

"She coming?" Bree asked, standing up. I shook my head.

"Sorry, Leo," Jenna said, giving me a hug. "I'm sure you don't want to hear this, but it's probably for the best. It's gonna be really dangerous."

"I know. Let's not talk about it. We have enough to worry about."

We waited another thirty minutes before the "Lights Out" call rang throughout Base Camp, which wasn't as effective as normal. Everyone besides us was ecstatic; the war was over, and many would be able to return home and see their families. They were safe. Life would go on as normal. They were completely unaware that their government was using war as an excuse to control them.

"Ignorance is bliss," Langston said. "They have every reason to be happy."

It was another fifteen minutes before a lieutenant popped inside to blow out the candles. We all stayed under our covers, hiding our clothes.

When the coast was clear, I threw on my backpack, weighted down with food, water, and more clothes—anything for the long journey ahead.

"You sure we shouldn't say goodbye to Memo?" Jenna said. She peered out the windows to see if any lieutenants were passing. "It doesn't feel right."

Memo had been there for us every step of the way. He was a mentor and the closest thing to a father I'd ever had. How did you not say goodbye to someone like that?

"Best thing we can do for him is get Peter out of here," I said. "That'll mean more than any goodbye ever could."

The fog had spread throughout Base Camp now. We kept low and quiet, silent as ghosts. On one hand, we were difficult to see. On the other, so were any patrolling lieutenants.

I did my best to keep up with Bree's bobbing backpack. My own, stuffed to the brim, was rubbing my shoulder blades raw and making my back ache before we even passed the Mess Hall.

We wound our way through the laundry building, along the side of the lavatories we'd cleaned our first week of Basic Training, and down a rocky path that ran along an inlet, through which water rushed.

One by one, we tossed our packs over the fence on the outer border and ducked into the inlet under the fence. Sopping wet, we collected our bags on the other side. No one complained about the cold.

Langston kept a quick pace up the hill, a far cry from when he was our worst runner on the obstacle course. When we came to a flat ridge at least a half mile outside of Base Camp, I finally had to ask him for a moment to catch my breath.

"How much further?" Bree asked when we had all taken a seat

in the dirt, resting against our backpacks.

Langston pulled out some water and passed it around. "Another mile or two."

"We'll need to drop off our stuff before we head in," Jenna said. "No way we can fight with our backpacks."

We marched on. I stayed hyper-alert to any movement or light up ahead, constantly searching through the dense fog.

The clouds subsided finally, and we stepped above the fog line and there was the pointed top of Mt. Brentwood. I'd never been this far up the mountain, and the dazzling stars felt close enough to touch.

As high as we were, though, the Orb's glow still reached us, casting the stars in a greenish tint. The fog line at our feet was an endless sea of green clouds.

A couple of mountain lions passed in the distance, but they didn't see us. We reached the top of a plateau in the mountain and, up ahead, a small light illuminated the entry to a cave—the Pit.

Langston led us away from the cave entrance and along the ridge to a huge pine tree. I set my backpack down—my back sighing in relief—and kept only my sword and bow. The others did the same. Langston also carried a jib—a metal poker he thought might come in handy.

When we were back within eyesight of the cave, we crept down the path until we were close enough to see torchlight flickering in the entrance. Voices echoed from it.

I slid by the others to the front. I tried to focus on my breath and channel my powers, but I managed only to slow my heart rate.

There was no warped vision, no way to collapse a tree or catch an arrow…

What was going on? Why had my power disappeared?

"We're going to have to do it the old-fashioned way," I whispered. None of them flinched.

"No worries, Leo," Langston said. "We've got this."

"You sure?"

"The entire plan wasn't dependent on you," Jenna said. Then she smiled. "Although it would've helped."

We crept up closer and I poked my head around the wall to see what lay behind. Two soldiers were sitting on top of a few stacked wooden crates, smoking cigarettes. Neither looked particularly attentive, swords hanging limp at their sides. Behind them, the path quickly dove out of sight—to what obstacles, we could only guess.

I held up my hand and signaled to the other three that there were two guards.

Quietly, I pulled out three arrows, sliding them between my fingers. I raised my bow and motioned to the others to follow on my count.

I nocked an arrow and took one last glance at the two guards on the crates. They were smoking cigarettes—I hoped they enjoyed them. They didn't deserve this. This wasn't their fault…

I sprang out, loosing the first arrow in the shorter one's chest, and quickly firing another in the bigger one's torso. The shorter one yelled and I charged him, yanking out my sword as I went. Behind me, I heard the *thwang* of more arrows and, before I could reach them, both guards fell motionless to the ground.

"Let's drag them behind the crates," I said. "In case someone comes by."

"If someone comes by and doesn't see the two guards they're going to know something is going on anyway," Bree said. "Not to mention, you know... blood." But she helped me drag the shorter one, whose body was surprisingly heavy, around the crates, leaving a dark red trail.

My hands shook with adrenaline. I steadied my breathing.

The cave was a solid ten feet high, lit up by torch-filled sconces that wound along the black, stone walls. Small red critters moved around the sconces, trying to soak up what little light was given.

"Fire ants," said Langston. "When one gets close to the light, it releases pheromones that attract other workers to the spot."

"They're everywhere," I said.

"Probably best to stay away from the walls," Langston said.

We jogged down the cave, our bows clanging slightly against our uniforms and swords.

"Slow down," said Bree. "They'll hear us a mile away."

I settled into a walk and followed the cave's steep trail down. I kept my sword in my left hand as the path twisted right, ready to stab at the first sign of movement. Jenna's breath swept through my hair, and I could hear Langston and Bree close behind.

The cave wall was smooth—something no pickaxe could've done. Down we went, spiraling past supply crates and MSP wrappers thrown on the cave floor. Could I actually hear the ants' feet pattering against the walls, or was that just my imagination?

The slope finally leveled out to reveal an iron gate that stretched across the entire passage, barring our way forward.

"How are we supposed to get through that?" Jenna asked. "It's solid metal."

"The gate isn't the problem," Langston said. "Those Supersoldiers are."

Sure enough, fifteen hulking masses dressed in the Verdean green and silver strutted toward us from the other side of the gate. They had the same crisscrossed shoulder straps as the Trusselian ones and arms as big as my torso. They pulled out their bows.

I hurtled back down the passage, sprinting along the straightaway, the others following. I turned my head around in time to see the menacing, enormous figures shoot a couple arrows as I turned the corner. Two loud clangs sounded off the cave wall, and the bent arrows fell down at our feet.

"You've got to be kidding me," Langston said, huddled down. "Supersoldiers? Again?"

"They're the exact same as the Trusselian ones," I said. "Guess those formulas we found were already in use."

"We can't kill them from this side of the gate," Bree said. "Probably can't do much damage if we're on the same side of the gate, come to think of it."

"Hold on," Jenna said. "I have an idea."

She took out her first aid pouch and removed a little aluminum cup. She pinched out a few different powders and poured two clear liquids into the cup. She added a few grains of red powder to the solution, which immediately turned a deep black.

"Give me your arrows," she said. "All of them."

One by one she dipped the point of each arrowhead into the black solution and returned it to us. "Be careful not to touch it," she said.

"What is it?" Bree asked.

"It's a sleeping solution. Melate powder mixed with some of these painkillers—it coagulates into a solution that should induce narcosis."

"Sounds good to me," I said, not understanding a word of what Jenna had said.

"Hit one of the super soldiers with an arrowhead coated with this stuff," said Jenna, pointing to the solution, "and he'll be knocked out within a minute."

"How'd you think of that?" Langston asked.

"Nurse's training," said Jenna. "I got bored a lot during the Base Camp training and experimented with different concoctions—mostly stuff from books Memo gave me. If one of my tablemates annoyed me, I'd just prick her with a small sleeping solution. A few minutes later she'd have her head on the desk, drooling."

"We still have to hit them with the arrows," Langston said. "There are fifteen of them, and they know we're here now."

"Seems like they don't know how to open that gate though," said Bree. "Let's keep our distance. And if they're close enough, we don't need to expose ourselves too much."

Careful not to touch any of the solution-coated arrows, we went back down the cave. Bree had been right. The Supersoldiers hadn't opened the gate—maybe they couldn't—and instead left a group of sentries there.

"Push some of those crates out, see if we can hide behind them when we're shooting," Bree said.

It took two of us to move even one box. We started with one right by the cave wall, and then placed two more alongside it. Each box took a few arrows on the side, but held intact.

We angled out diagonally, crouching low to stay hidden.

The Supersoldiers really were identical to those we'd seen in Brill, just in Verdean colors. They had the same overblown shoulders, abnormally small heads compared to the rest of their bodies, and they walked like they had no joints. To be fair, their rigidity and stiffness evaporated pretty quickly once they were sprinting full speed at you.

In front, Langston turned back to us, checking if we were ready. All three of us nodded.

"One..." Langston whispered. I knocked my melate-coated arrow and aimed it at a Supersoldier who had his hands on the bars, peering through the dim light. "Two..." My bowstring stretched tight, threatening to break. "Three."

I loosed and watched my arrow fly through the air, hurtling towards the Supersoldier. Three others joined it and, judging from the yells, apparently made contact. Before they could fire back we sent out another round and ducked behind the boxes.

Thud. Thud. Thud. The return shots came quickly.

"How many did we get?" Jenna asked.

"Three, maybe four," Langston said. "Tough to tell."

I stuck my head out around the side, and saw a few bodies on the ground, likely asleep.

I turned back to the Sphelix. "There are only a few there," I said. "Where did the others go?"

"Probably realized they don't need to stand at the gate since we're coming for them," Langston said.

When we all popped up again, the Supersoldiers were waiting and loosed a few arrows at us. A searing pain tore through my shoulder, and I reeled back behind the crate, screaming.

I pressed my hand down on the wound. The arrow was still sticking out, blood pouring through my fingers.

Jenna bent down. The arrowhead had pierced straight through my triceps, the tail poking out in front.

"Take it out!" I said. "It stings!" But a gentle tingling now spread out from the wound, and it didn't hurt nearly as much. "What'd you do?" I asked Jenna.

She shook her head, confused. "Nothing. Why? What are you feeling?"

"It feels fine now," I said. "Can barely feel a thing, really." My head started to lighten and my vision wobbled.

"Uh oh," Jenna said. Behind her Langston and Bree were trading shots with the Supersoldiers. I started swaying. Spots cropped up in my vision, and I tried blinking them away.

She dug around in her bag. "They shot you with one of the melate powdered arrows," Jenna said.

"Does that mean I'm going to pass out?" I said, registering that the absence of pain was a bad thing, but not entirely caring.

"One second," Jenna said. "Keep your eyes open." She pulled

out a few separate tubes and mixed them in a similar aluminum can as before. Every once in a while she'd look over at me and, if my eyes were starting to roll back, slap me across the face.

Jenna handed me the aluminum can, which was now filled with a light blue liquid. I swallowed the first sip and my head almost instantly cleared, paving the way for the pain to return. I drained the rest in one go. Jenna sliced off the butt end of the arrow with her sword and pulled out the other side. She applied a powdered rub to both entry points of my wound before bandaging it up.

Langston and Bree had taken care of the other Supersoldiers at the gate.

"You alright?" Bree asked, when I finally sat up.

"Peachy," I said.

"Now what?" Jenna asked.

"If we go to open the gate and the rest of the Supersoldiers come out, we're in no man's land," Langston said.

"So we need to take these boxes up with us," Bree said, matter-of-fact.

"One at a time?" Langston said. "We don't have long before the guard changes out front, and once they see the bodies, they'll come looking for us. We can't fight the Supersoldiers on one side and more guards on the other."

"I'm not seeing a better plan," I said. "Also, how are we supposed to get through that gate?"

"I told you, I have the jib," Langston said. I looked at the metal poker in his hand, and couldn't hide my disbelief. There was no way that little stick-like object was going to take down the steel gate. "It's all about applying pressure in the right places. I promise I can do it," Langston added. "Five minutes tops."

"Langston, there's no way that's going to work," Jenna said. "That poker is a couple pounds. The steel bars weigh about a ton."

"The Supersoldiers might think the same thing," Bree said. "They probably figure since they don't know how to open the gate, there's no way we'll be able to."

"You think they retreated?" Langston said.

"There's a good chance of it," said Bree. "They'll probably stay back and wait for the next guards to come. You sure you can open it?"

"Where's the faith?" Langston said. "You guys cover me while I work my magic."

I didn't know how much help I'd be in any more fighting—I could barely raise my arm above shoulder-level—but I agreed all the same.

We stood up above the boxes and kept an eye out for any movement, but there was nothing. Only the sleeping Supersoldiers.

Langston crept out into the open, where a Supersoldier could easily pick him off. Jenna, Bree, and I stood right behind, our bows raised—mine drawn with my left arm—ready to shoot. Aside from the random snore of a Supersoldier, there was nothing.

Once he reached the gate, Langston bent down and took off his jacket, wrapping it around two bars and tying the ends to both sides of his jib. Then, he started to twist the poker clockwise with both hands, slowly constricting the jacket. Before long, it was tightening around the bars. Amazingly, they started to bend inward.

When the bars were touching one another, Langston removed the jacket and rewrapped it, adding another bar to the fold. He did the same procedure, causing all three bars to bend towards each other until the two outside bars touched the middle one.

I scanned the other side of the cave for more Supersoldiers, but still nothing. Just a torchlit passage.

One by one Langston wrapped the bars in his jacket before twisting the poker. Soon there was a space between the bars big enough for us to crawl through.

Langston flashed a wide smile and reattached the jib to his waistband. "And you guys doubted me..." he said, shaking his head.

The path beyond the gate led even further down. How far did it go? I did my best to ignore the musty smell, like rotten vegetables, that grew stronger with each step we took. I drew my sword and held it out in front of me, hyperaware of every shadow that danced along the wall.

WHOOOOP! WHOOOOP! WHOOOOP!

I clasped my hands to my ears as a siren erupted. The noise was the exact same as the one Bree had set off on our first ranging. It ricocheted off the walls, magnifying the decibel level. Langston, Jenna, and Bree all glanced at me with the terrified expressions.

One of the Supersoldiers must have pulled a trip alarm. Would it notify everyone at Base Camp, or just the guards in the Pit?

I yelled over the noise to the others. "We've gotta move!"

They followed me in a dead sprint, the sirens shaking the fire ants off the walls around us. The distance grew between sconces the further down we went, casting most of the cave in darkness.

We needed to find Peter. We needed to get out of here before more soldiers came. I ignored the pain in my legs and continued pumping, faster, faster, and then—a scream came from behind, followed by a splash of water.

Trying to stop, I slipped and fell on the ground, scraping my elbows. I raced back and saw Langston and Jenna bent over a trench in the path. It ran along the side of the cave, about three feet wide, filled with water. Splashing out, barely managing to stay afloat, was Bree.

"It's biting!" Bree said. "Get me out!"

Langston quickly lowered the jib and Bree grabbed on. The drop was about three feet to the water, and between me, Langston, and Jenna we were able to hoist Bree up a few feet. She grabbed hold of the edge and pushed herself up, but clinging onto her pants were slimy, green fish with massive teeth, chewing violently at the wool.

Langston continued to drag her back along the path while Jenna and I took turns kicking the fish off her.

Bree didn't make the task any easier. "Get 'em off!" she kept yelling, frantically kicking her legs. The last fish finally hit the water with a splash and, aside from some torn pant legs, Bree appeared no worse for wear. She stood up and brushed herself off. "Thanks," she said.

"What were they?" Jenna asked, looking at Langston.

"Some type of piranha, I think," Langston said. "But they were more vicious than anything I've read about. Hey, do you hear that?"

I strained my ears. "I don't hear anything," I said.

"Exactly," said Langston. "The sirens are off."

We started walking again, but had taken only a few steps before booms rang out from up ahead. I stopped dead in my tracks. Another siren? No, they were different this time.

Were those from the Supersoldiers? I looked back at the others. Langston's face was paler than I'd ever seen it; Bree and Jenna both hardened their brows and urged me forward.

After one last steep dip, the narrow cave passage opened into a cavernous room, its ceiling out of sight. Candles rose along the sides, the highest ones little more than twinkling stars above. If I didn't know we were underground, I would have thought we were looking up at the night sky.

"Leo, look out!"

I turned just in time. A Supersoldier was feet away from me, his blade in mid-swing. I clumsily raised my weapon, but he was too close.

Out of nowhere, Bree parried the attacker's strike and countered with a lunge of her own that she buried deep within his ribs.

He grunted loudly, grabbing onto her blade with both hands and trying to keep it from digging itself any deeper. Bree yanked the blade out, and he collapsed to the floor.

"Stick together!" I yelled.

Langston and Jenna moved up next to Bree and me. All four of us stood shoulder-to-shoulder, covering an attack from any side, just like Memo had taught us in our training sessions. I could practically hear his voice saying, "Enclosed spaces with threats all around—stick together, like a foxhole, and trust each other's vision."

We slowly edged forward into the hollowed-out mountain, keeping our eyes peeled. The rancid, rotten-egg smell was now almost overpowering.

I felt awkward, useless, with my sword in my left hand. I quickly adjusted and took my bow out, slipping a couple arrows between my fingers. I ignored the wound in my shoulder, which opened up even more. I kept peering around, nerves frayed, reacting to every little sound.

But the surprise attacker had been the only Supersoldier in the hall. A smart idea, sticking him right where we would be distracted by seeing the hundreds of candles in the cave for the first time. I was only alive thanks to Bree's quick reflexes.

"Where do we go?" Bree asked, once it was clear no one else was going to charge us. "This looks like a dead end."

"Can't be," said Langston. "Where did all those other Supersoldiers go? I think it's just so big that we can't see another way out."

"What is this place anyway?" asked Jenna, keeping her sword held aloft. "How did they get all those candles up there? And how are they still burning?"

"No idea," I said. "But I'm with Langston. Let's split up and look around for another path. There's gotta be one, and we don't have much time to find it."

We quartered off the sections of the immense cave and walked the perimeter, searching for anything that might hint at another passage. I paced around my quadrant, bow at the ready, looking for a crevice in the jagged rock face, or maybe a hole in the dirt at my feet like the one Bree had fallen into.

But what I came upon was a far more obvious passage: a break in the cave wall completely covered with black steel.

I called the others over. There was a mixture of excitement at finding the way forward, and dismay because there was no way we would ever be able to penetrate through a steel door completely surrounded by stone.

"Well, we're screwed," Bree said, shaking her head.

"Langston can get us through," said Jenna.

Langston was our best and only hope. He stroked his chin while he considered the door. "My jib won't work," he said. "There aren't any bars."

"So we're screwed…" Bree said.

Langston held up a finger. "How did the Supersoldiers get through?"

"I don't know. They had a key or something," Bree said.

"It's completely solid, though," said Langston.

"Maybe there's a handle on the other side?" Jenna offered.

"That's what I think. Which means they have to have to a secret code they use to tell someone on the other side to let them in. A secret knock…"

"Well, we don't know about a knock. Oh…" I said.

The booms that had rung out right after the sirens. They'd

sounded more like lightning, but the Supersoldiers were so strong that when they'd given the secret knock it must have reverberated through the cave back to us.

"Knock-knock…wait a couple beats, knock-knock-knock," said Langston. "I'm pretty sure that's it."

So simple, yet different enough from a normal knock that there wouldn't be any confusion.

Langston walked up to the door. Bree stood right behind him, her sword raised high. Jenna and I were a few yards back, bow strings pulled back tightly.

Knock-knock… Langston's fist banged against the door. He waited a beat. *Knock-knock…* Sweat dropped from my head, landing cold onto my wrist. *Knock…*

Nothing happened.

Langston looked back at us and shrugged. "I guess I didn't—"

The door slowly turned inwards, revealing a guard in a Verdean uniform—not a Supersoldier. "Where are Dozerman and Victorino?" he asked. "And why are your swords—" He stopped short and Jenna and I wasted no time in piercing him with a couple arrows. He fell to the dirt and we rushed inside.

It was another huge hall, with candles stretching up as far as the eye could see. Across from us, the remaining Supersoldiers huddled together, a few turning at the commotion. Recognition slowly dawned on them.

They sprinted toward us, yelling.

I loosed arrows as quickly as I could. After a few Supersoldiers went down, the others wised up and took out their shields to deflect the arrows.

Jenna, Langston, Bree and I stayed side by side, not daring to split up against the larger group. We retreated quickly, trying to keep as much distance as possible between ourselves and the Supersoldiers.

They kept advancing. Behind their wall of shields, our arrows couldn't reach them.

They rushed at us like a careening truck. One broke off and lowered his shoulder into me. I flew back but managed to regain my balance. My bow fell aside, so I unsheathed my sword, flimsily wielding it in my left hand.

He raised his tree trunk arms and delivered a massive overhand blow with his sword. I reached up, preparing myself to withstand the blow.

When his sword hit mine, a shock of numbness split through my arm. The sword went limp in my hand.

The Supersoldier wound up for another blow. I clutched at my own sword, which was limp in my hand. A shot of pain coursed through my wrist just as I reached it up…

Whoosh!

An arrow soared by and lodged itself in the Supersoldier's neck.

I stood there, mouth open, and turned, expecting to see Jenna or Bree, but instead I found Langston lowering his bow.

"Leo!" he said, nodding at the guy.

"Oh yeah." I lunged, and the blade tore through flesh like a knife through warm butter. The soldier stared down in disbelief. He looked at me, eyes pleading for mercy, but I stabbed him again, and he collapsed to the ground.

A couple of injured Supersoldiers had rejoined the fight and were now outnumbering Jenna, Bree, and Langston. Bree flashed around like a hummingbird, dodging blows from two separate attackers.

I engaged one of them and quickly pierced him with my sword, the blade jutting out from his belly.

Bree took care of the other soldier on her own, using a nifty feint before taking out one of his Achilles tendons. He let loose a heinous scream that echoed off the cave walls, ricocheting up to the heavens.

Bree and I helped Langston and Jenna overwhelm the final two Supersoldiers. The last one breathing had a white speckled beard with lines around his face. His eyes glazed over while he lay on his back, bleeding through his uniform.

When Bree asked him—her blade an inch from his throat—where the prisoners were held, he slowly raised a finger and pointed up, a few candles reflected in his eyes. Then the light went out.

We were all alone again.

"What did he mean by that?" I said, confused.

"Shh..." Jenna said. "Listen."

A faint chattering of voices drifted down from above. I looked up, but there were just candles and crevices. Then a hand poked out of one of the crevices—a human hand.

"The cells are up there?" Jenna asked.

"Peter!" I yelled up. "Peter!"

A chorus of responses called back. Different prisoners answered, their voices blending together. "Peter Herbert!"

"Leo!" Peter screamed at the top of his lungs. His voice was unnaturally high-pitched, but it distinguished him from the others. "Leo, up here!" He sent two hands over the edge of a crevice that looked to be twenty feet high.

There was a ladder tucked to the side of the hall by the entrance. Beside it was a row of hooks with bows hanging from them—the Supersoldiers' bows. They didn't dream of anyone breaking in here, and we were alive because of their arrogance.

Langston dragged the ladder to where Peter's voice was coming from and climbed it as fast as he could, nearly slipping on a rung or two on his way up. Shortly after, he disappeared over the top of the crevice.

"Langston, is he up there?" Jenna yelled.

"There's another cell," Langston's voice called down. "Can you toss up my jib?"

Jenna grabbed the jib and climbed the ladder quickly, her hair bouncing from side to side until she was over the top and out of sight.

The gentle creak of bending bars reached me and Bree down below. Despite the blood coating her face, Bree's teeth gleamed with a bright smile, dimples in her cheeks.

A few minutes later, three bodies came climbing back down the ladder. Jenna first, a ginger-footed Peter second, and Langston bringing up the rear.

Peter landed and silently walked toward me. His face was

entirely blue from bruises. Massive clumps of his hair were missing, and his legs were teeming with bite marks and dried blood. Yet still he smiled as he collapsed into my arms. Warm, sobbing, and heavy.

Peter was back.

33. A HELPING HAND

"How did you guys find me?" Peter asked, using Jenna and me as crutches.

"Finding you was easy," I said. "Getting you out was a bit more difficult."

Blood dripped out of Peter's wounds with each step he took, and before long it became clear he wouldn't be walking far in this state. Jenna rifled through her backpack and pulled out a huge white sheet. She forced him to lie down on it and went to work bandaging his open wounds.

When she left Peter for a moment to get her first aid kit, I followed her. "Is he going to be alright?"

Jenna glanced over her shoulder. "Yeah, but he's weak," she said. "If he was in the hospital he'd be immobilized for weeks. We're about to go on a trip that's really long. If he catches a fever, or one of his wounds gets infected…"

We'd already taken a long time to fight off the Supersoldiers. The sirens had gone off what felt like days ago. If reinforcements came before we got out…

Jenna took an extra ten minutes to get Peter heavily bandaged, half-drugged, and ready to move again. Langston and I served as temporary crutches, with Peter's arms draped around our shoulders.

We briskly left the cell room littered with Supersoldiers and voices calling from above and made our way into the cavernous, candle-lit room. Every fifteen feet or so, Peter had to take a short break. Climbing the cave passage would have been impossible for him, so Langston and I carried him up.

"How are we gonna get him through the gate?" Langston asked. The jibbed gate barely had enough room for a healthy soldier to maneuver through. It took pushing and pulling on either end, with Peter biting his lips on multiple occasions to prevent from yelling out, but we got him to the other side.

Finally, we reached the cave's mouth where, miraculously, there weren't dozens of Verdean soldiers waiting to kill us.

"Maybe everyone celebrated the end of the war a little too much," Jenna said.

"More likely those sirens don't communicate with any in Base Camp," Langston said. "We got lucky."

Peter seemed to perk up a bit once the fresh air hit him. He looked down at his shoes. "I don't know what to say," he said. "But thanks. I'm sorry I deserted you in Brill, it's just—"

"Shut up," said Bree. "You didn't do anything wrong."

"If any of us were locked up in the Pit," Langston said, "You'd have been the first one to bust us out."

Peter went red. "Still… thanks," he said. "Where to now?"

"We're heading to the docks," I said. "Bree stole a pair of boat keys a long time ago. We're going to get out of here."

"Out of where?" Peter asked.

"Out of Arcton. For good."

"No," Peter said. "You can't do that. We can't leave Arcton forever."

"Can't exactly change our minds now."

I could see it dawning on him, what we'd just done. We couldn't go home. We couldn't even stay in Arcton. I wanted to tell him where we were headed, but thinking about the sheer length of the journey wasn't going to do much to lift his spirits.

Jenna put a hand on his shoulder. "We've got a trip ahead of us, Pete. Let us know what we can do to make it easier on you. I know you're exhausted, but we've got to keep moving."

Slowly, Peter inched along the trail toward where we left our backpacks. I stood next to him, keeping an eye and ear out for a truck hurtling along, bearing the next set of guards.

All was quiet until a flash of light burst through the fog line. Headlights blazed, accompanied by the deep rumble of an engine.

I shoved Peter off the trail into some brambles and dove after him. Crashes around me signaled that everyone else had done the same.

Had we been quick enough?

The engine roar slowed and then cut off completely, a silence falling over the mountainside. The fog must have blocked any sound the truck made from below.

Peter lay next to me. His teeth were bared against the pain from the fall, which had probably undone all of Jenna's work. He wasn't fit for this journey. He might never be. And we had more immediate problems to worry about.

A door creaked open and then shut. I reached for my sword. We could still make it out—just one more obstacle...

"Leo—Leo, is that you? Come on out. Quickly!"

I lifted my head up, and there was Oliver, peering some five feet above our heads, his hands in the air as though in surrender. I almost cried with relief.

"What are you doing here?" I asked, getting up and helping Peter to his feet. "Are you bringing the next group of guards?"

"Not a chance," said Oliver. He pulled out a cigarette and lit it carefully. "I heard my favorite squad might need one last ride."

"You're joking," said Jenna. "How'd you know?"

Oliver puffed out a cloud of smoke. "Take one guess," he said.

From behind the truck's headlights, a ponytailed figure moved towards us.

Memo smiled. "I had a hunch," he said.

Cool air rushed through my hair as Oliver guided the truck into the fog line. We had a legitimate shot at making it to the docks, and from there it was anybody's guess if we could disappear from the Verdean's search boats.

Memo, who sat in the front, asked us about the Pit over his shoulder. When we told him what we'd fought inside, he looked unsurprised.

"The Verdean had the formulas first," he said. "Makes sense they'd have Supersoldiers, too."

"There were more," said Peter. He took a sip from a canteen of water, but his hands were shaking so much he spilled all over himself. "There were way more."

"I don't like the thought of that," said Jenna.

Just as the words left her mouth, distant sirens erupted from below, echoing up off the mountainside towards us. There was no mistaking it this time. The Verdean knew what we'd done.

I shivered at the thought, but it was nothing compared to Peter's reaction. He started to bite his fist and curled up into a ball.

"I can't go back," he said, shaking. "I can't. They know you took me. They know."

"You're not going back," Jenna said. "Peter, look at me." She held Peter's face in her hands, staring into his eyes. "You're not going back to The Pit. We're right here, and we're not going to let you go. Got it? We're sticking together."

Oliver stepped on the gas. As we went around one hair-pin turn close to the bottom of the mountain, another Verdean truck whisked past in the opposite direction, presumably towards the Pit. Oliver jammed on the brakes, narrowly avoiding the other truck. For a split second I thought the fog might have concealed us. My relief was short-lived, though. Headlights appeared behind us within seconds.

The trailing car pumped the brakes around sharp bends while Oliver stepped on the gas pedal. A couple times Oliver pushed the car to its very limits, the wheels screeching right against the mountain's edge, but he always whipped the car back around just in time.

"Keep your heads down," Memo yelled back. "If they get close, they'll start firing."

The sirens blared louder as we got closer to Base Camp. When we came to a fork in the road—one leading back to Base Camp, the other around one of the sister mountains and over towards the docks—to my surprise, Oliver went right on the road towards Base Camp.

"Oliver!" I yelled. "We're getting on a boat!"

"I know," Oliver said. He backed into a little pullout and brought the truck to a stop before killing the engine. "We don't want them following us though."

The trailing truck came rumbling down the road. When it came to the fork, the driver swerved left toward the docks, zooming past without so much as a toe on the brake pedal.

Oliver inched out of the pullout and followed the same road the Verdean truck had just gone down. He didn't have the same sense of urgency as before, instead cruising along at a normal, comfortable speed.

Memo turned back to us. "You're not going from Silver Cove," he said. "There's a smaller one with less security—Witch's Cove."

"But our boat," Bree said. She held up the keys she'd gotten the night her parents died. "It's at the main dock."

"And that's where it'll stay," said Oliver.

"They'll expect you to take a boat from there," Memo said. "I've arranged for another one to be at Witch's Cove."

"Why are you doing this?" Bree asked. She wasn't looking at Memo, though. She stared at the back of Oliver's head.

Oliver turned around as though he could feel his gaze on her. I worried about the road, but Oliver kept one eye forward while he spoke.

"I was in the Verdean at the same time as your parents," Oliver said. "I wasn't anything special, and I certainly wasn't in the

Sphelix, or Squad 571. But everyone knew about them."

"Did they?" Langston asked. "How come we could only find mention in the Gilded Library? If the Sphelix was so special, they should've been in school textbooks, right?"

"It was my dad," I said. Memo looked back, surprised. "Lester told me and Jenna before the trial. Said he got caught as a traitor. That's why you're not in any of our textbooks, isn't it? Because of his treason."

Memo nodded. "I'm sorry you heard from Lester," he said. "I would've liked to have told you. But yes, the Verdean erased all records of our missions after your dad was caught. Except those in the Gilded Library."

I looked at Peter, Langston, and Bree—I expected them to be ashamed or embarrassed for me and Jenna.

"I never knew," Peter said.

"What was your dad caught doing?" Langston asked.

I shrugged and turned to Memo. He stared for a few moments, wringing his hands, before answering.

"I never found out," Memo said. "I think a rare few did. But he was labeled a traitor. Everything the Sphelix had done, all the missions completed, all the lives saved—they were all wiped away."

That must have been why Lester hated talking about his time in the Verdean so much— his name had been marred by what my dad had done. If all of my accomplishments, every achievement and medal, had been stripped from me, I'd be furious too.

But then again, what had they really accomplished, considering every war had probably been a fake?

Oliver shook his head. "No matter what your pops did," he said, "he did more good for this country than bad. I always thought the Sphelix got a raw end of the deal. And wiping names from the history books is no way to repay someone for decades of loyalty. Just like what happened with Peter at the trial."

Peter looked up at the sound of his name. He had been deep in thought but now was listening.

"It's not right, what they did to you, Pete," Oliver said. "You did the best you could under the circumstances. No one, not even your parents, did better. Even if you did run from the fight—and I'm not saying you did—but even if you had, that's fine in my book. Far as I'm concerned, y'all are too young to be fighting this war anyway."

Peter nodded and thanked him. I wanted to thank him too—for expressing what I wasn't able to.

We got to Witch's Cove and, just as Memo had predicted, there weren't any Verdean soldiers on the lookout for us. They had all apparently gone to Silver Cove.

Our boat was a tiny, scrappy sailboat with a black motor attached to the rear, but Bree gave it a nod of approval after examining it. She started pulling ropes tight around the sides, repositioning our luggage to distribute the weight evenly. Oliver helped us throw our backpacks onto the boat and then turned to say goodbye.

"Thank you," Bree said, running up and squeezing him tightly. "We'd be dead without you." She ran back to the boat to continue preparing.

Peter, Langston, and Jenna all said their goodbyes, and then, finally, it was my turn. Oliver, his barrel-chest and all, brought me in close and put his head to mine. "Your dad took the time to teach me how to shoot a bow," he said. "He was the best in the Verdean, and he helped someone who had no clue how to even string one. He was just being nice. He didn't know it then, but that saved my life more times than I can count."

"Oliver," I said, "this isn't goodbye. We'll see you again."

Oliver nodded, wrapping me in a bear hug. "You keep that attitude," he said, his voice gruff. "Even if you get burned every once in a while." He got in his truck, turned on the engine, and poked his head out.

"Oh, and there's one more note for you in there," Oliver said.

I nearly fell over. It was like getting hit in the head by a Supersoldier's fist.

"It was you?"

"Technically it was my daughter," said Oliver. "Somehow she attracts less attention than me."

Everyone – Langston, Jenna, Bree, Peter, and even Memo – was staring at Oliver.

"But why? How?"

"I'm not the only one your parents had an impact on," said Oliver. "You got friends in other places, too. And they know what you can do."

With that, Oliver pulled his head back in, but he didn't drive away like I expected him to.

He wasn't leaving alone.

"Memo..." I said, trying to stay standing. "You're coming with us, right?"

Memo had still been staring at Oliver, like all of us, but now he turned to me. Tears ran down his cracked cheeks, disappearing in his gray goatee.

"Memo," said Langston. "We need you. There's no way we'll survive on our own."

Memo's voice cracked. "I—I'm sorry," he said. "I would love to go with you."

"Then come!" said Bree. "Please... Why can't you?" Now tears were welling up in her eyes too. She had perhaps known Memo best. He'd broken the news to her about her parents, and then he'd naturally stepped into the role. He'd stepped in as a parent to all of us.

"This battle is no longer mine," Memo said. He stiffened up, arching his shoulders and taking a deep breath. "It's been my greatest honor to know you all. I don't say it lightly when I say you're the best people I've ever known. You'll be fine out there without me. You've been doing it for nearly six months now. Just remember: you're all a part of something greater than yourselves."

Memo hugged each of us. When it was my turn, he clasped a hand to my cheek and stared at me. I searched his brown eyes for some wisdom, something I could take with me.

But there was nothing. No last lesson; no final wise words. Memo shook his head ever-so slightly, and pulled back a few inches, taking the five of us in.

The pink sky of the early-morning sun shone on Memo's face,

and I could no longer see the cracks in his skin. His ponytail whipped behind him in the wind. He looked fifteen years younger.

Memo smiled and motioned to the boat. "I left something in there for you as well," he said.

"What is it?" I asked.

He laughed. "You've never been able to contain your curiosity, huh?"

"Sorry," I said. "Thank you."

"That's what I should be saying," Memo said. He patted me on the cheek and turned away.

I rushed to the boat, and Langston and I dragged it out through the first ten yards of water before climbing in. Bree started up the engine. When we were fifty yards out, I turned and looked back to shore. Oliver and Memo were still in the truck looking out at us.

Oliver flashed the lights a couple times as one last goodbye, and then they drove off.

I stood on the edge of the boat, doing my best to maintain my balance with the peaks and troughs of the waves. The truck skidded down the road, kicking up dust. Oliver had written the notes; Memo had known we'd try and break Peter out and he'd saved us.

The truck started up a steep hill, but up ahead, blocking their path forward, was a swarm of Verdean trucks...

Memo and Oliver didn't put up a fight. Soldiers surrounded the truck, yanking both of them out and throwing them into the back of another one.

The car carrying Memo and Oliver turned back towards Base

Camp. The other seven or so raced towards Witch's Cove, where a long line of archers sprinted out along the sand, aiming their bows toward where we floated, well within range.

34. THE FOXTAILS

A volley of arrows shot out from the archers, sailing high into the crisp sky and growing bigger by the second.

I can stop these. I can block them. I lifted up my hand, focusing on my breath and moving outward from there. No warped vision, no arrows. Nothing. I couldn't see the obsidian or the wood. I couldn't *see* anything.

Still they flew.

I strained harder, expanding my mind until my body was shaking from the effort. *I've done this before. Stopping arrows is the one thing I can do.*

Still they flew. Zipping cleanly through the air, seconds from hitting us… Feet away…

I ducked behind one of the railings.

One by one they whizzed by and nailed our boat, digging themselves deep into the woodwork like beaks of a woodpecker. All of them somehow missed me. I lifted my head and looked around. They'd missed everyone.

Peter screamed. He grabbed his leg, crying in pain. An arrow was lodged in his thigh.

Jenna dove down next to him and set to work. She tried to dislodge the arrow, but it had pierced entirely through his leg and dug deep into the wood. Blood gushed out onto the boat deck.

Everyone gathered around him. "Give me your sword," Jenna

said. I handed it to her, and she began sawing off the fletching. Meanwhile, the archers were readying a second round.

"Leo," Langston said, turning to me, "You've got to stop them! We're sitting ducks!"

"I tried!" I said. "I can't do it anymore. I don't get it."

I was pissed, flustered. How could my power abandon me right now? How could I let Peter get hurt?

Langston grabbed me by the shoulders. "You can do it," he said. "I promise, you can do it."

A second round of arrows catapulted into the sky. I closed my eyes again, but still no luck. I kicked the side of the boat. Why wasn't it—I—working?

I blinked my eyes open just as our sailboat passed out from within the green glow of the Orb. It was like a backpack had been taken off me. The Orb's glow wasn't the main source of light anymore; the sun was. My head cleared and, focusing outward, I was able to *see* the arrows—the warped vision.

A wave of relief crashed over me. I spread my consciousness outward and halted them in the air. I thought for a minute about throwing them back at the archers, but I instead guided them safely down onto the boat. More ammunition should we need it for later.

There was a collective sigh when they landed harmlessly at our feet. Bree patted me on the shoulder. Jenna was still tending to Peter, who was fighting to stay awake and didn't seem to be aware what was going on. Langston was the only one that caught on.

"The Orb," Langston said. It wasn't a question.

"I think so," I said. "I guess it was sucking my power from me."

But before I could try to explain further, Peter yelled out again in pain.

"I'm sorry, Pete," Jenna said, continuing to wrap a bandage around his leg. Blood soaked his uniform, wet and black. The arrow still stuck out from his thigh. "I've got to keep wrapping it though."

"Can't we take it out?" I asked.

"Not yet," said Jenna. "If we do, it'll cause even more bleeding. I've done my best to wrap it up and disinfect the areas around it." She had cut away the pant leg from the thigh and was still dabbing at it with a stained cloth. "We have to get him to shore as soon as possible and give him rest and water."

"Is he going to make it?" Langston asked.

Jenna looked up at him, her eyes red from tears.

She didn't answer.

Another volley of arrows was on its way, but we were so far away now that only a few soldiers had the strength to reach us. I stopped the arrows easily, once again saving them for ammunition.

Bree steered the ship directly towards the Foxtail Islands—or where we thought they were. We'd seen them when we first arrived into Base Camp so many months ago, barely visible on a clear day, and impossible to see with the fog now. But Bree assured us we were going in the right direction.

Back on shore, the first Verdean ships set sail from Base Camp. They'd finally been alerted that we'd left from a different cove, and now thirty or forty boats were after us. Why so many for a few stray fugitives?

We were a good distance away, and our small, raggedy boat was bound to be tough to find. The Verdean ships were bigger. Some even looked to be cargo ships. They were all easy to see, but I wasn't so sure they could see us. In fact, if we were lucky, they might think, given all the rounds of arrows that had just been shot, that we were dead.

A half hour later the massive rocks of the Foxtails came into view. The burnt-red stone towered over our miniature boat as we passed below. The Foxtails were infamously treacherous, with loads of hidden rocks and quarries. We carefully maneuvered around the first giant rock and shortly thereafter entered into a minefield of rough whitecaps and burnt-red boulders.

Bree killed the engine and we wound our way through, cautiously, at a snail's pace.

We bumped into a rock—or what I thought was a rock. An enormous white head popped out of the water.

"Look out," Bree yelled, quickly turning the rudder to take us in the opposite direction. The shark splashed down into the water without pursuing us, but ominous dark shapes still swam underneath.

"Don't worry," Langston said. "If we don't disturb them, they won't attack us. They're just looking to mate."

"Won't that make them more aggressive?" Jenna asked.

Langston didn't answer.

A few minutes later, another loud thump sounded from underneath, but this time it really was just a rock. The boat held strong and Bree was able to steer us onto a small, red-pebbled beach.

We quickly off-loaded Peter, setting him down on a bed of rocks that appeared clean. While Jenna tended to him, we took out the cargo and set to work dragging the boat itself halfway up the cliff face, concealing it behind a clump of bushes.

Jenna knelt over Peter, her hands working vigorously.

"Anything we can do to help?" I asked.

"Bandages and water," she said. Bree ran to get Jenna's backpack. I handed Jenna my canteen. "I'm still too scared to work on that arrow until he has more strength."

"I'm alright," Peter said, slurring his words. "Save your water."

"Shut up, Pete," Jenna said. She felt his forehead with the back of her hand. "No need to try and be the hero. We've got plenty of water."

I peered out into the ocean nervously. The fleet was coming. We'd be dead if they found us.

But we couldn't move Peter. He needed as much rest as possible.

"And warmth," Jenna said. "We need to build a fire so I can heat the needles and sew up the wounds."

Langston, Bree, and I hiked up one of the dirt trails to try to find some wood.

Langston pulled out a dead branch from behind a clump of bushes. "They sacrificed their lives for us," Langston said. "Memo and Oliver. They knew we were never going to see them again."

I hadn't thought about it until then. I'd only spared thoughts for Pete. But now that Langston said it, I knew he was right. There was no way the Verdean would let them off the hook. My stomach dropped when I thought about Memo and Oliver.

"I wish they'd come with us," I said. I stomped my foot on the middle of a dead branch, breaking it clean in two. "Or at least left more quickly. Maybe they could've escaped."

Bree shook her head. "They didn't have a chance," she said. "We should've tried harder to get them to come with. But Memo probably didn't want to slow us down."

"He wouldn't have slowed us down!" I said. "We need him."

"I'm with you," said Bree. "But maybe he thought he'd be taking up too much of our food and water. I'm also not sure he sacrificed himself for *us*."

"Who else was he saving?" I said.

Langston answered. "She means Memo and Oliver weren't trying to save me and her," he said. "They did it for you."

"What?"

"Leo, come on," Langston said. "Think about what you just did with those arrows. You're something beyond what we all are—you have a power no one else has. And what did Oliver say to you about your dad's friends? *They know what you can do...*"

"I'd be dead if it wasn't for Bree saving my life in the Pit," I said. My triceps throbbed in agreement. "And we would've never gotten Peter out of there if you hadn't come up with the jib."

"You're being modest," said Langston. "Memo and Oliver know what you're capable of. Arcalaeus and the government may know too, or at least suspect. They sent half their fleet after us. They wouldn't do that for just a few random soldiers."

"We're not just any group of random soldiers," I said. "We're the Sphelix. We're a part of something bigger than ourselves—that's what Memo said was important."

Bree shrugged. "Sounds pretty corny to me," she said. She went over to another branch and started sawing at it with her sword.

"If you think Memo wouldn't risk his life to save either of yours," I said, "you're out of your mind."

Peter was in a bad space when we returned. He was feverish and sweating, losing water fast.

Jenna sat next to him, force-feeding him nutrient pills and sips from the canteen. His jacket and shirt were cut open, and his pants removed so that all he was wearing was underwear. She wiped him down with a cool, wet cloth while another rested on his head. His tan skin shone brightly against the rock.

"The fever is okay, actually," Jenna said. "It means his immune system is working, but it also means there's an infection or one developing. I need to get the arrow out."

I expected her to be more flustered, but she was stern and businesslike, staring uncompromisingly at me. The blue emerald reflected the sun beautifully against her neck.

"Tell us what to do," I said.

Jenna jumped into action. She told Langston to hold down Peter's leg. Bree retrieved some numbing medication. I began wiping the blood off Peter while Jenna prepared.

I massaged the dark red streaks of blood away with the damp cloth, wringing it out every few minutes while we waited for Jenna.

Peter was awake but didn't talk much until he put a hand on my arm and said, "I always knew you wanted to give me a massage. Glad I could finally make your dreams come true."

I let out a laugh and hit him in the face with the cloth.

"Oh, sorry," I said. "Forgot."

"Nah," Peter said. "I needed to get hit by someone after ditching you guys."

"It's alright, Pete," I said. "Seriously. We all understand." He didn't look me in the eye. "What was it like in that hell hole?" It was an attempt at changing the subject, though probably not the best choice.

"We dug day and night," Peter said.

"You dug?"

"With shovels. Into the ground. We literally did it all day. And if you slacked off, they tortured you."

"That sounds awful. Why digging?"

"There was some mineral they wanted," Peter said. "Some of the prisoners had been in there for years…

"Hey, did you talk to my mom and dad before you left?" Peter asked. "Let them know you were coming after me?"

"No," I said. "I spoke to them before the trial, but there wasn't any time afterward. And I don't think it would've been smart to tell anyone what we were about to do. We didn't even tell Memo."

"I'm worried about them," Peter said. "You, me, and Jenna all deserting… Arcton wouldn't take it out on my mom and dad, or Jexter and Flora, would they?"

"Your dad is well-connected enough that that shouldn't be a

problem," I said. "Everyone will be fine."

But would they? The last twenty-four hours had gone by so quickly that I'd never stopped to consider the impact our escape would have on those we loved.

Lester, despite his drunkenness, had still put a roof over my head and food on the table. Losing me, Peter, and Jenna would hit Helen hard, but hopefully that'd be the worst of it. And what *would* happen to Jexter and Flora?

Then, of course, there were Memo and Oliver. They'd given their lives for us. Memo had done more for me in the last six months than anyone else. Was it just out of love? Or, like Bree and Langston seemed to think, was it because of my power? And Oliver's daughter...

Jenna returned with a pair of white gloves.

"Now, Pete," Jenna said, "I'm going to count to three and then remove the arrow, okay?"

"Okay," Peter said. His voice betrayed his nerves.

"One..." Jenna said, and then she pulled out the arrow, quickly but carefully.

"Ow! What happened to going on three?"

"Changed my mind," Jenna said. Blood started to spout from the wound. "Gauze," she said to Bree, who handed it to her. Jenna poured rubbing alcohol on it before pressing down on Peter's wound.

Peter groaned in pain. "Give me some warning, will ya?"

Jenna did the same thing on the exit wound, lifting Peter's leg up and holding gauze in place underneath. Next, she set to work wrapping the wound with a dressing. Peter clenched his teeth through the entire thing, but eventually, once his leg was properly wrapped and he had drunk some water, he relaxed. His normally curly hair was matted down with sweat, but his eyes looked revitalized after the operation—more aware, and moving around in short bursts.

"Not out of the woods yet," said Jenna. "But it's a start."

Bree and I went to go explore the rest of the island and look for food. Jenna, who hadn't slept all night, took a hard-earned nap while Langston watched over Peter.

The Foxtails were covered entirely in reddish dirt—the same color that made up the island's base. Despite the rocky habitat, plenty of wildlife thrived. Jackrabbits and beetles were seemingly in endless supply, and there were a number of birds—both flying and ground-bound—that lived on the island, in addition to a couple foxes.

I wanted to get a view and see if we could find the Verdean fleet, so we climbed the steep face until we reached a plateau that gave us a panoramic view.

Two other main islands comprised the rest of the Foxtails. Smaller, jagged rocks jutted out from the water, creating the treacherous path that Bree had navigated earlier that day.

"Your dad's friend must have been a master sailor to teach you how to navigate something like that," I said.

"He let me captain the boat every once in a while," Bree said. "But my mom was the one who told me to trust my instincts and demand more responsibility."

"Sounds like my mom," I said.

"I'm sure they would've liked each other."

"You think Langston and Peter's parents will be alright?"

Bree ran a hand through her neck-length hair. "Honestly?" she said. "I think they're in trouble."

"But they didn't do anything," I said. "It was us that escaped."

"Leo, it doesn't matter," Bree said. "There's no use pretending."

"They won't be killed…" I said. I needed something.

"If not killed," Bree said, "their lives are going to be much worse. They might take Peter's place in the Pit."

"How can you say that? Did you know that going into this?"

"I knew it was a possibility," Bree said. "But my parents, if they were alive, would understand my decision. What happened to Peter was…that trial was a joke. The things we saw… The things we did… All for a phony war."

"But Flora and Jexter can't be thrown in the Pit. They're too young."

"I hope you're right," Bree said. "Langston has a sister too, remember. And Oliver has a daughter. But this just means we can't fail. We've sacrificed too much now."

I wanted to cry. I'd unknowingly jeopardized the lives of not only all my friends, but their families. I started breathing heavily, hyperventilating again.

"Leo," Bree said, putting a hand on my shoulder, "It was all worth it."

"How can you say that?"

"We weren't *living* in Arcton. We were doing the government's bidding, whatever it was. Think about it."

And I did. Every moment of our life had been regimented. Go to school at this hour, practice war tactics at that hour. Did you eat more than your fair share of rice? Well, then you get to go hungry for two days.

But one thing Bree said stuck with me. *We weren't living in Arcton.* It was similar to something my dad used to say to my mom. *This isn't living.*

"But if Jexter and Flora are dead because of what we did..."

"Stop," said Bree. "Screw Arcton. Your dad was killed because he was a traitor – maybe he wanted to take the government down, too."

"That doesn't make this any easier," I said.

Arcton's massive west coast stretched out before us. The barracks and buildings in Base Camp were barely visible from the Foxtails. The ships the Verdean had sent after us were nowhere to be found, most likely still searching for what they thought would be a shipwrecked boat.

We took it easy the next couple of days, eating DMPs and taking turns watching over Peter who, slowly but surely, regained his strength. We started to befriend some of the animals, who had likely never encountered humans before.

By the end of the second day, Peter's fever broke and he was actually moving around on his own—just a few guided steps, but still progress. Jenna said that we could even take him on the boat and continue our journey, but that was the problem—we didn't know where to go. We'd taken off and escaped Arcton, but that was as far as we'd gotten in our planning.

The fourth night, we all gathered underneath a slanted rock face where we could start a fire without being seen by passing boats. Bree stuck a whittled stick through her DMP vegetables and chicken pieces to roast over the fire. Peter rested on a blanket while Jenna re-dressed his bandages.

For what seemed like the millionth time, Langston and I debated about where to go.

"We could make pit stops in Vacson along the way," Langston said. "We could stock up on supplies and be okay to make the month-long journey with just two stops."

"We shouldn't be in any of the countries in the Combination," I said. "They'll be looking for us."

"Not if they think we're dead," said Langston. "That has to be their rationale right now. We didn't turn up; our boat wasn't found. No one's sending them a secret message saying, 'Hey, Squad 19 is actually alive and traveling through Vacson.'"

"Wait..." I said, wondering how I forgot.

I sprinted off to where the boat was hidden, throwing off the branches and leaves covering it.

"What are you doing?" Jenna asked when she caught up.

I didn't look back. "Oliver said there was one last message for me," I said. "Remember?"

Langston and Bree, with Peter using them for support, finally caught up, and together we pulled the boat out. I crawled inside and poked around.

"You see anything?" Jenna asked.

"Just our backpacks," I said. I tossed bags out of the boat without caring where they landed.

As I threw my own bag aside, I saw something buried underneath the stern. I crawled down to get a better look... Sitting snug against some loose boards sat the mahogany chest from Brill.

"Of course," I said. I pulled it out for the others to see.

There was no mistaking it was the same chest with the gold-plated lock.

None of us said a word. We just stared in awe. Memo and Oliver were gone, Peter almost executed—all for the documents inside this chest.

I opened it and, sure enough, the letters from General Magner to General Nygaard were there, neatly stacked, along with the diagrams and formulas for creating Supersoldiers.

Memo's last gift to us.

Jenna pointed to the lid of the chest. "What's that?" she asked.

On the wood, in silver ink, were a few words...

I bent down to get a better angle. The handwriting was scratchy and almost childish, just like Oliver's notes from before.

Head West to Notitius.

Langston leaned down and smiled. "Looks like those discussions about where we needed to go were moot," he said. "Oliver solved it for us."

"Where's Notitius?" I said.

"Beyond Lewent," Langston said. "It's far."

"Hey, check this out," said Bree. She reached into the chest and pulled out the letters from General Nygaard and General Magner. Hidden beneath was a blue, leather-bound book.

She held it out. "Memo left us this, too. *Retrieval Tactics in Late 21st Century Vacson...*"

My palms started to sweat, and my whole body began to overheat. "Let me see that," I said. I fumbled it a few times, knowing, but not believing, what could be inside. The spine of the book was loosely attached to the pages within. I flipped open the front cover...

Gestalt Diary

"No..." I said.

"What?" Jenna said. She looked from the book to me. "Leo, what's wrong?"

"It's the book. Dad's book."

"What book? Leo?"

I told her—told all of them. How dad had read it to me every morning, how he'd said it was important. I flipped through the pages, unable to comprehend the thousands of words written there. Blood rushed to my head. I couldn't think. I needed to read this, right now, and I said so.

Jenna put her hand on me. She smiled sadly. "Leo, that's incredible," she said. "I'm excited to read it, too. But we need to get everything ready to leave. Okay? We don't have that much fresh water left, and who knows how long the trip will be. You'll have plenty of time to read, but right now we need to get going."

I opened my mouth to argue, but when I met Jenna's gaze I

couldn't. She understood, of course. She knew I wanted to read this more than anything, but right now we had other things to worry about. Peter's health, where we were going, avoiding Verdean ships...

The sun was close to setting. Cover of night was the perfect time to set sail.

We loaded the boat quickly and took off within an hour. Bree guided us slowly through the treacherous rocks. Thankfully, the moonlight was strong enough for her to see most of the whirlpools and even some shadows swimming beneath.

Oliver's last message had given us direction again; it breathed new life into us. And there was *Gestalt Diary*.

Who knew what was in the Nefa, or what Notitius would bring? All I knew was that I had Langston, Bree, Jenna, and Peter. Right now, that was more than enough.

ACKNOWLEDGEMENTS

To all my friends and family, thank you. This book would not have been possible without your love and support. There are a few that I need to pick out by name: Michael Hlebasko, for helping turn this into a full-fledged story, rather than a stream of incoherent thoughts. Sheldon Siegel, a brilliant and generous author in his own right, whose guidance gave me the confidence and roadmap to actually write *The Sphelix*. Tanya Egan Gibson, an editor extraordinaire who played as large a role as anyone in making this something that might be worth reading. My mom, Alice Flaherty, for her inexhaustible nuggets of wisdom. Conor and Matt Flaherty, two of my biggest supporters and cheerleaders. All of my teachers and professors over the years, namely Ralph "Ralphie" Williams, whose insight into a number of books provided much of the inspiration for this story. Tish O'Dowd, who graciously allowed me into her writing class when she didn't need to, and then went on to show me how to write into the heart of characters. Linda Siegel, for her marketing tips and tricks. Arthur Mansbach, for checking to make sure I was actually doing something with my life. Dom Fusco, for his succinct and perfect suggestions. And lastly, thank you, whoever you are, for giving *The Sphelix* a read. There's more to come.

Made in the USA
San Bernardino, CA
28 June 2018